BROTHERS IN ARMS

By

G.S. WILLMOTT

Copyright

CONTENTS

He's a Rebel

Chapter 1

As the young Boer warrior was being led to his execution, he passed the newly dug grave that was to be his for eternity. He placed his manacled hand over the badge on his hat; on it was inscribed the word for love: "Liefde".

'Don't you bastards pinch this badge as a souvenir. It stays with me in the grave.'

'Mate, you won't know if we do or we don't.'

'I'll haunt you.'

The execution party reached the chair strategically placed for the firing squad; they secured him to the chair.

'No need to tie me to the bloody chair, lads! I'm not going anywhere.'

'Sorry, mate, we have to; it's the rules.'

They bound his wrists and ankles with white cloth and placed a blindfold around his head. His hat had been removed.

There he sat in a large quadrangle with many British soldiers and the majority of the town of Graaf-Reinet looking on. The British had ordered there be a large audience.

Two men in the crowd were talking in whispering tones, they were the condemned's brothers; 'brothers in arms' they had followed their leader in many raids against the British and admired his bravery and his intelligence also his wit. They had hoped that they could save him from his fate but realised that would be impossible, too many British soldiers. They had to stand by helplessly and watch the execution of the man they loved.

The young woman was standing in silence her head slightly bowed; this would be her first experience of a public execution. She looked around and saw a sea of people from her town. Some she recognised, most she didn't. They all seemed to be craning their necks to get a good view of Scheepers being tied to the execution chair. The young rebel about to be executed had been her lover, her confidant and her best friend.

The day was hot, very hot and the eternal buzzing of flies was the only sound she heard. The musty smell of sweat permeated the air: sweat from the overpowering heat, the excitement and the fear. It was British settlers who seemed to be excited; they were finally getting rid of this criminal who had

1

caused so much havoc in their town. The Boers comprised the majority of the crowd; they were sad to be witnessing the death of a true hero.

The chaplain stepped forward and read the 23rd Psalm and blessed the Boer rebel.

The air was thick with anticipation. The only noise now was the flies and women sobbing into handkerchiefs.

The Execution Scene

Scheepers was in a black void. He thought about his sweetheart, Johanna, his mother and the "brothers in arms" he would leave behind.

He heard the order to present arms.

'Shoot straight, you bastards!'

They did. Every bullet splintered the chair directly behind his heart. They untied him, placed him on a stretcher and carried him to the grave where they lowered him down. The sergeant threw in his hat with the badge still attached before he was covered in lime and the dusty brown soil of the Veldt interred him forever.

The condemned Boer rebel (mostly obscured by his guards) tied to a chair for execution.

The Boer rebel slumps backward in his chair.

Who was this twenty-three year old Boer commando who departed this world in such a horrifying and public way? His name was Gideon Scheepers.

He was a soldier from the still-independent Boer states, which were being reduced in this war to British dependencies.

In 1901, late in the Boer war, Scheepers took a column of irregulars into the British Eastern Cape Province and wrought havoc behind the lines.

Commandant Scheepers had a group of about one hundred men under his command. He would ride into a town like Murraysberg and cause absolute havoc. He liked raiding Murraysberg. He had raided the town fourteen times and the locals started calling it Scheepersberg!

Before one such raid he gathered his men before him.

'OK men, here we go again! Just follow my lead and see if we can upset the "Khakis" a little bit.'

They rode off into Murraysberg heading straight for the POW camp.

'Let them all out, lads.'

Scheepers, and two of his men rode to the magistrate's house.

'Come out here, you bastard. I hope we don't have to look for you under the bed.'

The British Magistrate, James Holsworthy, stepped out onto the veranda looking petrified.

'Don't worry old man we're going to keep you as a bargaining chip. Tie him up, lads, and put him on a horse.'

'Sir, look what I found.'

'Good on you, Hans, a bloody Union Jack. We can cut it up into little squares and wipe our arses on it!'

He would spend that year giving the British much better than he got, but the war was also infamously dirty. Scheeper's men also flogged and shot natives who helped the British, looted as well as burned farms, and executed Boer 'traitors'.

Was he a criminal?

Since Scheepers was over enemy lines, the Boers who joined him could be held liable for treason … but that didn't hold for Scheepers himself. His execution was based on war crimes, or so the British said: his thirty-count charge sheet included seven arsons, seven murders, and various and sundry abuses of prisoners and blacks. Scheepers was really annoyed about the last; natives were supposed to be kept out of the fighting; he insisted that the ones he "murdered" were under arms as scouts for the British, therefore fair game.

Many brave men lost their lives in this war. The difference between the two sides was that the Boers fought a guerrilla war and the British didn't shoot until they saw the whites of their enemy's eyes.

Why did this brutal war begin in the first place?

How did 27,000 women and children die at the hands of the British?

Scheeper's Commando Troops

British Troops Marching to Meet the Boers

This is a Real Boer

Chapter 2

The Boers were the descendants of the Dutch farmers who settled in South Africa from 1652. They used South Africa as a stopping point for ships on their way to the East Indies. Fruit and vegetables were grown here to battle the problem of scurvy. The Dutch first settled the area that was to become Cape Town and with time, expanded across the entire tip of southern Africa.

After the Napoleonic wars in 1815, South Africa changed hands and became a British colony. Many of the Dutch went north to get away from the English. Here they encountered tribes that, over time, had moved south from central Africa. There ensued a period of war between the Dutch Boers and the Zulus, a powerful tribe led by "Shaka". The Boers eventually won and created an Afrikaner state in the north.

The trouble between the English and the Boers began for a number of reasons. Two of the major factors were the resolution of the British to abolish slavery in their territories, and their failure to protect the outlying Boer farms from raids by the natives (while refusing to allow the Boers to deal with the problem in their own manner).

The Boers were a rugged and fiercely independent race while the British were civilised, idealistic and very officious.

The Boers resented the British and objected to being told how they should live.

Trouble was brewing!

1889 South Africa

The first Boer war was very brief; the British were defeated at every turn. The British government had lost its will to continue and it conceded independence to the Boers after a particularly humiliating defeat at Majuba Hill. The concession to the Boers was seen as controversial; many British leaders felt it was a disgraceful defeat and that Britain should have continued until victory was won.

Five short years later, an enormous quantity of gold was discovered in the territory of the Boer's Transvaal Republic. As thousands of British citizens and other foreigners flocked to the goldfields, the conflicts between the British and the Boers increased. There were arguments over taxes, rail transportation, and the rights of British settlers. But there was also the vision of Cecil Rhodes and many other imperialist Britons. They dreamed of a unified South Africa

7

governed independently and part of the British Empire. The very existence of the Boer Republics threatened this vision. One of Rhodes' cronies, Leander Starr Jameson, attempted to incite an uprising in Johannesburg in order to overthrow the government of the Transvaal. The attempt failed, but at that point the Boers prepared for war. When negotiations broke down, the Boers did not wait to be invaded, but went immediately on the offensive.

This was war!

Cecil Rhodes and Alfred Beit, planners of the Jameson Raid

Sir Leander Starr Jameson

Danie Boy
A True Hero

Chapter 3

Danie Theron had ridden out to see what the British were up to at Fochville, a strategic area in Gautung Province in South Africa. It was unusual for him to be alone. The norm was, at least half a dozen of his loyal band that made up the TVK (Theron Reconnaissance Corps) would accompany him. He dismounted and crawled up a stony hill only to be confronted by seven soldiers from the "Marshal's Horse", a South African cavalry unit formed to fight along side the British.

Danie knew there was no alternative; he had to take all of them out. He had been in enough situations to know the element of surprise was in his favour and that gave him the edge. He aimed his Mauser rifle at the officer in the lead and shot him through the forehead. He fell from his horse his left foot still caught in the stirrup. By the time the cavalrymen knew what had happened two more had been killed. Danie then used his pistol to shoot the remaining four. They were lucky they survived with serious wounds.

The element of surprise had gone: he knew the Brits down below would have heard the shooting.

Danie decided the only way to survive was to fool the British into thinking a Boer platoon was their opponents and not a single soldier.

He began firing his rifle at the enemy, his pistol too, reloading as fast as he could and firing again. He wasn't sure if he had hit any of the bastards but the trick worked.

The British had been deluded into thinking there was a Boer force to deal with. The British column's escort, alerted by the firing, immediately charged the hill. Danie continued firing while the column's artillery (six field guns and a 4.7-inch naval gun), opened a heavy barrage on the hill. The legendary Republican hero was killed in an inferno of lyddite and shrapnel.

Danie Theron

Theron's Commandos in Action

Just Concentrate

Chapter 4

Johannesburg, South Africa, 1900

Melrose House, Lord Roberts' Head Quarters 1900

Lord Roberts, and his second in command, Lord Kitchener, were finishing their evening meal with a fine Portuguese port.

They had both arrived in South Africa on the "RMS Dunottar Castle" the previous year.

'Kitchener, do you know the biggest problem we have with these blasted Boers?'

'Well Sir, I would imagine the biggest problem we have is that they keep killing our men, although we taught them a bloody good lesson at the Battle of Paardeberg. They lost half their fighting men. The POWs are now on their way to Ceylon and India, well out of harm's way.'

'You're right to a certain extent, but the way I see it, the biggest problem we have is that unlike our men, the bastards go home to their farms, see their wives and children and stock up with fresh provisions. They're fresh and revitalised ready to do battle again.'

'I see what you mean. But what in the hell can we do to stop it, Sir?'

'Well, I've been giving it some thought; I think we need to get rid of the incentive to return home. I suggest we burn their homes, destroy their crops and

12

slaughter their stock. That should stop the bastards.'

'What happens to the women and children?'

'We take them into temporary refugee camps until this bloody war is won.'

'Sir, I think your plan might just work.'

'It has to.'

British Concentration Camp

The "Scorched Earth Policy" was initiated with great vigour and enthusiasm.

Lord Roberts was soon to be recalled to England for higher duties; Lord Kitchener took over High Command. He accelerated the "scorched earth" policy and under his leadership, the number of farms destroyed and women and children as well as black Africans in concentration camps grew rapidly.

Eventually, there was a total of forty-five tent camps built for the Boer internees and sixty-four for black Africans. Of the twenty eight thousand Boer men captured as POWs, twenty five thousand six hundred and thirty were sent overseas to Ceylon, India, Portugal and Bermuda. The majority of Boers remaining in the local camps were women and children. Over twenty six thousand women and children were to perish in these concentration camps. This figure is even more horrific when compared to the casualties of war.

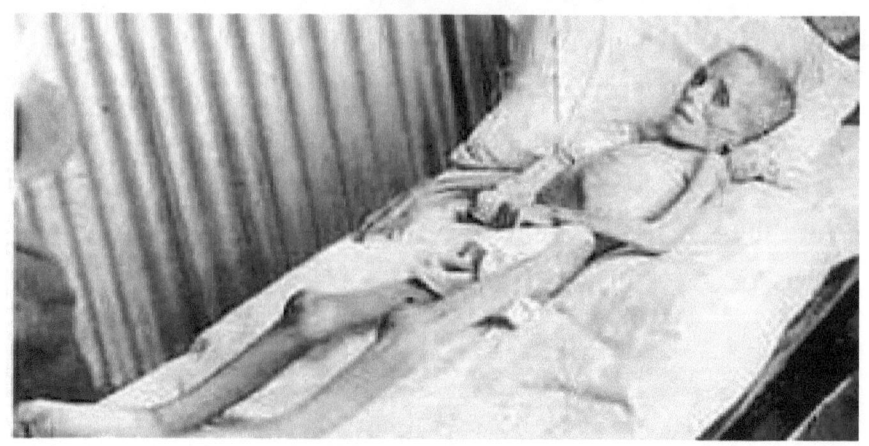

Boer Child in a British Concentration Camp

British Military casualties

7,894 killed in battle

934 missing

Boer Military casualties

4,000 in battle

The camps were poorly administered from the outset and became increasingly overcrowded when Kitchener's troops implemented the internment strategy on a vast scale. Conditions were terrible for the health of the internees, mainly due to neglect, poor hygiene and bad sanitation. The supply of all items was unreliable, partly because of the constant disruption to communication lines by the Boers. The food rations were meagre and there was a two-tier allocation policy, whereby families of men who were still fighting were routinely given smaller rations than others. The inadequate shelter, poor diet, inadequate hygiene and overcrowding led to malnutrition and endemic contagious diseases such as measles, typhoid and dysentery to which the children were particularly vulnerable.

As the war raged across their farms and their homes were destroyed, many Africans became refugees and they, like the Boers, moved to the towns where the British army hastily created internment camps. Subsequently, the "Scorched Earth" policy was ruthlessly applied to both Boers and Africans. Although most black Africans were not considered by the British to be hostile, many tens of thousands were forcibly removed from Boer areas and also placed in concentration camps.

Africans were held separately from Boer internees. Eventually there were a total of sixty four tent camps for Africans. Conditions were as bad as in the camps for the Boers.

Young Winston

Chapter 5

Johannesburg, 1899

Winston Churchill

In 1899, Winston Churchill headed to South Africa as a newspaper correspondent for the Morning Post to cover the Boer War. Another English correspondent joined him; his name was Richard Lamont, heir to the Lamont estate including "The Observer" newspaper, which he was now representing. His father, Lord Lamont, thought it would be good experience for the young Richard Lamont: he was 23.

'Winston, what are your plans for tomorrow?' asked Richard Lamont.

'Why?'

'I was just curious, I have an opportunity to ride with the "Death or Glory" lads on a raid against the Boers at Elandslaagte.'

'Actually, I'd love to ride with the 17th Lancers who've earned their "Death or Glory" title, however, I am already committed to another assignment.'

'Never mind, another time. Where are you off to?'

' I'm travelling on an armoured train to report on a reconnaissance mission. We will be heading towards Colenso North. Apparently some Boer patrols have been spotted.'

'Good luck! I'll catch up with you a bit later when you're back.'

Winston was in the front carriage with the officers when he heard rifle shots and lots of yelling from Boers chasing the train. The train's engineer opened the throttle to outrun the horseman. What he didn't realise was the Boer commandos had placed rocks on the track at a blind bend. The train had no hope of stopping. It hit the rocks and the front carriages derailed.

A firefight began and both sides lost significant numbers. Winston was captured, along with the surviving soldiers and was marched off to prison in Pretoria.

He didn't stay long.

Winston Churchill (on the right) as a Prisoner

The Observer.

December 27th, 1899

Correspondent Richard Lamont

My good friend and fellow correspondent Winston Churchill has made a daring escape from the clutches of the Boer enemy.

On the night of December 12th, when several prison guards had turned their backs, he took the opportunity to climb over the prison wall. Wearing a brown flannel suit with £75 in his pocket and four slabs of chocolate, Churchill walked on leisurely through the night in the hope of finding the Delagoa Bay Railway. So began his great escape and journey to freedom.

Churchill jumped onto a train and hid among soft

sacks covered in coal dust. Leaving the train before daybreak, he continued on his escape. Lady luck was on his side, Winston happened upon the home of Mr. John Howard, manager of the Transvaal Collieries. He knocked on the front door, Mr. Howard's response to his plea for help was "Thank God you have come here! It is the only house for twenty miles where you would not have been handed over. We are all British here, we will see you through."

Mr. Howard first hid Churchill in a coalmine, which made the young Winston quite ill, Mr Howard then transported him to safety. Churchill had to squeeze into a hole at the end of a train car loaded with bales of wool. This was a very uncomfortable journey.

Once he arrived in Durban, a British stronghold, he was heralded as a hero.

I look forward to working with my good friend again.

Winston Churchill and Richard Lamont remained close friends until death separated them.

Winston on his Horse

News of the World

Chapter 6

London, England, 1913

Richard Lamont, was sitting in his large office overlooking Fleet Street in London; he was regarded as one of the most powerful newspaper barons in Britain. He had come a long way from being a war correspondent in Africa: he had inherited a fairly insignificant newspaper, "The Observer", in 1905 from his father, George Lamont.

He now owned three significant and influential newspapers, the "Guardian", "The Times" and the "Observer". Every morning at 8am precisely the paper's editors arrived at his office to discuss what stories they were intending to publish. If Lord Lamont disagreed with running a particular story, it would not be published. Lord Lamont had very strong views including on whether women should be allowed to vote.

He believed if women were on an equal footing as their male counterparts they could end up in Parliament and start influencing the way the country was run.

The editor of the "Guardian" submitted a story about the German General, Bismarck influencing the Kaiser to become more aggressive and expand the German Empire. George approved the story; he too was concerned about Germany's expansionist ambitions.

The "Times" front-page story centred on large insurance claims being filed against the Cunard Line for the lives lost on the Titanic. One woman had submitted a claim for £1,000,000; her name was Mrs Irene Harris, from New York City and she was travelling with her husband on the Titanic when it sank, drowning her husband. She was a beneficiary of the ship's policy, 'women and children first'.

The editor of "The Observer" submitted a story supporting the Suffragettes in their bid to allow women the vote. Women, after all, had won the right to vote in New Zealand and Australia, why not the United Kingdom or the United States?

Lord Lamont, brought the meeting to a close and the three editors left the meeting room: two were happy, one was dejected.

He summoned his secretary, Sophie, to take some dictation.

Lamont dictated several memos to senior staff and two letters, one to his lawyers and one to his good friend, Winston Churchill, who at the time was First Lord of the Admiralty.

12th February 1913

The Times Newspaper

Editor in Chief

Dear Winston,

I trust you are keeping well and not smoking too many cigars!

I am writing to you because I am very concerned about your favoured policy in relation to "The Feeble-Minded" and the proposed legislation to be introduced to Parliament.

I understand you are in favour of sterilisation of all men and women who have been classified as feeble-minded, idiots or imbeciles.

I can assure you that my papers will vigorously campaign against forced sterilisation.

I am in favour of 'containment' in a humane environment.

I look forward to your response.

Lord Richard Lamont

Sophie entered his office and informed him that his wife and two sons were waiting in the boardroom.

Richard Lamont was very proud of his family. His wife, Elizabeth, was a very beautiful woman, well educated, and came from very good stock, the Rothschilds. This family was one of the most powerful banking dynasties in England.

Elizabeth's father was Charles, a very gentle man who, as a naturalist, would rather work with butterflies than high finance, however he was a very good banker. Elizabeth's mother, Rozsika, was a stunningly beautiful woman who adored her husband and their four children.

Richard entered the boardroom and kissed his wife and greeted his two sons, identical twins Charles and Harold.

Nobody could tell them apart, particularly when they were dressed in identical outfits, which they usually were. Even their parents had trouble; Richard would quite often play a game where he had to pick who was who. If he was correct, the boys had to wash his Rolls Royce but if he was wrong, they each received a pound. Even with the odds stacked at 50/50 he was out of pocket.

The family was going on a two-week vacation to their castle, "Torwood" in Scotland near Edinburgh; It had been in the Lamont family for over three hundred years and family tradition dictated the eldest son inherited the estate.

"Torwood" was positioned on a three hundred acre estate, which was abundant with deer; it also had a trout stream meandering through it.

The castle had twenty bedrooms, ten bathrooms and a number of living areas, including a formal lounge room, a library, and a billiard room. The billiard room was used to display the estate's trophies.

The two brothers had always loved holidaying at Torwood; they grew up running around the magnificent gardens and horse riding through the forests. Things had changed now they were seventeen; much of their time was spent shooting deer as well as pheasant, partridge and grouse. Both Charles and Harold enjoyed watching their dogs retrieving as much as the actual hunting. The dogs consisted of three Golden Retrievers and three Curly Coated Retrievers. These dogs were cared for in their absence by the estate's resident gamekeeper, Jack Black.

On the morning of their first day of holidays, the family gathered in the second dining room for breakfast.

'Well, lads, are you looking forward to a good day's hunt?'

'Sure are,' answered Charles.

'I went over to Jack's cottage and saw the dogs early this morning They all look fit and well, ready to go,' said Harold.

'How did you identify them, Harry?'

'Dog tags, father; the three Goldens are Lucy, Molly, and Katie.'

'The Curleys are Jock, Jimmie, and Hamish.'

'Well, maybe that's what I need for you two it would save me money!'

'Unfair Father.'

When they stopped laughing they checked their guns.

Richard had invested in the latest and best technology for all of them, the Boss

& Co "Over and Under" shotgun, which was regarded as the best money could buy.

Richard had taught both his sons to treat a gun with respect and not to skylark with a loaded gun. He also had them properly trained in marksmanship by the pre-eminent marksman in Scotland, John McKenzie. Both Charles and Harold were now regarded as crack shots. Jack had their horses ready at the front of the castle.

The hunting group was due to ride to the edge of the estate, where Jack had spotted a magnificent stag with his harem of does only the day before.

Richard mounted his steed as did all the others and Jack led the way to where the deer was last seen.

'My Lord, if you don't mind me asking, have you decided who will take the first shot?' asked Jack.

'No, not at all Jack. It will be Charles, he is the elder of the two boys.'

'If Charles does not take him down, Harry can try and I will have the last shot in the unlikely event they both miss.'

Harry felt a pang of jealousy, 'Fifteen minutes older than me and he gets all the privileges including the estate.'

Harry loved his twin brother, but sometimes it was hard to bear, knowing that

Charles would be Lord Lamont one day with all the wealth and influence that title brings whereas he as the youngest would inherit an estate in Cornwall, and ten thousand pounds a year.

'May I suggest we dismount and continue on foot so we can get close enough for the shot,' Jack whispered to the hunters.

The party dismounted and gave the reins to Jack's son, Billie to tether. They crept through the Golden Castle Ash and Hermitage Douglas Pines which grew on the estate until they came to a clearing.

'There, do you see him on top that ridge?'

Richard, and the two boys looked up and saw a magnificent stag with huge antlers and a coat that shone in the sun. He was surveying his domain but did not sense the hunters.

Jack led the group closer down wind so the stag would not detect their scent.

'All right Charles, here is your chance to put his head in the trophy room', whispered his father.'

Charles lay on the soft, fern covered ground and took aim.

He squeezed the trigger, missed, immediately fired again, but missed again.

Nobody realized it had been a deliberate act.

By the time Harry could have his shot, the stag sprinted off, scared by the sound of the gunshots.

Richard looked at Charles.

'I can't believe you missed. Never mind, we all have our bad days I suppose'.

Jack sent Billie back to get the dogs and arranged to meet them all at the wetlands area for some bird shooting. Riding to the wetlands, Harry was musing over what had just happened. He had seen Charles shoot many times; he did not believe it was an accidental miss.

'Gentleman, I suggest we do some shooting in the wetlands and bag us some water-fowl,' Said Lord Lamont.

Charles and Harold both shot six fowls each, the dogs performed superbly.

The Lamonts retired back to Torwood and gave Jack the birds to prepare for eating. Lord Lamont and the twins retired to their respective suites to bathe and dress for dinner.

Charles reclined in his bath thinking about the day: why had he refused to shoot the stag? He had no problem shooting deer in the past, nor waterfowl, nor any other game bird for that matter. He probably would never know. What he knew though was that he was pleased he didn't shoot the beast.

He was drying himself and once again admired the only feature which distinguished him from his brother, Harold: it was a port wine birthmark on his left buttock, which he called his "map of Tasmania". It was roughly the same shape as the island to the south of the Australian mainland. He had visited Australia two years earlier with his parents and brother when Lord Lamont was looking at investing in an Australian newspaper.

As soon as he was dressed and refreshed he met Harold on the grand staircase; they descended together and entered the dining room where their mother and father were already seated.

'Well, boys, I hear you had a mixed day of fortune? Did you enjoy it nonetheless?'

'Well, Mother, I think if I had been allowed the first shot, that stag would be in the barn now waiting for the taxidermist to weave his magic' sneered Harold.

Charles glanced at his twin brother. He could understand Harold's anger, but knew he would get over it by breakfast next morning.

The family enjoyed their holiday together but like all holidays, it came to a close too soon. The brothers were due back for their final term at Eton after which Charles would attend Oxford University.

Harold would attend the Royal Agricultural College in the Cotswolds.

Both had no choice about which course they were to be enrolled in: their father decided for them.

Charles would undertake a degree in English Language and Literature; Harold would undertake Agriculture.

Both did extremely well in their final year at Eton; Charles just pipped Harold for dux of the school.

It was August 1913; they had two months off before they started at Oxford and R.A.C.

Richard and Elizabeth decided they would take the twins to Europe beginning in Paris. They owned a seventeenth century three storey villa close to the Champs Elysees. Their intention was to stay in Paris for the first three weeks, then tour France and Italy for a further four weeks. This would give the twins a week back in London to prepare for the start of their first term at University.

Charles and Harold were usually inseparable but during the three weeks in Paris there were a few days where they saw each other only for breakfast and dinner.

Charles used this time alone to visit the Louvre and various other museums including museum d'orsay.

Harry, on the other hand, spent most of his time around the Montmartre red light district learning about things of which he was still ignorant about. After Paris, they drove to Ypres in Belgium and Lille in northern France as Elizabeth was keen to purchase some lace and fine cotton cloth for her dressmaker to tailor her some new outfits. The twins, although not particularly interested in the fine cloth, were impressed with the medieval architecture of both cities, particularly the Cloth Hall in Ypres.

Down the west coast of France they then travelled to reach Bordeaux on their fourth day of touring.

Richard felt it was important that the twins were introduced to the good things in life including premium wine and fine food. The Lamonts ate in some excellent restaurants and drank some superb wines in Bordeaux before travelling to the Perigord where they tried foie gras and ate duck until they could not look at another duck, let alone shoot one.

Richard's Rolls Royce performed beautifully although some of the country roads were a little precarious. They drove through Provence stopping at Arles and then hit the Côte d'Azur at Nice.

The next port of call was Cannes where they stayed for a few nights and then followed the coast to Italy, their destination Venice.

Charles and Harold really enjoyed Venice; the Gondola through the canals was followed by a visit to St Marks Square and the Doges Palace. The family ate in various Venetian restaurants of high renown.

Before they knew, it was time to go home on a magnificent small ship belonging to one of Richard's business associates. The Rolls got loaded in the hold.

Once they arrived back in England there was a week before the twins were to begin their first year at University. This would be their first time apart. Neither was sure how he would cope.

University Days

Chapter 7

Lord Lamont arranged for both boys to be met at their respective train stations by a senior member of the University staff. Harry had a short train trip to Cirencester in Gloucestershire where he was met by the Dean of the School Professor Henry Lassiter, and was driven to the University campus where he would begin his Bachelor of Science-Agriculture.

This was the first time he had spent away from his family and in particular, his twin brother. It felt like a part of him was missing. They had often commented on the occasions where they both knew what the other twin was thinking or even feeling.

The Dean showed him to his room, which although small, had a good atmosphere. There was a single bed with a polished timber bed-head, a timber wardrobe and a desk and chair with matching bookcases. It overlooked a beautiful garden and fields with cattle and sheep beyond.

He felt quite at home, although it lacked the luxury of his parent's Pall Mall townhouse.

Dean Lassiter informed him dinner would be at six pm.

Oxford

Charles took the train to Oxford having been waved off by his parents The trip was uneventful and he sat with two of his Eton schoolmates, Tim Harris, and John Thompson who were also starting at Oxford albeit in different courses.

He was met on the station platform by the captain of the Rugby team; Oxford did not send senior university staff to meet new students regardless of who their father was.

George Simmonds was very friendly and showed Charles around the campus and then showed him his room. It was a very similar layout to Harry's but a little larger, although the view was of a grassed square with a sandstone pathway around the perimeter certainly not cows and sheep!

Charles's reputation as an excellent rugby player had reached the Oxford coach. Apparently, he was very quick and agile with superior tackling skills. Harry played on the opposite flank and wore the number six when they both played

27

for the Eton firsts.

George was keen to know if Charles was interested in trying out for the Oxford team and was not disappointed.

Harry was also approached by the rugby coach and asked if he would consider playing for the RAC team, he too was enthusiastic. Thus the scene was set for a competitive grudge match between the two brothers when the two universities clashed.

Charles had settled into University life and was enjoying the English course he had undertaken albeit at his father's insistence. He was sitting in the grounds on a beautiful summer's day, when a very attractive girl sat down beside him and commented on the weather.

'It will be difficult to go back to lectures when it is so nice sitting in the sun, don't you think?'

'Yes, I know what you mean'.

'You're Charles Lamont aren't you?'

'That's right, how did you know?'

'My father knows your father quite well; in fact I have been to your Scottish Castle when I was a little girl and played in the grounds with you and your twin brother. Is your brother attending Oxford too?'

'No, he's at the Royal Agricultural College; he is going to be a farmer. So, what is your name?'

'Oh, I apologise, I should have introduced myself, Emily – Emily Scott.'

'Scott? are you the daughter of Sir Edward Scott of the woollen mills fame?'

'I am.'

'Well, I'm afraid I don't remember you coming to Torwood, but it would be a different matter if you had come more recently.'

'Why do you say that?'

'If you don't mind me being so bold, you are a beautiful girl! I would have remembered you'.

'Charles, you embarrass me.'

Such was their first meeting at university and the start of what was to follow.

Royal Agricultural College

Harry was enjoying his lectures, particularly all the outdoors practical work. He had made some good friends; they would go into the village on a Saturday night and have a few pints at "The Fleece Hotel". He also made the rugby team and tennis teams, so life was pretty full for Harry.

Toward the middle of Harry and Charles's first year something significant happened.

Britain declared war on Germany after Germany had refused to withdraw from Belgium which it invaded on August 3rd 1914.

Britain declared war on the next day August 4th 1914.

Times

AUGUST 5, 1914   1 D.

BRITAIN AT WAR

Lord Lamont approved this simple front page

Although, the consensus of opinion was that the war would be over by Christmas, both brothers agreed in secret if the war was still going in 1917, they would both enlist.

At the end of each semester, they would return home and each time the brothers were delighted to see each other after such a long absence. Once a year, at the long break, they would go to Torwood and hone their shooting skills. On the shorter breaks they would go back to London.

On one Torwood visit, their father produced two Enfield 303s.

'You'd better learn to shoot these boys; I don't think this cursed war will end any time soon.'

'What are you saying, do you expect us to enlist?'

'I know you both better than you may think.'

Charles looked at Harry, and gave him a wink.

John McKenzie, who taught them how to shoot their shotguns, gave the twins tutelage.

At the end of the summer break, the twins were regarded as expert riflemen by both McKenzie and their father.

'If they are required to serve their country, they'd better be well prepared,' thought Lord Lamont.

The event the brothers had keenly anticipated had arrived – the match between Oxford and RAC. It was Oxford's turn to host the match. Harry and the RAC team travelled by train to the hallowed grounds of the Oxford rugby ground.

The team was anticipating a very tough game: RAC had not beaten Oxford for a decade.

At 2.00 pm both teams ran on to the field and at 2.15 the game began. At half time, the score was Oxford 5 – RAC 0.

The RAC team was determined to win this game; two tries, both converted, gave Oxford a score of 19 to RAC 3.

Twenty minutes before full time, Harry Lamont ran from the halfway mark for a try under the posts. The normal kicker had gone off the field injured. Harry converted the try.

The scores were now, Oxford 19 – RAC 10.

Five minutes later, the RAC Number 8 scored another try from a scrum pack bringing the scores to 19 – 17. Harry converted the try. The two teams were now 19 – 19.

It looked like it was going to be a draw; with only two minutes to go, Harry received the ball from his captain and told to kick a field goal. Harry was thirty metres out. He took his shot, which sailed between the posts. Oxford 19 – RAC 21.

There was much merriment on the return trip; the local pub was overflowing with well-wishers.

This would not be the first time Harry had beaten his brother. The rivalry was about to become more intense.

Fortune Favours the Brave

Chapter 8

England 1915

Both Charles and Harold had completed their first two years of University and were now ready to complete their final year. The brothers had made a commitment to their father; they would complete their degrees, before taking up arms for their country. It had been difficult. The news filtering back from the battlefront was disconcerting, to say the least. Their father had been instrumental in getting Winston Churchill demoted after the debacle at Gallipoli in 1915.

Ashmead Bartlett was the senior war correspondent for Lord Lamont's premier newspaper, "The Times". He had been stationed on the Gallipoli Peninsula since the landing in April 1915. He was appalled at the way the British High Command had conducted the campaign and, appalled at Sir Ian Hamilton who was Commander in Chief of the Mediterranean Expeditionary Force.

Hamilton spent six fruitless months unimaginatively bombarding the Turks at Gallipoli, making little progress, but incurring severe casualties.

He nevertheless remained optimistic with regard to the overall success of the plan, to the point of opposing Cabinet moves in London to initiate an evacuation.

Gallipoli Turkey September 1915

Keith Murdoch was a tall lanky Australian war correspondent. He arrived on the Gallipoli Peninsula on the 2nd of September 1915, and soon established a relationship with the senior British correspondent, Ellis Ashmead-Bartlett. Murdoch and Ashmead-Bartlett would sit in their dugout, drinking and talking about the Gallipoli campaign.

Murdoch was infatuated with the British newspaperman and drank in every word he said. Ashmead-Bartlett was extremely critical of General Hamilton, and in fact was determined to try to get rid of him, any way he could. He persuaded Murdoch, to help him in his quest.

'Keith, I believe you will be returning to London shortly. Would you be prepared to carry a very important letter back to Mr Asquith for me? It may just help end this bloody campaign.'

31

'Ellis, you know I would do anything to end this stupid bloody fracas. Can you show me the letter?'

'Certainly.'

Keith read the letter, impressed with the level of detail and the overall sentiments it portrayed.

'So, I take it that you want me to take this letter to Asquith because if you went through the normal channels it would be heavily censored, or confiscated by the British authorities?'

'Dead right, Keith; I also want to make sure a copy goes to David Lloyd George. I figure he will be our next Prime Minister in the very near future.'

Overhearing their conversation, was Henry Nevinson, a British correspondent from a rival newspaper.

He reported what he had overheard to the British command, who asked the French authorities to intercept Murdoch, who was travelling to London via France. The French accosted Murdoch, and confiscated the letter when he reached Marseilles.

Keith had an extremely good memory: he replicated the letter, with a very high degree of accuracy.

He contacted Mr Asquith's office once he arrived in London and requested a meeting. The meeting was granted; Mr Asquith, very much aware that Murdoch had just returned from Gallipoli was keen to hear a first hand account.

Keith Murdoch was sitting in the Prime Minister's anteroom at number 10 Downing Street, waiting to meet with the Prime Minister, when Asquith's secretary asked him to follow her into the P.M.'s office. Murdoch was surprised at the size of the office, which really wasn't that big, certainly not what he expected for the most powerful man on the globe.

The Prime Minister was reading a report of some sort, but put it down when Keith entered.

'Hello Mr Murdoch. Please take a seat.'

'Thank you, Sir.'

'Well, I believe you have just returned from Gallipoli. That's a long way from Australia.'

'Yes, sir, a bloody long way!"

Asquith gave a chuckle: only Australians would dare to swear in front of the British Prime Minister in the first minute of conversation.

'What are your impressions on how things are going over there in

Turkey?'

'Sir, I believe a letter written by Ellis Ashmead-Barlett, whom I believe you know, will sum up the situation very well. May I ask you to read it? Then hopefully, I can answer any questions.'

The Prime Minister took the letter, and started to read it. Every now and then, he would look over his reading spectacles at Murdoch, with a very concerned look.

September 8th 1915

Dear Mr Asquith

I hope you will excuse the liberty I am taking in writing to you but I have the chance of sending this letter through by hand and I consider it absolutely necessary that you should know the true state of affairs out here. Our last great effort to achieve some definite success against the Turks was the most ghastly and costly fiasco in our history since the Battle of Bannockburn.

Personally I never thought the scheme decided on by Headquarters ever had the slightest chance of succeeding and all efforts now to make out that it only just failed owing to the failure of the 9th Corps to seize the Anafarta Hills bear no relation to the real truth. The operations did for a time make headway in absolutely impossible country more than any general had a right to expect owing to the superlative gallantry of the Colonial Troops and the self-sacrificing manner in which they threw away their lives against positions which should never have been attacked.

The main idea was to cut off the southern portion of the Turkish Army by getting astride of the Peninsula from Suvla Bay. Therefore the whole weight of the attack should have been concentrated on this objective, instead of which, the main attack with the best troops was delivered against the side of the Turkish position which is a series of impossible mountains and valleys covered with dense scrub.

The Staff seem to have carefully searched for the most difficult points and then threw away thousands of lives in trying to take them by frontal attacks. A few Ghurkhas obtained a lodgement on Chunuk Bair but were immediately driven off by the Turkish counter attacks and the main objective Koja Chemen Tepe was never approached. The 9th Corps miserably mishandled having failed to take the Anafarta Hills and is now accused of being solely alone responsible for the ultimate failure of the operations.

The failure of the 9th Corps was due not so much to the employment of new and untried troops as to bad staff work. The generals had but a vague idea of the nature of the ground in their front and no adequate steps were taken to keep the troops supplied with water. In consequence, many of these unfortunate volunteers went three days in very hot weather on one bottle of water and were yet expected to advance carrying heavy loads and to storm strong positions.

The Turks having been given ample time to bring up strong reinforcements to Anafarta, where they entrenched themselves up to their necks, were again assaulted in a direct frontal attack on August 21st. The movement never had the slightest chance of succeeding and led to another bloody fiasco in which the unfortunate 29th Division who were brought up especially from Helles, and the 2nd Mounted Division (Yeomanry) were the chief sufferers. As the result of all this fighting our casualties since August 6th now total nearly fifty thousand killed wounded and missing.

The army is in fact in a deplorable condition. Its morale as a fighting force has suffered greatly and the officers and men are thoroughly dispirited. The muddles and mismanagement beat anything that has ever occurred in our military history.

The fundamental evil at the present moment is the absolute lack of confidence among all ranks in the Headquarters staff. The confidence of the army will never be restored until a really strong man is placed at its head. It would amaze you to hear the talk that goes on amongst the Junior Commanders of Divisions and Brigades. Except for the fact that the traditions of discipline still hold the force together, you would imagine that the units were in an open state of mutiny against Headquarters.

The Commander-in-Chief and his Staff are openly spoken of, and in fact only mentioned at all with derision. One hates to write of such things but in the interests of the country at the present crisis I feel they ought to be made known to you. The lack of a real Chief at the head of the army destroys its discipline and efficiency all through and gives full rein to the jealousies and recriminations which prevail amongst the Divisional Leader.

At the present time the army is incapable of a further offensive. The splendid Colonial Corps has been almost wiped out. Once again the 29th Division has suffered enormous losses and the new formations have lost their bravest and best officers and men. Neither do I think even with enormous reinforcements that any fresh offensive from our present positions has the smallest chance of success.

Our only real justification for throwing away fresh lives and fresh treasure in this unfortunate enterprise is the prospect of the certain cooperation of Bulgaria. With her assistance we should undoubtedly pull through. But as I know nothing of the attitude of Bulgaria or Greece or Italy I am only writing to give you a true picture of the state of the army and the problems with which we are faced in the future if we are left to fight the Turks alone.

Already the weather shows signs of breaking and by the end of this month we cannot rely on any continuous spell of calm for the landing of large bodies of troops at some other point on the coast. In fact the season will soon be too late for a fresh offensive if another is contemplated. We have therefore to prepare against the coming of the winter or to withdraw the army altogether. I am assuming it is considered desirable to avoid the latter contingency at all costs for political reasons owing to the confession of final failure it would entail and the moral effect it might have in India and Egypt.

I am convinced the troops could be withdrawn under cover of the warships without much loss far less in fact then we suffer in any ordinary attack. I assume also that the future of the campaign out here must be largely dependant on the measure of success that attends our fresh offensive, in conjunction with the French, in the West.

It is no use pretending that our prospects for the winter are bright. The Navy seems to think it will be able to keep the army supplied in spells of calm weather provided a sufficient reserve of food, munitions and ammunition is concentrated while the weather holds at the various beaches. The outlook for the unfortunate troops is deplorable.

We do not hold a single commanding position on the Peninsula and at all three points Helles, Anzac and Suvla Bay we are everywhere commanded by the enemy's guns. This means that throughout the winter all the beaches and lines of communication to the front trenches will be under constant shellfire. Suvla Bay is especially exposed. The Turks are firing a fair amount of ammunition but it is obvious they are feeling the shortage or else are carefully husbanding their supply otherwise they could shell us off the Peninsula at some points altogether.

But it must be remembered that as soon as they are absolutely certain our offensive has shot its bolt, and that we are settling down in our positions for the winter, they will be free to concentrate their artillery at certain points and also to bring up big guns from the forts and therefore we must expect a far more severe artillery fire on the beaches during the winter months than we are exposed to at present.

A great many of the trenches which we hold at present will have to be abandoned altogether during the winter as they will be underwater, and preparing a series of defensive works which will ensure us against sudden surprise attacks. We could thus hold our positions with fewer men and rest some of the divisions from time to time in the neighbouring islands.

We ought to be able to hold Helles without much trouble but, even if we commence our preparations in time, we shall be faced with enormous difficulties at Anzac and Suvla Bay. Our troops will have to face the greatest hardships from cold, wet trenches and constant artillery fire. I believe that at the present time the sick rate for the army is roughly 1000 per day.

During the winter it is bound to rise to an even higher figure. I know one general, whose judgement is usually sound, who considers we shall lose during the winter in sickness alone the equivalent of the present strength of the army. This may be an exaggeration but in any case our loss is bound to be very heavy. The whole army dreads beyond all else the prospect of wintering on this dreary and inhospitable coast. Amongst other troubles the autumn rains will once more bring to view hundred of our dead who now lie under a light covering of soil.

But I suppose we must stay here as long as there is the smallest prospect of the Balkan alliance being revived and throwing in its lot with us even if they do not make a move until next

Spring. I have laid before you some of the difficulties with which we are faced in order that they may be boldly met before it is too late.

No one seems to know out here what we are going to do in the future and I am so afraid we shall drag on in a state of uncertainty until the season is too far advanced for us to make proper preparations to face the coming winter in a certain measure of comfort and security. At the present time some of our positions gained by the Colonial Corps high up on the spurs of the hills on which the Turks are perched cannot be considered secure.

A sudden counter attack vigorously delivered would jeopardise the safety of our line and might lead to a serious disaster. There will have to be a general reshuffling of the whole line and some of our advanced posts will have to be abandoned during the winter months.

I have only dealt with our own troubles and difficulties. The enemy of course has his. But to maintain as I saw stated in an official report that his losses in the recent fighting were far heavier than ours is a childish falsehood which deceives no one out here. He was acting almost the whole time on the defensive and probably lost about one third of our grand total.

You may think I am too pessimistic but my views are shared by the large majority of the army. The confidence of the troops can only be restored by an immediate change in the supreme command. Even if sufficient drafts are sent out to make good our losses we shall never succeed operating from our present positions. A fresh landing on a grand scale north of Buliar would probably ensure success but the season is late and I suppose the troops are not available.

If we are to stay here for the winter let orders be given for the army to start its preparations without delay. If possible have the Colonial troops taken off the Peninsula altogether because they are miserably depressed since the last failure and with their active minds, and positions they occupy in civil life, a dreary winter in the trenches will have a deplorable effect on what is left of this once magnificent body of men, the finest any Empire has ever produced. If we are obliged to keep this army locked up in Gallipoli this winter large reserves will be necessary to make good its losses in sickness.

The cost of this campaign in the east must be out of all proportion to the results we are likely to obtain now, in time to have a decisive effect on the general theatre of war. Our great asset against the Germans was always considered to be our superior financial strength. In Gallipoli we are dissipating a large portion of our fortune and have not yet gained a single acre of ground of any strategical value. Unless we can pull through with the aid of the Balkan League in the near future this futile expenditure may ruin our prospects of bringing the war to a successful conclusion by gradually wearing down Germany's colossal military power.

I have taken the liberty of writing very fully because I have no means of knowing how far the real truth of the situation is known in England and how much the Military Authorities disclose. I thought therefore that perhaps the opinions of an independent observer might be of value to you at the present juncture. I am of course breaking the censorship regulations by sending this letter through but I have not the slightest hesitation in doing so as I feel it is absolutely essential for you to know the truth. I have been requested over and over again by officers of all ranks to go home and personally disclose the truth but it is difficult for me to leave until the beginning of October.

Hoping you will therefore excuse the liberty I

```
have taken.

Believe me

Yours very truly


E. Ashmead-Bartlett


The Rt. Hon. H. H. Asquith

10 Downing Street
```

The Prime Minister arose from his desk, the same desk so many British Prime Ministers had used over many years. He started to pace the room, asking Murdoch questions about the campaign and how accurate was Ashmead Bartlett's account of the situation.

'Mr Prime Minister, I would not have delivered this letter, if I did not agree with its content and its conclusions.'

Mr Asquith called his deputy, David Lloyd George, to join them.

'David, I have just read a letter written by Ashmead-Bartlett, "The Times" correspondent, stationed at Gallipoli; he paints a very bleak picture indeed.'

'To be perfectly honest, Prime Minister, I am not surprised. I have, as you know, been very sceptical about the whole operation for some time.'

'Yes, I know you have, David; God, do I know that.

Read the letter and give me your opinion.'

'When would you like me to get back to you?'

'In about fifteen minutes. I am going for a walk in the gardens with young Murdoch, and when we return, we can discuss what we should do about this bloody campaign.'

'Use my office, but not my desk. You are not Prime Minister yet!'

David Lloyd-George sat down on the Chesterfield lounge, and read the letter. He could see that this could be a very powerful tool, to change things at Gallipoli, in particular, getting rid of General Hamilton whom he never liked or agreed with.

The Prime Minister and the young Australian returned from their stroll around the rose gardens and found Lloyd George sitting on the couch with a smirk on his face.

'So, I take it from the look on your face that this letter meets with your approval?'

'Sir, you know my views on this campaign. I believe they have been vindicated by an independent source, as in Ashmead-Bartlett.'

'Mr Murdoch, thank you for bringing the letter and sharing your candid views. Mr Lloyd George and I now need to have a private discussion.'

Murdoch left the Prime Minister's office, knowing he had achieved his objective.

Hamilton was recalled to London on 16 October 1915, effectively ending his military career. He was replaced by General Sir Charles Monro, who echoed Hamilton's belated recognition of the futility of the campaign and immediately recommended evacuation.

The Guardian

Monday 20 December 1915

Allies retreat from Gallipoli disaster

In a laconic, single-sentence communiqué, the War Office in London this afternoon revealed that the ill-fated Gallipoli expedition had been abandoned after ten months of bad luck, muddle, indecisiveness – and outstanding heroism by British, Australian and New Zealand troops.

The final act of evacuating some 90,000 men, with 4,500 animals, 1,700 vehicles and 200 guns was carried out with great skill and ingenuity, under the very noses of powerful Turkish forces. Not a single life was lost. Some 30,000 beds had been prepared for the wounded in Mediterranean hospitals, but these were not needed.

The evacuation was carried out by night. During the day, however, ships riding at anchor under Turkish observation could be seen disembarking troops and unloading guns and stores. The trick was that more men and materials were evacuated during the night than had been ostentatiously brought ashore during the day.

In the last stages, at Anzac Bay, when it seemed the Turks could not fail to hear what was going on, a destroyer trained its searchlight on the enemy's trenches. While the Turks concentrated their fire on the destroyer, the troops were lifted off the beaches.

As the last men were leaving, having set thousands of booby traps, a huge landmine in no-man's-land was exploded. The Turks, thinking the Australians were attacking, began a furious barrage of fire that lasted forty minutes.

It was a better end than might have been expected to a sorry story that began when the Russians appealed to Britain and France for munitions. Ministers and military men in London agreed to let the Royal Navy try to get to Russia's Black Sea ports by forcing the passage of the Dardanelles; they also decided a back-up force of land troops would be needed.

Kitchener said he could not spare the men from the Western Front. Three weeks later, he changed his mind and said he could send a division to join Royal Marines and troops from Egypt.

But by the time the combined land and sea operation was mounted at the end of April, a full two months after the navy had first bombarded the Dardanelles forts, all advantages of surprise had been lost and the Turks had heavily reinforced their positions.

When Bulgaria came into the war, a clear route was opened for Germany to keep Turkey supplied.

Britain decided to pull out and use the men, as today's announcement says, in "another sphere of operations".

The Commons has been told the casualties were 25,000 dead, 76,000 wounded, 13,000 missing and 96,000 sick admitted to hospital.

The slaughter had begun in Turkey; it would end in France. How many young men would die by the time the "War to end all Wars" was over?

They're in the Army Now

Chapter 9

Charles completed his first class degree in English in the December of 1916. He was looking forward to his new career, not working for one of his father's newspapers, but enlisting as a junior officer, in The Duke of Wellington's Regiment. He looked forward to going to France and having a damn good go at the bloody Germans.

He had been an Officer Cadet in the Oxford Officer Training Corp, for the three years, while he attended University. Each Tuesday afternoon, they would be trained in marksmanship, of which he was the best in the Corps, as well as battle tactics, and of course, marching.

He had spoken to Harry, who also had completed his degree in Agriculture; he was equally keen to join the regiment.

Harry, too, had been a member of the Officer Training Corps at the Royal Agricultural College and had excelled.

Charles and Harry had both made an agreement with their father, Lord Lamont. They would not only finish their degrees, they would also consult with their father, prior to enlisting.

An appointment was made with their father's secretary, for a meeting at his Fleet Street office, on Friday the 5th of January 1917. The plan was to seek his approval, then join him at his club for lunch. "The Brooks Club" in St James was regarded as the club for the aristocracy.

Both twins waited in the waiting room for their father, who had been on the telephone to David Lloyd George, the Secretary of State for War, a position that was first established in 1794.

Lord Lamont was on very good terms with Lloyd George and they often spoke about the war and the implications for Britain.

'David, I am calling you to ask a favour… well, actually, two favours.'

'Well I will try to grant them, Richard, if it is within my jurisdiction. What are they?'

'My two sons have just completed their degrees at Oxford and The Royal Agricultural College.'

44

'Did they? Well done. That's what the Empire needs, qualified young men to rebuild the nation when this bloody war is over.'

'Both of them are about to turn nineteen and they are intent on enlisting and getting involved in this "bloody war" as you put it. They graduated from their respective Officer Training Corps with flying colours.'

'So what are the favours you would like me to grant, Richard?'

'Firstly, I would like them to be in the same regiment, so that they can look out for each other. The regiment both they and I would prefer is "The Duke of Wellington's Regiment".'

'Bloody good choice, I am sure I will have no problem in getting them a place. And the other favour?'

'I would like both of them to enter the regiment as Second Lieutenants.'

'I see. Look, Richard, that would be unusual but having said that, it has happened on occasion in the past. Let me see what I can do.'

The telephone call was completed with an agreement that David Lloyd George would contact Lord Lamont, with an answer in the next few days.

Lord Lamont left his office to welcome his two sons; he still could not identify who was who, so God help the Germans!

After the initial hand shakes, they all went into Lord Lamont's luxurious and spacious office.

Charles and Harold both sat down on one couch and their father sat opposite them. His secretary entered, asking if they would all like a cup of tea; they all declined.

Charles started the conversation.

'Father, as you are aware, Harold and I are very keen to fight for our country. As agreed with you and Mother, we have completed our tertiary education. The time has come to enlist, with your blessing of course.'

'You are aware that it is not going to be a picnic over there. You have read the papers, mine I hope: things are not going all that well. The "Battle of the Somme" was a disaster and smaller battles at Fromelles, and alike have reduced our fighting forces dramatically. When I say "reduced our fighting forces dramatically" I mean many thousands of our officers and men have been slaughtered and those that were wounded have lost limbs or sight and hearing or have lost their minds. If you both want to face hell on earth, who am I to stop you?'

'We are going into this with our eyes open, Father, but we believe we

45

are obligated to do our duty.' explained Harold.

'Well, if that is your position, so be it. You can understand that your Mother and I are very worried about you both and we both love you, so keep your bloody heads down for God's sake.'

That was the first time the brothers had ever heard their father proclaim his love for them.

The next day David Lloyd George telephoned Richard to give the good news but was it good news?

'Hello Richard, David speaking. I have been successful in getting both your sons into "The Duke of Wellington's Regiment". Additionally, they will both enter as Second Lieutenants.'

'Thank you, David, I really do appreciate what you have done. I can assure you they will not let down you or their country.'

'Well, Richard, some good press would not go astray at the moment. I believe we will have a change at the top sooner than later. Asquith is not the person we need to help us win this bloody horrible war.'

'I agree, David, you know you have my full backing.'

Richard asked for both his sons to meet him at his club in London for lunch and to discuss their future military careers. This meeting took place two days after Richard's telephone call from David Lloyd Jones.

Charles and Harold arrived at the Brooks Club in St James at noon, where they waited in the foyer for their father, who was running late.

Lord Lamont arrived at twenty minutes past twelve and welcomed both his boys with a firm handshake. The Lamont party went into the Members' Dining Room and were allocated a table in a secluded corner; Richard did not want any other members to overhear their conversation.

'Well, lads, I have pleasure in informing you both that you have been accepted into the Officer Training School at Balliol, Oxford.'

'Wonderful news, Father.'

'When do we start?'

'The next course commences on February 5th and will conclude on June 30.

'The other good news is that when you both graduate, you will become junior officers in The Duke of Wellington's Regiment.'

'This is wonderful news, Father, I can hardly wait; I just hope the war is still going by the time we graduate.'

'Well Charles my son, the way it is going, this war has a while to run yet,' said Richard, hoping he was wrong.

A hearty roast beef and Yorkshire pudding was presented and washed down with an excellent French red wine.

Finally Richard bade his sons farewell and returned to his office on Fleet Street.

Charles and Harold decided to go down to the "Black Friar" pub in Queen Victoria Street and have a few pints where they could discuss their future as Army Officers and reflect on the war in general.

'Well Charles we are on our way.'

'We are, and although I am looking forward to the training, I wish it was not so long. I want to get over to France, Harry, and give it to the bloody Germans.'

'I know what you mean, Charlie. Me too.'

Before retuning to their Pall Mall home the brothers had consumed several pints.

They, like all the other recruits, had no real idea what life and death was like along the Western Front. They would find out soon enough.

We'll Make an Officer of You Yet

Chapter 10

The day came when Lord and Lady Lamont took their two sons to the Oxford campus to begin their officer training at Balliol College. This was the college where the British Prime Minister, Herbert Asquith, completed his education.

An Officer, Captain Riley, showed them their dormitory which they would share with thirty-eight other officer cadets. No private rooms here, but the twins were allocated bunks side by side, so they didn't feel totally isolated.

'Get your bag unpacked, use the locker next to your bunk. Inspections will take place when you least expect them, so make sure your locker is always neat and tidy and your bed is made to army standards. You are permitted to walk the grounds and familiarise yourself with the terrain. Mess call is at 6pm. Make sure you are in the mess hall by that time, or you are excluded and you do not eat. Is that clear?' Captain Riley spoke in a very stern tone.

'Yes, sir,' they both replied.

The twins did as they were instructed. Then as the captain suggested, they decided to "familiarise themselves with the terrain."

As they were walking along the pathway to the sports oval, Charles, commented.

'I think we're in for a pretty tough time here, Harry, but I suppose we need toughening up before we go over there to fight.'

'Yeah, I agree with you Charlie, but it is only for a few months and then the real fight begins.'

Charles looked as his watch: it was 4.45pm, time to return to the dorm and dress for dinner. Both headed back at a lively pace arriving at the Mess Hall at 5.55pm.

The adjutant was Brigadier General Henry Morphet, a retired career soldier who came out of retirement to ensure Britain had an adequate supply of highly trained officers to lead their men into battle.

He addressed the cadets.

'Gentlemen, it is my task to ensure that you all graduate from officer training, ready to lead your troops into battle and ensure that as many of them

48

as possible survive the experience. You will be trained in marksmanship, tactical studies, weapons management, infantry tactics, tank tactics, artillery tactics and communications.

You will also be taught how to act in all circumstances, like an officer of the British Army, the finest fighting force in the world.

I now ask you to enjoy your meal and sleep well, your first day of training begins at 7am tomorrow morning.'

Lights were out at 9pm but, before they went to sleep, the brothers discussed the day and how both would throw themselves into training and top the class.

Charles and Harold made some good friends over the coming months and enjoyed most of their classes; they also revelled in the rugby matches played on the Oxford Oval.

Every Saturday night, a few of the cadets would go down to their favourite watering hole, "The Perch", and drink the odd pint and play a little billiards.

Charles, Harold, Percy Gates, Jack Pearson and Dave Roberts, all decided they should try for a change, a new pub on this particular Saturday night. Percy suggested "The Bear", a tiny old pub, with a collection of Oxford and Cambridge ties on the wall.

The Oxford boys walked into the lounge bar and found themselves a table close to the open fire.

'Harry, you and the rest of the lads order your drinks. I will mind the table,' said Charles.

A new law brought in by the Government, forbade the shouting of drinks. The person consuming the drink had to pay for it; the penalty was up to six months jail if you bought somebody else an alcholic drink. The idea behind it was to ensure the workers did not consume too much alcohol during the war years.

The group of cadets went up to the bar and ordered their pints and brought them back to the table. Charles purchased his and joined them.

The group was in a deep conversation about the war. The topic was whether they would make it to the front, when Charles noticed a group of girls sitting across the room. He recognised Emily Scott, and waved to her.

Charles excused himself from the table and approached Emily.

'Hi Em, how are you? Its been a long time since I saw you last.'

'I am just fine Charlie, how are things with you?'

'Good! Just one month to go before I graduate from officer's school.'

'That's wonderful. Then I suppose it's off to France and the great

49

adventure?'

'I'm not so sure I would call it 'an adventure', but yes, we'll be going to the western front.'

'Are you worried?'

'I know things are rather grim over there from what you read in the papers.'

'My cousin was killed in France. We are all very sad.'

'I'm sorry to hear that Em.

I would be lying if I didn't admit to being a bit worried about going over.'

'Changing the subject, are you having a graduation ceremony?'

'We certainly are. Would you like to be my partner, Em?'

'I would love to Charlie.' Her face lit up and her blue eyes were sparkling.

'It's being held on the July 7th. How about I get in touch in a week or so?'

'Splendid! It was so nice to see you again, Charlie.'

'You too, Em. It won't be so long before the next time either.'

Emily did not realise that this chance meeting would change her entire life.

An Officer and a Gentleman

Chapter 11

Charles and Harold were meeting their parents, Lord and Lady Lamont, at Oxford, six days before they graduated; it was Sunday the June 24th 1917. Richard Lamont had chosen the best French restaurant in Oxford for lunch; "Le Manoir aux Quatre Saisons".

He and Elizabeth, knew this would probably be the last time the boys would be eating in such an establishment for some time.

Richard chose his favourite wine, a bottle of "Baron Philippe de Rothschild Mouton".

'You look so smart in your uniforms'. Elizabeth smiled proudly at her twin sons.

'Well, if you think they look smart now, just wait until their graduation when they will be wearing the uniform of "The Duke of Wellington's Regiment" with a Second Lieutenant's star.' boasted Richard.

'Father, I think you may be a little over confident. Cadets don't normally graduate as Second Lieutenant.'

'We'll see.'

The last week at Balliol College was merely to finalise things, packing bags and polishing brass.

The latest news from the front was about the battle of Arras, and although it was seen as a success by the British press, the casualty count was more than 87,000 British troops.

All the young cadets were keen to get over to France and Belgium where they were itching to give the Germans a good flogging. They were also nervous about what lay ahead.

They then began talking about the graduation ball to lighten things up. The discussion centred on invited partners.

The parents of most of the cadets were also going to be present, all but the parents of David Roberts, who had only just been informed that his father, Lieutenant Colonel Geoffrey Roberts, had been declared 'Missing in Action'. David, knew that this really meant 'killed in action but no body found'!

His group of friends, including Charles and Harold tried to convince him to attend the graduation, in honour of his father, but he was too grief-stricken to consider attending.

Lord Lamont, published a story about the battle of Arras. As a favour to his good friend the Prime Minister David Lloyd George, he put a very positive slant on it without mentioning the casualty count.

THE ✠ TIMES

View in Feuchy, three miles east of Arras. Careful to avoid waste—though within limits disregarded by the Germans—our soldiers built a sentry-box out of German ammunition carriers.

April 10 1917

This is an account of the battle of Arras by one of Great Britain's finest Commanders.

The Times editorial staff believe our readers should have the opportunity of reading it.

Today began another titanic conflict which the world will hold its breath to watch because of all that hangs upon it. I have seen the fury of this beginning, and all the sky on fire with it, the most tragic and frightful sight men have ever seen. The bombardment which went before the infantry assault lasted for several days and reached a great height yesterday, when, coming from the south, I saw it for the first time.

Those of us who knew what would happen today - the beginning of another series of battles greater, perhaps, than the struggle of the Somme - found ourselves filled with a tense, restless emotion. Some smiled with a kind of tragic irony because it was Easter Sunday.

Easter Sunday, but no truce of God. The bombardment was now in full blast, a beautiful and devilish thing - and the beauty of it, rather than the evil of it, put a spell upon one's senses. All our batteries, too many to count, were firing, thousands of gun flashes were blinking from hollows and hiding-places, and all their shells were bursting over the German positions with long flames which rent the darkness and waved sword-blades of quivering light along the ridges.

The earth opened and great pools of crimson fire gushed out. Star shells burst magnificently, pouring down golden rain. Mines exploded east and west of Arras and in the wide sweep from Vimy Ridge to Blangy, and voluminous clouds, bright with a glory of infernal fire, rolled up to the sky.

The hour for attack was 5.30am. Officers were looking at their wrist watches as on a day in July last year. The earth lightened. A few minutes before 5.30 the guns almost ceased fire, so that there was a strange and solemn hush. We waited, and pulses beat faster than the second hands.

"They're away," said a voice by my side. The bombardment broke out again with new and enormous effects of fire and sound. The enemy was shelling Arras heavily, and black shrapnel and high explosive came over from his lines, but our gunfire was 20 times as great. Around the whole sweep of his lines green lights rose. They were signals of distress; his men were calling for help.

It was dawn now, but clouded and storm-swept. A few airmen came out with the wind tearing at their wings, but could see nothing in the mist and driving rain. I went down to the outer ramparts of

Arras. On the higher ground beyond, our men were fighting forward. I saw two waves of infantry advancing against the enemy's trenches, preceded by our barrage of field guns. "Grand fellows," said an officer lying next to me on the wet slope. "Oh, topping!"

Fifteen minutes afterwards groups of men came back. They were British wounded and German prisoners. They were bloody and exhausted, but claimed success. "We did fine," said one. "We were through the fourth lines before I was knocked out."

"Not many Germans in the first trenches," said another, "and no real trenches either after shelling. We had knocked their dug-outs out. Their dead were lying thick, and the living ones put their hands up."

The Battle of Arras is the greatest victory we have yet gained in this war, and a staggering blow to the enemy. He has lost already nearly 10,000 prisoners and more than half a hundred guns, and in dead and wounded his losses are great. He is in retreat south of the Vimy Ridge to defensive lines further back, and as he goes our guns are smashing him along the roads. It is a black day for the German armies and for the German women who do not know yet what it means to them.

The Belle of the Ball

Chapter 12

The 7th of July finally came. Both Charles and Harold looked resplendent in their officer's uniforms on which the Second Lieutenant stars were shining bright. Their ambition to be Dux of the academy was realised: Harold, was given that much-sought-after title, to the huge disappointment of Charles.

The Great Hall at Oxford looked magnificent; long tables with white table cloths and the best silver and crystal were laid out as though it was a Royal Banquet.

The Black Rod announced each regiment, while the officers and their partners were seated at the appropriate regimental table.

Finally, he announced "The Duke of Wellington's Regiment".

Harold, and his partner, Jane Kirby, was to lead the group in, as it was his honour as Dux of the Academy.

Unfortunately, at the last minute Jane could not attend. Harold arrived at her door in the chauffeur driven Rolls Royce his father had loaned to him, as a reward for being Dux.

Jane's mother informed him that Jane had fallen ill and would not be able to partner him.

Harold was devastated, and immediately decided not to attend the graduation, instead travelling alone to Soho to get drunk, and see what mischief he could get up to.

Another group of tables was reserved for the graduates' parents, who were seated first, so they could welcome the graduates to the Great Hall.

After the speeches from the Academy Commandant and the special guest speaker, David Lloyd George, the five-course meal was served including the beef, which was piped in by the Oxford University Pipe Band. It was a wonderful and stirring sight.

Charles was very concerned about Harold not turning up and hoped nothing untoward had befallen him. He knew his little brother did have a propensity to act impulsively and maybe this was one of those instances.

Emily looked stunningly beautiful in a long black ball gown with just the right amount of cleavage showing, certainly enough to draw the attention of the other young officers at the table.

The plan had been for a select group of friends to return to the Pall Mall townhouse for a post-graduation party. Charles' parents were due to leave on the midnight train to Scotland, so the place would be theirs for the night and indeed for the next few days.

Charles decided to stick to the plan and no doubt Harold would either be there when they all arrived or would turn up eventually.

Charles and Harold had organised several boxes of Dom Pérignon Champagne as well as local and imported beers. Also a couple of boxes of their father's best French red wine Château Rothschild were borrowed from his private cellar.

More and more graduates and their partners arrived and by midnight Charles found himself entertaining over one hundred people.

Harold was nowhere to be seen but Charles had had enough to drink not really to care.

'Emily, have I given you the grand tour?'

'No Charlie, you haven't. How thoughtless. She smiled affectionately.

'Well I think I should. Take my arm and off we go…'

The young couple climbed the grand staircase and Charles proudly displayed his room and Harry's room and his parents' master suite.

'Charlie, this is beautiful! I love the colour scheme and the four-poster bed is superb. Where does this door lead?'

'That's their ensuite. Go in. It's OK.'

Emily entered and was amazed. It had twin baths and twin basins. The mirror over the basin was gold leaf and very large. It even had a bidet, which she had never seen before and Charles was reluctant to explain its use.

'Charlie, I need to use the bathroom. Would that be OK?'

'Of course, Em. That's what it's there for…'

Charles sat in one of the Victorian chairs at the bay window and thought about his new life in the military and his looming transfer to France.

Eventually the door opened: Emily emerged naked.

Charles did not say anything at first. He was speechless.

She approached him smiling seductively and held out her hand.

'Charlie, I have a 'going away' present for you.'

She led him to the four-poster bed and gradually undressed him. His regimental uniform ended up on the floor and they ended up in the bed.

Their lovemaking seemed endless; Charles eventually rose and dressed.

'Em, I should go downstairs and see if the apartment is still in one piece. When you come down, we can have champagne before I take you home. I will never forget tonight or you my love. The memory of you will be with me always.'

Charles descended the grand staircase and found a few drunken stragglers lying on couches and the floor. He was able to convince them to leave and looked around to assess the damage. Apart from what you would expect, with the odd broken glass, all seemed OK.

Harry was nowhere to be seen; Charles checked his room and the other bedrooms apart from the master bedroom: no Harry.

He decided to wait until mid morning and if he still was missing he would report it to the police.

Charles escorted Emily home then returned to Pall Mall and crashed on his bed awakening at 9am with Harry blowing in his ear.

'What the hell are you doing, you stupid bastard, and where have you been?'

Harry explained what had happened and Charles empathised.

'Nevertheless Harry, it was your graduation and you were Dux. I hope you have an adequate excuse for the Commandant.'

'Don't worry, Charlie, it will all be sorted.' Ultimately it was.

And so Harry graduated as a Second Lieutenant in The Duke of Wellington's Regiment.

Orders came down that they were sailing to Marseilles in three days' time.

Three days remained before their lives would become dominated by gunfire, mud and death; three days before the twins' relationship would be tested like never before.

The Horror of War

Chapter 13

Troop Ship Viper

The troops from The Duke of Wellington's assembled on the wharf at Plymouth. They were sailing to Marseilles on the "The Viper", then by train up to Ypres in the north of France. It was a short trip and the troops enjoyed the break playing cards and the odd game of chess.

From Ypres to Belgium

Things certainly changed when they arrived in Lille. There were soldiers marching out the City Gate to join the front at Ypres. Horses and trucks were carrying ammunition and hauling cannon. It was a hive of activity and any observer would know there was a war going on.

Harry and Charles organised their men to assemble outside the train station and marched them one kilometre outside the city where a tent city had been assembled.

On the march they saw the wounded returning to the Lille hospital. They were a very sad looking lot, some with legs and arms shot off, others with what looked like horrendous burns. The lads from the Duke of Wellington's could not help but be horrified by the injuries and began to wonder what they would be marching into the next day.

They would soon discover the horrors of war.

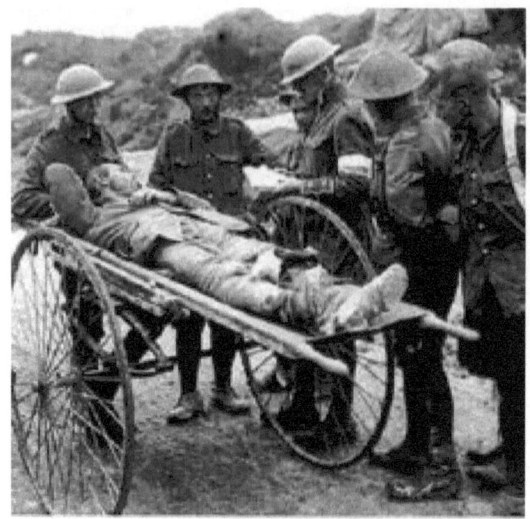

One of the Wounded

At dawn they were awoken by the bugler. After breakfast the troops were assembled and began their march to the battlefront. The procession of wounded continued stumbling on in the opposite direction and the officers, including Charles and Harry, attempted to play it down, but it was difficult to sound positive.

The rain was relentless, turning the muddy road into a total quagmire so that it was almost impossible to make any headway. An officer told Harry that there had not been a day without torrential rain since he had arrived four weeks ago. Charles and Harold wondered what their first taste of battle would be like and felt apprehensive about how they would cope.

They knew only too well that the two previous battles at Ypres had failed. Why would this battle be any different?

London, 1917

Lloyd George, the British Prime Minister, sat in his office at number 10 Downing Street, the same residence as Sir Robert Walpole who had received the home as a present from King George II in 1735. Number 10 had also housed Henry Pelham, who put down the 1745 Jacobite Rebellion. Robert Banks

Jenkinson who was Prime Minister in 1815 when the Battle of Waterloo took place, ending the Napoleonic Wars, had also used this office.

Lloyd George felt the history of the office and the history of the position he held.

The year was 1917; he had been in power for a year and what a year it was. He had taken over from Herbert Asquith, who had mismanaged the first two years of the war or that's how Lloyd George saw it. The majority of the Cabinet agreed with him.

David Lloyd George was not an aristocrat; unlike Herbert Asquith, he tended to 'say it like it was', just as when he had practised law.

The first action he took was to create a "War Cabinet" to oversee everything concerning the war, including munition supply, approval of battle plans and the logistics of moving men into battle.

He was reading a report from General Haig, and he was not particularly happy with what he was reading. Haig and his entourage were due at number 10 in thirty minutes. He intended to propose to the War Cabinet a plan for a new battle in Flanders. Lloyd George felt the best way to redeploy the troops from the Western Front was to help the Italians defeat the Austrians.

'It will be in Italy where this war will be won or lost,' he thought.

The President of the War Council, Lord George Curzon, knocked and entered the Prime Minister's office.

'Good morning, Sir.'

'Good morning, George.'

'General Haig, General Robertson, and General Gough, along with their support staff are waiting in the cabinet room, Sir.'

'So be it. They can wait a little longer. I want your opinion on Gough's plan for Ypres, George.'

'Well, Sir, having read the brief, I am doubtful it will succeed. I certainly don't want to see another Somme.'

'I bloody well agree, I think we should be diverting the resources we have at our disposal to fighting the Austrians in Italy.'

'Sir, I think you should be prepared for a fair amount of opposition to that proposal.'

We'll see. Come on let's get it over with.'

Lloyd George and Lord Curzon entered the cabinet room.

61

'Sit down, gentlemen.'

'Well, General Haig, would you care to present your plan?' Lloyd George sounded gruff.

It was obvious to all that these two men had little regard for each other.

'Sir, I believe we have the Germans on the back foot. We have worn them down through attrition. Now is the time to strike the deathblow.'

'And how do you intend to do that, General?'

'Sir, we will bombard the German lines for ten days straight, with three thousand guns. They will be decimated. We will then launch our ground attack across an eighteen-kilometre front.'

'That sounds like a similar plan you used at the Somme with the loss of over four hundred thousand men.'

'Prime Minister, this plan will work. General Gough and I have spent many hours preparing it. I think you should give it due consideration.'

'Go on, General.'

'We will move through Flanders and capture the submarine pens on the coast. Too many of our supply ships are being sunk. If we don't stop them, it will threaten our victory over the Germans.'

There was a lot of discussion and argument, but in the end, Lloyd George had no alternative but to approve Haig's plan.

The name 'Polygon Wood' was a farce. Shelling had reduced the 'wood' to little more than stumps and broken timber.

Polygon Wood 1917 (note the cross)

The British artillery barrage commenced at 5.50 a.m. on 26th September, just as the Polygon plateau became visible.

French mutinies were increasing. It was decided that the British Forces would need to take control of the Western Front.

This provided General Haig with an opportunity to launch an offensive, which is what he wanted all along. He bombarded the German positions for ten days prior to the attack, using 3000 guns, which expended 4,250,000 shells. With that intensity the Germans certainly knew a land attack was imminent. Thus, when the attack was launched across an 18-kilometre front, the German Fourth Army was in place to hold off the main British advance around the Menin Road. This restricted the Allies to fairly small gains to the left of the line around Pilckem Ridge. Similarly, the French were halted further north by the German Fifth Army.

Menin Road 1917

British attempts to renew the offensive over the course of the next few days were severely hampered by the onset of heavy rains, the heaviest in thirty years. The entire area had become a thick muddy swamp. Tanks found themselves immobile, stuck fast in the mud. Similarly, the infantry found their mobility severely limited. They were crawling through thick smelly slime that buried them and their horses to the point where they could not move. The bodies of their comrades littered the terrain. If there really was a hell, they had discovered it. The massive bombardment had destroyed the drainage systems and the millions of shells had created a moonscape difficult for the Allied forces to advance. Finally, with the army stuck in the muddy fields, the bloody offensive came to an untidy close. Many would call this offensive after the name of the village that had become the last objective – 'Passchendaele.'

Menin Road

The Third Battle of Ypres was a bloodbath resulting in 310,000 Allied casualties and an estimated 400,000 Germans. These numbers represent fathers and sons who would not be returning to their families, soldiers who had farewelled their sweethearts with the promise of returning safely.

Passchendaele, Belgium, August 1917

'If there was a hell on earth, it was here at Passchendaele,' thought Harry. There was not a tree left standing – only charred remains, no birds singing, no small animals scurrying around looking for their next meal. No grass, no flowers, no wheat or barley in what were once fields of gold.

Tank in badly shelled mud area. Battle of Passchendaele. November, 1917.

Passchendaele Mud

For most of the day, there was no sun as the smoke from the artillery and guns blotted out its existence.

Passchendaele

What there was, Harry observed, was mud, mud that could suck a tank down to the point where only the gun turret could be seen, mud so thick, a soldier could be drowned in the slimy ooze.

The corpses of fallen soldiers littered the horrific landscape. The smell of decomposing flesh was omnipresent. The British High Command would not permit the retrieval of badly wounded or dead soldiers, so they remained in no-man's land, slowly rotting and being devoured by the bloated rats. War was very good for the rats.

Harry and Charles arrived in this God-forsaken environment in August 1917, ready to fight for their King and country. A far cry from officers' school, no amount of training could prepare them for this. Charles and Harry were in charge of a platoon of fifty men and were assisted by a platoon Sergeant.

It was the 17th August at 5 am. The night had been relatively uneventful, just the odd flare from both sides to ascertain if there were any imminent attacks on their trenches; there were not, just the odd angry shot.

Charles spoke to his men for the first time as their commander.

'Men, we all know this is not going to be easy, but most of you have been involved in previous attacks and you know what to expect. For the new soldiers in our group, if Sergeant Walsh, or myself, are not available for whatever reason, follow the lead of the experienced men in the platoon. There will be no retreat unless ordered by me; if I see any soldier retreating, I will shoot them with my own revolver; is that clear? We are due to go over the top at 5.15; I will blow my whistle three times. When you hear the final whistle, 'Charles paused', climb the ladders and make your way. Our objective, as I am sure you all know, is the village of Passchendaele.'

Harry gave his platoon very similar instructions. The two platoons commanded by the twins would be fighting side by side.

Both Harry and Charles looked at their fob watches and blew their whistles for the final time. The men started to scramble up the ladders. Many did not make three metres before they were mown down by the German machine guns. There were a few soldiers so terrified by the noise and the screams, they froze. Charles approached one of the soldiers in his platoon.

'OK, soldier, I want you to start breathing very deeply and when I say go, I want you to climb that ladder.'

Unfortunately this method did not work.

'Right, the alternative method is, I shoot you between the eyes right now; I don't have time to fuck about. I will count to three and if you are not over the top when I finish counting, I will shoot you.'

The soldier looked at Charles; he knew he wasn't kidding: although petrified, he climbed the ladder and started crawling through the mud. As the soldiers crawled through the slime, bullets were whizzing above their heads. Many poor unfortunates were shot. There were body parts all over no man's land; it was impossible to avoid them. Passing one of the many bomb craters filled with water, Harry saw a soldier dead at the bottom and judging by the state of decomposition, it had been there for some time.

Tommie Soup

A German Pill Box pinned down Charlie's platoon; the Krauts inside were relentless in their firing. He knew the only way to move forward was to take it out. This would entail someone getting close enough to hurl some hand grenades in through the gun slits.

German Pill Box After Battle

He knew that person was himself; he had to lead by example. He looked around for a soldier. He needed protection while he threw the grenades. The soldier next to him was firing his 303 with great enthusiasm. He would do. Charles crawled over and realised that the soldier was the same one he had threatened to shoot in the trench.

'Soldier, I am going to try to get rid of that Pill Box. I want you to come with me; are you up for it?'

Yes, Sir, I take it that's an order?'

'No it's not, I want a volunteer.'

'Well sir, I am your man.'

'Right,good. Well, what we need to do is get close enough to blow the bloody thing to bits. You need to be to my left and don't stop firing; here is my pistol. Use that too. I will crawl to the right of it and hopefully get close enough to throw these eggs in on the Kraut's laps. You understand?'

'Yes,Sir.'

'What's your name, private? I would like to know in whose company I am probably going to die.'

'Private Christopher Harmsworth, Sir.'

'Nice to meet you Christopher, now let's go and kill some Germans, shall we?'

Charles slid on his belly towards the German position; he had to sweep away various bloody body parts. He needed to keep low and out of the line of fire. He looked over to where Private Harmsworth was crawling and firing as quickly as he could load his own rifle and Charles' pistol. Charles was satisfied that they were both advancing at the same pace. Charles and Harmsworth were about twelve feet from the gun emplacement when Charles decided he needed to run to the base and throw in the grenades. He signalled his intention to Harmsworth who seemed to understand. The time had come. Charles did not feel any fear, just pure adrenalin. He was pumped.

He half ran, half crawled, until he reached the concrete base of the German machine gun, which was firing at rapid pace and slaying as many Tommies as they could.

Charles slowly stood up and, at the count of nine, threw in two hand grenades. At the count of ten, they exploded.

He then threw in two more just to make sure. He called for Harmsworth to run around the back of the Pillbox from his side and Charles did the same from the right. Carefully they both peered into the concrete fortress and found four Germans dead.

Charles took the machine gun and instructed Harmsworth to carry as much ammunition as he could. The Germans stationed behind the box were now starting to retreat, knowing the silence of the machine guns could mean only one thing.

Charles and Harmsworth set up the machine gun, firing at the Germans in retreat. Charles was relentless. He fired until the gun became so hot that it was blistering his hands. Harmsworth held the gun and Charles kept firing until they ran out of ammo.

Carefully they returned to their trench with a German machine gun and twenty-five confirmed kills.

Charles was nominated for, and received, The Victoria Cross. Private Harmsworth received a Military Medal for Bravery in the Field. What a far cry from the young kid who was too petrified to go over the top.

The other significant event was the promotion of Charles to Captain. This of course made him Harry's commander.

Train Wreck

Chapter 14

For Richard and Elizabeth Lamont, it was customary to holiday in Scotland for four weeks in September each year. Richard handed over the affairs of the newspapers to his chief editors, picked up Elizabeth in a taxi and went straight to Kings Cross station to catch the train to Edinburgh where they intended to stay at the family castle, "Torwood".

The train left on time for once and was travelling at great pace through Yorkshire when it failed to make a turn. The engine and the first few passenger carriages hurtled off the track and down a steep ravine. The majority of carriages were separated from the engine and stayed on the tracks, sparing many lives. The first few carriages were always first class and naturally that's where Lord and Lady Lamont were seated.

The rescuers arrived to find all the first class passengers and the driver and his engineer were killed, probably instantly.

It was left to Richard's secretary to inform the War Office of the tragedy so they could inform Charles and Harry. She expressed the hope that they could get leave to attend the funeral.

Ypres, Belgium 1917

Both Charles and Harold had survived the Battle of Passchendaele; they were sitting in the officers' quarters at Ypres.

Charles and Harold were playing cards with two other officers when a messenger asked permission to enter, delivering them a message. He passed an envelope to each brother.

The brothers read the telegram and looked in horror at each other. Both in shock, they left the quarters immediately without uttering a word.

The two brothers started walking, speechless, through the devastated town until they stopped. Both broke down, crying uncontrollably and hugging each other still without saying a single word.

Leave was granted to attend their parents' funeral in London. They travelled by train to Marseilles, then boarded a ship to Plymouth, and took a train to London. It was a very sombre trip with little talking and a lot of contemplation.

Charles felt the burden of responsibility that had been handed to him, including the title of "Lord Lamont". He knew, as first-born son, he would inherit the lion's share of the estate, but decided he would share 50/50 with his twin brother. He also decided he would not inform Harry of his decision until they returned from the front: after all, they may not return.

London 1917

The Funeral was held at Westminster Abbey after a cremation service at the Golders Green Crematorium in London.

The notable attendees included David Lloyd George, the Prime Minister, The Prince of Wales, representing the Royal Family, as well as many Lords and Ladies and various industry leaders. All in all, over two hundred people attended. The Lamont newspapers covered the funeral as their front-page story, with the war relegated to the later pages.

Charles and Harold hosted a wake at the Pall Mall townhouse and, despite the occasion, enjoyed seeing many of their parents' friends and their children, many of whom they grew up with.

Charles was surprised that Emily Scott did not attend and asked her mother where she was.

' Emily decided she would like to live in America for a while. She is living with some very good friends of ours, the Ashworths.'

'Really? My goodness, she never expressed to me a desire to live there. Where in America is she living?'

'In New York… Manhattan, to be exact. The Ashworth's have a beautiful home there.'

'What is she doing there? Is she studying?

'Well, yes. She is she is studying medicine; Emily always wanted to help others.'

'When you are next in touch with her, could you ask if I could write to her from the front? I would love to hear from her.'

'Yes, of course, Charles, I will ask her. She is very busy, as you can imagine, but I will ask her.'

Emily, her mother and father were all eating their evening meal in the formal dining room of "Cliveden House" in Berkshire where the ancestors of the Scott family had lived for the past three hundred years.

Emily was extremely nervous and had been delaying announcing her news but she knew it was time. She could not put it off any longer.

'Daddy, Mummy, I have some rather important news,' she said meekly.

'Yes, darling, what is it?' her mother asked.

Her father said nothing, just looked at Emily, waiting for Emily to divulge her news.

'I don't really know how to tell you this, so best I just come out with it. I am going to have a baby.'

'What! You can't be serious!' yelled her father.

'Darling, there must be some mistake you couldn't possibly be pregnant. You are too young and not even married."

'I am afraid that I am, Mummy. The doctor confirmed it yesterday.'

'So who is the father?' demanded her father.

'I am afraid I can't tell you, Daddy.'

'What? You certainly will, young lady. Who is he and where is he?'

'I am not saying who and, as for where, he is in France, fighting in the war.'

'This is not good enough Emily, leave the room.'

'I am not twelve, Daddy! I am twenty and I will not go to my room but I am leaving the house and I will return when you have had time to discuss it with Mummy.'

Emily left them to their grief and walked the three miles into the village to visit her best friend, Sarah Dawes.

Emily trudged up the long driveway to "Radcliff House," where she knocked on the door, asking to see Sarah.

'Emily, how are you? Come into the sitting room and we can have tea.'

Once the servant brought them tea and cake, Emily divulged her news.

'Oh my God, Emily! It's always the quiet ones. Who is the father?'

'Sarah, you are as bad as my parents. The father remains my secret.'

'Why, aren't you going to marry him? You cannot raise a baby alone.'

'Who says so? I am perfectly capable of raising a child.'

'Why won't you tell anyone who the father is?'

'Because he is fighting in France or Belgium and the last thing he needs right now is this news.'

'He doesn't know?'

'No, and he won't know until he returns from the war.'

'What if he doesn't come back?'

'Then I will raise it alone.'

'Emily, what are you going to do? You can't have the baby here. Your parents will surely send you away somewhere.'

'I don't know what is going to happen, Sarah, we will just have to wait and see.'

Emily returned home and went straight to her room and wrote in her diary what had transpired that fateful day, then she hid the diary beneath a loose floorboard under her bed.

Five days had passed when her parents called her into the drawing room and asked her to be seated. She knew this was not going to be a light-hearted chat.

'Emily, your mother and I believe it would be in your best interests if you moved to America to stay with our very good friends, George and Sophie Ashworth. They have agreed to take you in and care for you until the baby is born. They will also help with arranging the adoption.'

Emily knew it would be futile to argue with her father now but she had no intention to put her child up for adoption. She would raise the child.

Emily sailed for New York on 24th January 1918.

America had been involved in the war for the past nine months and the Atlantic crossing was a perilous one but she arrived safely in New York harbour on 31st January 1918. Her new life had just begun.

Cain and Able

Chapter 15

Charles and Harold had come to terms with their parents' death and were now waiting on their orders from High Command.

Those orders would be determined by General Von Ludendorff, who was planning the German "Spring Offensive". This offensive would win Germany the war, or so thought Ludendorff.

He was sitting in his office in Mons, contemplating his plan to use all the Divisions that had returned from Russia since the Bolsheviks negotiated the Treaty of Brest-Litovsk.

This would free up fifty Divisions, which were available to him for the Western Front.

The basic concept was to overwhelm the British Army with sheer numbers.

He knew he had a small window before the full might of the American forces were deployed along the Western Front. At this stage they were arriving in small numbers but he anticipated there were going to be over one million fresh troops looking for a fight against his battle weary troops in the very near future.

Ludendorff had planned four separate German attacks, code-named 'Michael', 'Georgette', 'Gneisenau' and 'Blücher-Yorck'. 'Michael' would be the first and most important attack which was intended to break through the Allied lines, outflank the British forces which held the front from the Somme River to the English Channel and defeat the British Army.

The "Spring Offensive" (or as some called it "Ludendorff's offensive" or as others called it the "Kaiser's Battle") was Germany's final opportunity to win the war. The Kaiser was obviously impressed with the plan and turned up at Ludendorff's Head Quarters with his entourage to receive a final briefing.

Ludendorff's true objective was to bring Britain and France to the peace treaty table. This was a great underestimation of the Allied objectives; one large battle would not turn the direction of the war.

Meanwhile, back in Berlin, General Hindenburg who, together with Ludendorff, governed Germany (despite what the Kaiser thought), was hoping that a decisive win would lift the morale of the German people. His total lack of knowledge about human nature had surfaced. A military win was not going to put food on the table or heat homes or bring back fathers and sons.

On the 21st of March 1918, Germany launched fifty eight divisions up against sixteen British and colonial divisions.

Charles and Harold were in the firing line of this massive German onslaught. Both were now fighting in the same platoon, with Charles as commander and Harold as his second in command. The two young officers were located beside the Lys River, only about five miles from Ypres where they had been stationed since arriving in Belgium.

A German attack was not expected at this point, so they were just killing time writing letters and playing cards.

Charles heard a shell scream over their heads and explode about one hundred yards behind them, hitting a medical dressing station. That was the start of the mayhem; the German artillery was firing over three thousand shells a minute, over one million in all, over five hours.

Charles could only order his men to keep their heads down but over seven and a half thousand British and Allied troops became casualties during the horrendous bombardment.

The cacophony ceased. There was silence. Charles whispered to Harold:

'This is going to be bad, Harry! Tell your men to be prepared for a full front on charge.'

The last shells from the bombardment contained mustard gas, a devastating weapon that caused shocking burns and a painful death.

The call went out "GAS"! This call was relayed to the troops along the trench line and all the troops donned their gas masks. The gas would settle on their uniforms as a sticky mist and would penetrate anything, including leather. The gas would burn their skin and, if allowed to get into their eyes, cause blindness.

Vickers Gun Crew with Gas Masks

Charles heard the war cry of German troops running towards them.

'Fuck, how many bastards are there!' Harry yelled.

'The Krauts are throwing everything at us.' Charles sounded desperate.

The troops were firing their Vickers machine guns and Enfield 303s as fast and as hard as they could. Germans were falling like flies but the bastards just kept coming.

Men were dying in large numbers in the trenches, blocking access both to the troops and to desperately needed supplies.

'Harry, get some men together and get rid of those bodies over the back of the trench.'

'I would rather stay and fight the Huns if it's all the same to you, Charlie.'

'Well, it's not all the fucking same to me! I gave you an order, now get on with it and fast.'

Harry reluctantly gathered half a dozen men together and started the gruesome task of picking up the bloodied corpses and heaving them over the back of the trench. Eventually, they cleared a reasonable access, having disposed of over one hundred men from a couple of hundred yards of trench line.

The battle raged on and the casualties mounted, requiring Harry and his men to repeat the exercise three more times in the space of a couple of hours.

Charles knew that even though they had all fought gallantly against overwhelming odds, they would not be able to hold their line.

The British communications had been destroyed by the bombardment so he summoned a runner to take a message back to General Plummer's command post, informing him of the dire situation.

The runner took thirty minutes to reach HQ.

General Plummer and his staff were well aware of the situation from the reports received from other officers involved in the battle.

'This is getting out of hand, Henry. We either try and stick it out or pull the troops back to fight another day'

'I agree, General Henry,' said Henry Horne his trusted second incommand.

'These bastards are making one hell of a push. If we don't get Lloyd George to release the reinforcements we have been asking for, we will lose this bloody war.'

'In the meantime, we need to retreat and consolidate our resources.'

The decision was taken to withdraw their troops back ten kilometres.

God Help Me

What Have I Done?

Chapter 16

The runner made it back to Charles without incident and delivered Plummer and Horne's reply. He was relieved and immediately passed on his order to retreat to his second-in-command. Harry moved down the trench informing his men that they were making a tactical retreat and instructing them how it was to be conducted. The plan was that groups of ten men would go back over the trench every five minutes, so that Fritz would not notice they were leaving.

Eventually, all but the last ten remained. Each one had a Vickers machine gun which they were firing with great gusto to give the Germans the delusion that the trenches were fully manned. This plan was implemented right along the British frontline. Eventually, they retreated one by one, taking their precious machine guns with them. Now, there was the last man standing: Sergeant Wilson from the Yorkshire Regiment. He fired his last shots and then bade a hasty retreat. It took the Germans some time to realise what had happened and by then it was too late: the British were gone.

The Germans, when made aware of what had happened, blasted the retreating British with shellfire, killing many. Generals Plummer and Horne were surprised at the sheer numbers the Germans had thrown into their assault. They knew the enemy had gained many more battalions from the Eastern Front but did not expect them to be deployed so quickly. The Generals sent an urgent request to the British Prime Minister to release the many thousands of reserves he was holding back. Even if Lloyd George released them, it would take a couple of weeks to get them to the Front.

It was decided by General Plummer that accurate intelligence was badly required. He needed to know how many enemy troops faced them and where they were located. There was no doubt in his mind that the British and colonial troops would face another major attack on the morrow. An order was issued to all the battalion leaders to meet at Head Quarters for a briefing. Each battalion would be required to select two officers to penetrate the German-held territory and determine their strength and exact location. They could then ascertain where to place their resources when the attack came.

Major Baker was Charles and Harold's commanding officer. He returned from the briefing and asked, rather than ordered, Charles and Harold to undertake the perilous task. Both agreed without hesitation. It was decided that each officer would take the minimum amount of equipment and, to that end, they carried only their service revolvers as weapons. The only other piece of equipment they carried was field binoculars.

Charles, as the senior officer, was in charge of the operation.

Charles and Harold climbed the trench ladder and made their way out to what was a very large expanse of land, estimated to be five miles from the German line, the line that the British had occupied up until that very day. The brothers kept low and made their way, avoiding the many bomb craters and the thousands of dead bodies strewn around the battlefield. Eventually, they made it to within one hundred yards of the new German line and could see through their binoculars a hive of activity behind the trench. The artillery was being dragged into position by horses and there seemed to be an endless number of tanks.

Judging by the tents that had been erected, there were many thousands of soldiers ready to launch another deadly attack. Charles and Harold were amazed and horrified by what they saw and what it meant to their own defensive line. Slowly, they started to make their way back to their line, however, German snipers attacked them; they quickly jumped into a bomb crater and kept their heads low. It seemed the snipers had lost them in their sights due to the heavy mist and the darkness.

'We can't stay here forever, Harry. We are going to have to make a move.'

'Don't be daft, Charles. As soon as we show our heads, they will blow them off our shoulders.'

'We have to get back and report our observations.'

'No fucking way, brother. I am not moving, not now, anyway.'

'I think you are forgetting who gives the orders here, brother. If I say we go, we bloody well go.'

'I'm telling you, I am not moving.'

'I will give you one chance and one chance only: you will get your arse out of this crater or I will arrest you for disobeying an order. You will be court-martialled and shot. Is that what you want? Now, I order you to vacate this crater immediately.'

Harry looked at his brother. He raised his revolver and shot Charles through his left eye. He fired off another round that hit Charles in the forehead.

Charles slumped to the bottom of the trench. He was dead.

Harold was stunned.

'Oh my God what have I done?'

He lay down beside his dead brother, hugging his still twitching body and removed Charles' helmet. He stroked his hair and sobbing uncontrollably, he kissed his cheek.

"I am so sorry, Charles, I don't know what got into me. Will you ever forgive me?" he whispered.

He laid his twin brother's head down on the sodden earth and thought about what he must do. He knew he had to act quickly. He took off Charles's dog tag, replacing it with his own. He retrieved his brother's wallet containing his identification papers, again replacing them with his own. Finally he removed Charles' jacket. For all intents and purposes, he was now Captain Charles Lamont, *Lord Charles Lamont*. Harold slowly looked out from the crater. He took one last look back at Charles. All was quiet, thus he crawled his way back to his line and reported to Major Baker.

'Sir, I am devastated to report that my brother, Captain Harold Lamont, was shot and killed by a German sniper.'

'Good God, man! Are you all right?'

'Not really, sir. I would like thirty minutes alone before I make my report to you.'

'I am sorry, Captain Lamont, I need that information immediately. Make your report, then grieve.'

Harold wrote his report and then retreated to the officers' dugout to be alone in his mind at least.

'I need to stay alive for the rest of the war. If I do, I am Lord Lamont, owner of three newspapers and three magnificent properties. God knows how much money Father kept in various banks. That's got to be better than being a farmer in Cornwall.'

The German attack recommenced at five am the next day. Again, heavy artillery was used to soften up the British army and then a full frontal attack supported by an armada of tanks.

Again, the British were required to retreat to lessen their losses and again the Germans occupied the British trenches.

The stench from rotting corpses was unbearable and the German command was worried about their troops catching disease from the dead and from the thousands of feeding vermin. It was decided to dig large pits and also utilize some of the bigger bomb craters to bury the dead. Charles remained where he was murdered, accompanied by thirty other British warriors, never to be found.

I'm the King of the Castle

Chapter 17

Harold was sitting in his dugout contemplating how he would continue to masquerade as Charles, not only in the immediate future but for the rest of his life. He knew his voice was the same and he obviously was the mirror image of his dead brother. The only problem he had was the lack of a distinguishing port wine birth mark that had been on Charles's buttock, not that most people would see that; however, plenty of the rugby players knew about it from the showers in the change room. He wasn't sure if Charles had been a virgin, but if not, there were some girls out there who knew about it as well.

In his solitude, there came to him a brilliant idea. He would travel to Paris while on leave and find a tattoo artist who could replicate it from a drawing he had made.

'Right,' he thought, that's my appearance sorted. Now I have to practise my writing before I take over the newspapers. Charles was the one with the degree in English.'

For a non-premeditated murder, he had all the boxes ticked, or so he thought.

All leave was cancelled because of the German offensive; Harold would have to wait to get his tattoo. The only remaining issue was how to survive the war. How could he guarantee he would return to Britain and take over the Lamont Empire?

He was aware that not all the men under his command came from honest hardworking backgrounds: some were outright criminals before the war.

He decided to approach one particularly unwholesome character, Sid Black. Sid had volunteered in order to get away from the police who were looking for him in connection with a rather gruesome murder on the East side of London in 1914.

Harold pulled him aside, putting to him a proposition.

'Private Black, I have a business proposal for you. I will pay you two thousand pounds to shoot me in the leg.'

'What! You'll pay me to shoot you, a bloody officer? Some would do that for nothing.'

'The condition is this: if you divulge this to anybody whatsoever, I will have you killed. Understand? I am an extremely wealthy man; believe me, it would be easy to have you shot.'

'OK, Governor, I understand. I take it you are rather keen to get back home?'

'You don't need to know why I want it done. Just do your job and we can leave it at that.'

'When do you want the deed done, Gov?'

' I will let you know. And don't call me Gov. You call me 'Sir'.'

'Yes,Sir.'

 Harold organised a German rifle and bullets for the shot and hid them in a timber box in his quarters, commonly known as "the rat hole". Now he could approach his Commanding Officer, Major Baker, with the suggestion that he and a soldier under his command sneak out under cover of darkness and gather some reconnaissance about what Fritz was up to. Major Baker approved the plan and wished them well, praising their courage and initiative.

'Brave man, that Lamont. His brother was killed doing the same thing a few days ago and here he is volunteering again. Bloody good show.'

Harold grabbed Black and whispered the plan.

'Sir, how do I get my money then?'

'I will arrange for it to be deposited in your bank in London.'

But, I don't have a bank account in London. I don't have a bloody bank account anywhere!'

'All right, I will make all the arrangements when I get back to England. Don't worry, you will get your money.'

'I'd better.'

Now, we are going over the top in fifteen minutes. Take this G98 rifle. It's loaded and don't make a fucking mess of it.'

'Don't worry, Sir, I'm a crack shot.'

'OK, let's go.'

The two men climbed the ladder and started to crawl over the pock-marked landscape, where not a tree was left standing and where the mud caked their uniforms. They had arrived at about two hundred and fifty yards from their trench when Harold decided they had gone far enough. They were out of sight of their own line and not too close to the Huns.

'Right. Let's do it, Black. You need to shoot me from about ten yards and you need to be in front of me, so on your way! Let me know when you are ready to fire.'

Private Black crawled the ten yards and turned. He could hardly see the Captain, let alone shoot accurately.

He crawled back to within whispering distance.

'It's too far to shoot in the dark. I need to be closer or I might end up killing you.'

'Alright, how close do you need to be?'

'I think five would be about right.'

'Do it.'

Black crawled back the distance and put Harold's left leg in his sights. Slowly he pulled the trigger. Harold collapsed with a searing pain and blood gushing from his leg.

Private Black crawled back and wrapped a bandage around the wound to try to slow the bleeding.

'Are you all right Sir?'

'Of course I'm not all right, Black. Now get me back to the trench so I can be treated.'

As the two soldiers were making their way back, they heard the German artillery firing at the British positions. It was gas. Private Black donned his gas mask and looked for Captain Lamont's but Harold didn't have one. He had disposed of it as 'superfluous' before they went over the top.

Private Black buried the German rifle and carried Captain Lamont back to the trench. He was immediately taken to the dressing station where they assessed his wounds. The medical officer was not so concerned with the leg wound; the bullet had entered at the front of his thigh and exited cleanly. He was far more concerned that the captain had been exposed to mustard gas; Lamont was starting to scream, his eyes were burning and he could not see. The MO knew the blindness would only be temporary but what concerned him was the blistering forming on Lamont's face. Mustard gas caused terrible burns and the scars would never disappear. This young captain could be horribly scarred for life.

The MO ordered the ambulance to take Lamont to the field hospital in Ypres where he was reassessed and declared serious.

Harry stayed in hospital for two weeks before being shipped back to England where he was admitted to the King George Hospital in Waterloo, London. This facility was regarded as the premium wartime hospital and had pioneered plastic surgery for officers and soldiers with facial wounds. After careful examination and consultation with his colleagues, Dr. Francis Bates decided that they could operate, but with the proviso that the skin grafts may not work. Skin was taken from his buttock and transferred to his face. He was closely monitored for the next few weeks to ensure no infections took hold. Eventually, Dr Bates gave the all clear. The next step was to fashion a mask manufactured from wafer thin tin, which would hide the horrible scarring. Charles Lamont, formally Harold Lamont, left hospital in January 1919 to begin his new life as Lord Lamont.

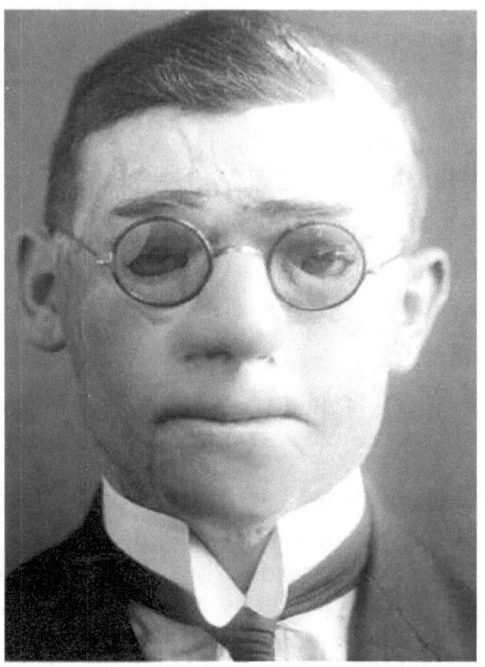

Lord Lamont 1919

Charles would need many months recuperation at his Pall Mall apartment. He could afford a private nurse and paid Dr Bates a retainer to visit him once a week.

There were also ten domestic staff members to cater to his needs.

Charles would often sit in his study by the fire and contemplate what his life would have been if he had not murdered his brother. He would be sitting in his beautiful sixteenth century farmhouse in Cornwall and would still have his brother, whom he dearly loved, but without as much power and money.

One of the first tasks he undertook on his arrival at Pall Mall was to arrange a beautiful monument to his dead brother next to the family crypt where his beloved parents were buried.

In June 1919, Lord Lamont decided he would donate the use of his Scottish estate, "Torwood", on a twenty-five year lease to the Government in order to help British and Colonial officers and soldiers who had suffered facial injuries to convalesce while attempting to get their lives back together.

Torwood Castle

He created a Board of Directors, chaired by Dr Bates and five other prominent medical professionals, including Hugh Crichton-Miller, the famous psychiatrist who developed psychological treatments for shell-shocked soldiers during and after the war.

He also donated a figure of five hundred thousand pounds to operate the facility.

He was applauded by all in Great Britain for his philanthropy and received many accolades including a personal thank you from the King.

Lamont thought he was well on his way to making amends for his brother's murder.

He named the facility "The Harold Lamont Rehabilitation Centre."

Paris 1919

Christmas was looming and Lamont decided he was well enough to make the trip to Paris alone to finalise his transformation to Charles.

He booked his passage on a ferry to Calais and caught a train to Paris.

He remembered in his youth, trolling around the unsavoury district of Montmartre when visiting Paris on holiday with his parents and brother. He observed many tattoo parlours on that trip but one that stood out was located in a small alleyway leading from the main street. It was called "Tatouage".

He walked the streets looking for the parlour and at last came across the laneway where it was located.

He entered the parlour, decorated with all the tattoo designs customers could choose; there were naked ladies, dragons and an assortment of grotesque-looking characters, along with the standard love-hearts.

The man behind the counter looked quite normal, not the criminal type Lamont had expected.

'Bonjour monsieur.'

'Bonjour,' replied Lamont. 'I was wondering if I could get you to give me a tattoo, monsieur?'

'Why not? That is what I do.'

'This is not a normal tattoo, it is unique.'

'Can you show me? Have you sketched it?'

'Oui'

Lamont showed the man the sketch; he looked over his glasses.

'This is an unusual shape. Where do you want me to tattoo it?'

'On my left buttock.'

'May I be so bold as to ask you why that shape and why on your that part of your anatomy?'

'My brother was killed in the war. He was my identical twin and he had a port wine birthmark on his left buttock. I wish to replicate it in his honour.'

'Oh, I see. Well it is not a difficult tattoo. If you would like to follow me to the back of the parlour, we can get started.'

Mr Dubois asked Lamont to remove his trousers and lie on a table that resembled a massage table.

'Monsieur, you have some significant scarring on the left side.'

'Yes, I needed skin for a graft on my face, I also suffered in the war.'

'I am sorry, monsieur, I cannot tattoo that skin. I can tattoo the right side, no problem.'

Lamont reflected, deciding that no one would remember which side, except his parents and they were both dead.

'Go ahead and tattoo the other side, monsieur.'

The tattoo took over an hour to complete and was quite painful, but at last his transformation was complete. He would live and die as Charles Lamont, Lord of the Manor.

The Good Life

Chapter 18

November, 1920.

Lord Lamont, as he was now known, followed his father's routine of meeting with his chief editors each morning to discuss the lead story each paper was intending to run.

He felt very comfortable behind his late father's enormous oak desk with the three editors sitting facing him. The editors were impressed with Charles' ability to decide quickly which stories had potential and which would never see the cold light of day.

The stories they were discussing this morning included the Polish Soviet war and the shocking events in Ireland.

Bloody Sunday 1920

"Bloody Sunday" 21ˢᵗ November 1920

```
The Dublin football team was scheduled to play
Tipperary, in Croke Park, on the 21st of November
1920; the proceeds of this 'great challenge
match' were to be donated to the Irish Republican
Prisoners Fund.
```

IRELAND UNDER SINN FEIN.

V.—DUBLIN.

A COMPLEX OF FORCES.

(By Our Special Correspondent.)

There is reason to believe that Dublin is the capital of Sinn Fein. If so the fact is hopeful, for it implies that there is in that Ireland—so often wrongly called revolutionary—a central organization capable of discussing a situation in view of facts, shaping or managing a policy, and pursuing that policy into effect.

If such an organization exists it can only exist in Dublin. Unless it exists and has really the power to discuss, decide, and give effect to its decisions, it appears to me absolutely certain that England will find itself committed to undertaking the reconquest of Ireland by armed force. It is no instance of mine to examine here the probable consequences of such an enterprise; but presumably for one is simple enough to think that they would be limited to Ireland or to England's relations with Ireland. What I have to note is the uncertainty of finding at any given moment such an organization in power. Many observers hold that owing to the driving of disaffection underground, the suppression of Dáil Éireann and proclamation of Sinn Féin, there has ceased to be any central control, a short that Dublin is not the capital, and that there is now one rebel Government, but many. To a certain extent this is unessentially true. The forces arrayed in opposition to the British Government are complex. The main body, which is generally known as Sinn Fein, has of course two wings, one of which believes conservedly in physical force while the other regards physical force at best as an adjunct to other methods. Allied with these is the distinct and, separately organized body of Irish Labour, whose has spare of a revolutionary and less of a purely nationalist character.

At the present moment it is probable that a proposal from the British Government designed to avert real war might be discussed and effectively accepted. There is no assurance that such a possibility will exist in a month. The balance of forces shifts from week to week according to the success which any one of the three groups can claim. But at present the offer of a settlement within the British Empire might bring about peace.

AN ISSUE OUT OF HAND.

There is nothing like universal agreement on this point even among the older leaders in Sinn Fein. One very prominent man said to me the other day:—"The issue is no longer in any man's hands to decide; it is in the control of the nation. And this meant to join, in the control of the young men—for whom there could be no half-way house. No man, no leader, has the power to negotiate or decide for them. Fear I neither Mr. de Valera, Mr. Griffith, nor any other. But a body exists, at present, which might conceivably control for the acceptance of an offer which would mean a sacrifice of the republican ideal for the sake of peace.

Such a proposal as is outlined in Lord Monteagle's Bill would, I think, be almost cordially accepted by Sinn Fein. Quite certainly, however, it would be rejected by Ulster, and could not be imposed on Ulster by the present Government; and this is fully recognized by Sinn Fein, which, so far as I can discover, does not anticipate any proposal from this Government to which it will be obliged to give serious consideration. Yet individual members of the Government have been declaring to prominent Irishmen a willingness to go to lengths which would make such a contingency quite possible.

It is as well to be plain on this matter. Many men have been told that there are only two limiting conditions. First, no Irish Republic, that is no cessation; secondly, no coercion of Ulster, that is no joining of Belfast under a Dublin Parliament unless by Belfast's own consent. If these things are not seriously meant, they should not be said; and if they are seriously meant, they should receive effect in action.

OFFER OF SETTLEMENT.

There is no use in discussing the provisions of the Bill now before Parliament as affording a possibility of settlement. The Times has very justly pointed out that Sinn Fein cannot be expected to accept what two out of the three English parties repudiate as wholly insufficient. Nor, again, is there any use in asking Sinn Fein to say what it is prepared to accept as a compromise. Mr. Redmond's fate is too fresh in memory. Nothing can be done by negotiation; Sinn Fein will not and can only deal with definite facts.

What Sinn Fein would do if confronted by a proposal which put Ulster and the rest of Ireland in the position which, for instance, Victoria and New South Wales occupies before the rest of Australia, is, of course, uncertain. But certainly a new situation would be created. There are no doubt men who will tell you that such an offer would not receive or deserve a moment's consideration. This means no more than that there would be a strong current of emotional defiance against it, and that many men would decline the attempt to breast that current. If Mr. de Valera secured a great success with the Democrats in America, hopes from that quarter might lead Sinn Fein as a whole to resist on a fuller realisation of national aspirations. If indications from the Labour world in Great Britain pointed to the chance of direct action in Ireland for a political purpose operating effectively in England itself, Sinn Fein might well militate against the chances of acceptance. Yet the best brains in Sinn Fein—and there are very good brains in it—do not count with any confidence on the realization of the extreme hopes held out by men at the rank and file, and have thought that for their present mood to think that they would be limited to Ireland or to England of its reduction at thought that they would be limited to Ireland or to England's relations with Ireland.

A DISTRUST OF FORCE.

Trust in ourselves for the physical force men means, I think, an acceptance of the view that their influence destroyed at once if they ever attempted to negotiate. The same is with the Government. They can offer Ireland peace, on terms which Ireland would not feel it easy to accept, yet which if they are ever to be offered Ireland should have the full responsibility of considering before the reality of war is upon her.

The alternative is that this Government should undertake the task of beating down Ireland by force, leaving the task of settlement to some successors of theirs. The Government that makes war here will never make a settlement of war.

ARREST OF ALLEGED MOTOR THIEVES.

Charles Langley, 33, and Henry Johnston, 27, motor drivers, of New Kent-road, S.E., were charged with being concerned with other men not in custody in breaking and receiving the Austroman Garage, Vauxhall, and stealing a motor-lorry, valued at £750, the property of Harris Charles Robinson. In consequence of information which reached the police, Detective-sergeant Downer and other officers have kept observation on the garage, and the suspect on Wednesday evening, at about 9 o'clock, saw Johnston lift Langley up over the gates, and then the latter admitted Johnston through a wicket gate. About 10.40 a motor-lorry was backed out by the two men, who were arrested. Mr. Chartres requested the prisoners in custody.

A young widow who was to be married at the Aldgdal, Bedfordshire, register office yesterday, after waiting two hours, received a message that the bridegroom saying that at the moment of starting out on the ceremony he had yielded to the advice of a friend and had changed his mind.

WELSH COTTAGE MURDER.

INQUEST VERDICT AGAINST THE NIECE.

The inquest on the Craig Police Court on Mrs. Sarah Ann Watts, the widow who was murdered at Rose Cottage, Abermawddwy, Rhaymdir-shire, on June 16, was concluded yesterday. The jury returned a verdict of wilful murder against Princess Catharine Alice Whiteman, the 19-year-old niece of the dead woman.

Mrs. Whiteman, the girl's mother, made some fresh statements to her evidence. Kallie, she said, complained that her aunt was not very kind to her, and that their life together had not been happy. She had not, however, given any reason.

The foreman of the jury asked Mrs. Whiteman if she did not knock and burgle her a bicycle quite recently.—Mrs. Whiteman agreed, and said that Mrs. Watts was very kind to her niece at times.

Did not she felt too that her aunt was not going to buy anything to do with her, and that she had to go back home.—No, Sir.

When was your divorce given to Mrs. Whiteman and Raymond Hatherall as to the five.£1 notes which Kallie had in her possession.—The mother said that she was aware that the girl's purse about the week after, and about Wednesday evening, at about 9 o'clock, saw Johnston up over the late and said I found the five.£1 notes by my bed when Kallie brought me the supper last month. She said, I think I went to bed and I want to do something for you.

Chief Inspector Haldan, questioned by the Coroner, said that the only money found in Rose Cottage was two new halfpennies.

Dr. Salisbury, the Motts Office analyst, gave evidence with regard to the bloodstain on Mrs. Whiteman's dress.

Mr. Lloyd, Abergavenny, said that the fact that there were no bloodstains would be due to the diversion of the blows and the shape of the bottle.

THE WEATHER.

GENERALLY UNSETTLED, WITH FURTHER RAIN.

General Situation, based on the Meteorological Office 7 p.m. (10h. G.M.T.) Reports of Thursday, July 1, 1920.

The fall of the barometer which was in progress over our south-western districts on Wednesday evening heralded the approach of a deep disturbance from the Atlantic. This centre was moving somewhat beyond the Scilly coast of Ireland on reaching observation yesterday, and spread slowly eastward during the day, occasioning rain at many stations. The area of depression embracing the greater part of the country, rain has been heaviest over the southern and midland counties of England. Readings over the British Channel district, Somersetshire and Brittany have often exceeded one-tenth of an inch. The barometers are moving quietly over all parts except over Scandinavia, where it has risen again, and between the westward of Scotland and Iceland, off France and a new depression has developed over the British Channel district, Somersetshire and the Bay of Biscay. Falmouth and Penzance 79mm. 13.4; Aberystwyth 84mm. 17.5; Holyhead 2.0mm. 18.3; the thermometer registered 79mm. 18.3; Lowestoft, Margate, Ramsgate, and several stations in Scotland ranged altogether. Locally on the north-eastern coast of the latter country the day was hot. Roll returning to the middle country. Simdue to Lincoln. Tour readings of a thousand feet by rain in the valleys, north-west and westward of Ramsgate and Colwyn Bay, unless conditions vary widely. The barometers over the moorland range from 8mm. of snow. In the district, one along the temains angle from 42mm. 84m. Andover, Maidap. at Moretane and Bournemouth 48 to 65mm. at Tenterden. By night the thermometer fell little, except in sheltered spots inland, falling generally in the south. Coastal runs at the widespread hails in England. Ireland.

It is anticipated in most districts on Friday, and conditions are likely to remain generally unsettled for at least a day or two.

Forecasts for Friday, July 2.

(16 Hours from Midnight, Thursday.)

(Issued last evening by the Meteorological Office.)

ENGLAND, S.E.   Wind south to south-west, N.E., MIDLANDS, E.   fresh; mainly overcast; S. Wales, E.   some rain or thunder; fair intervals, but more would be warm.

ENGLAND, N.W., S.E., MIDLANDS, N., S. Wales, W.   Moderate or fresh westerly to south-west wind; some rain; cooler.

SCOTLAND, E., S.W., Irish of Man   Moderate south-westerly or westerly winds; unsettled, fair; but locally; moderate temperature.

S. ENGLAND, N. N.W., HEBRIDES, ORKNEY and SHETLAND.   Light winds from south and east, variable; fair to fine with hazy. Moderate or warm.

IRELAND, N.W.   Wind south-east, moderate; cloudy or overcast; some rain; mainly unsettled; moderate temperature.

IRELAND, S.E., S.W.   Light variable winds; mainly overcast; some rain or local thunder; moderate temperature.

AMPLIFIED LONDON FORECAST.

Surface wind south-westerly, 14 to 20 miles; weather changeable, periods of warm bright intervals. Temperature ranging from about 52deg. to 64deg. or slightly higher.

LONDON OBSERVATIONS, KENSINGTON PALACE, 7 p.m. (10h.)—9mm. mean sea-level, 1.2mm.; Wind N.W.; light. Temp. 58deg. Humidity, 80 per cent. Weather dull, rain.

Wednesday, 7 p.m. (10h.) to Thursday, 10 a.m.—Min. temp. 57deg. (8.45 a.m.); rain 0.00in.

Thursday, 10 a.m. (9h.) to 7 p.m.—Max. temp. 64deg. (rainfall); rain 0.00in.

Sunshine to 6 p.m. (17h.), at a New Observatory (Richmond), nil.

Mean temperature for 84 years at Greenwich for July 1.—Max. 72deg. min. 52deg.; afternoon-mean, 16deg. to 18.5, 10deg. to 16.0.

London observations for July 1, 1856.—Max. 66deg., min. 58deg.

FLYING PROSPECTS TO-DAY.

ENGLAND, S.E. and CHANNEL.—Winds will be fresh, with rain at times, or thundery at 5.10, 14 to 18 m.p.h. near the surface, rising to higher levels at times. The sky is likely to continue mainly overcast by cloud at 1,500ft. or below, with a chance of improving tendency during the latter half of the day.

Drifting fog or mist-bank may be anticipated over the Channel, on the coasts, and in the higher inland regions, but over the mainland in general visibility should exceed some miles. There will be no serious impediment to cross-country flights, but the trans—

AVIATION WEATHER.

Thursday, July 1, 1920.—Wind Direction and Velocity in the Upper Air.

District & Time	1,000ft.	2,000ft.	5,000ft.	10,000ft.

HEALTH RESORTS.

The following reports of the weather yesterday at health resorts were received last evening:—

	Max. Temp.		Weather.

NEW INSTITUTE OF FOREIGN AFFAIRS.

AN OUTCOME OF THE PEACE CONFERENCE.

At the Royal Society of Arts, John-street, Adelphi, last Monday evening, the British Institute of International Affairs will be founded as the outcome of Unionist Grey of Fallodon, supported by speeches from Mr. Balfour and Mr. E. R. Glynn. Lord Robert Cecil will preside.

The idea of founding such an institute, which should serve as an exchange or clearing house for expression of opinion and the communication of knowledge of affairs in foreign countries, originated in the course of the Conference at Paris last year. There several of the delegations, notably those of the British and American Commonwealths, were for the moment fashions for the study of foreign affairs. Out of the meetings arose the plan of a joint association which was originally proposed. The movement, it has been among the younger members of the British and American delegations, and was strongly supported by such men as Lord Robert Cecil, General Smuts, and others who appreciated the educational importance of the work. The project was divided in two sections, and the British and American investors are to establish institutes separately.

The first will be known as the British, and the sole money issued in Rose Cottage will be two new halfpennies.

Dr. Salisbury, the Motts Office analyst, gave evidence.

NEWSPAPER DEADLOCK IN DUBLIN.

THREATENED SUSPENSION TO-DAY.

Negotiations for the settlement of the dispute between Dublin newspaper proprietors and their staffs broke down yesterday. Failing a renewal of the negotiations an evening paper will appear this afternoon, but no morning newspaper will be published to-morrow. The staffs claimed an increase of 25s. weekly. The proprietors have offered an advance of 14s. and substantial increases to the higher paid.

The men were working last night, but at a late hour our Dublin Correspondent telephoned that the situation was still uncertain, and it was not known whether the staffs would agree to accept the advance of 14s. and continue at work till fresh negotiations take place.

IRISH JUDGES' ESCORT OF SOLDIERS.

EFFECTS OF THE RAILWAY DISPUTE.

(FROM OUR OWN CORRESPONDENT.)

DUBLIN, July 1.

On the Great Northern Railway there has been trouble at Dundalk to-day over the question of the shunting of a war-train which broke up on the British troops and munitions and the men are reported to have been disciplined. The clerk of petty sessions, and the carters who shunted the train at Ballymcot. The men declined to accept it. The matter was referred to a committee of the Workers' Union, which advised the men to carry out the ordinary duties in connexion with the train. The train subsequently went north, in ordinary. Trains were running, and the men are doing normal work, except in the case of this train. In Dublin the position is that the drivers of the train refused to work, and the engine was placed alongside a platform.

It is reported to have been a general meeting of the Irish Bar to consider the Council's recent regulation preventing trains from being run if they contained armed forces. Under the Republican Courts would constitute unprofessional conduct.

FOOT-AND-MOUTH DISEASE.

NORFOLK OUTBREAK SPREADING.

A further outbreak of foot-and-mouth disease is notified from Norfolk. The disease is this instance bearing made its appearance on a farm at Great Yarmouth, Southrepps district, Rockham, where infection was confirmed a week ago.

DEATH OF LADY SOMERSET.

The death occurred at her residence, Rockhill Court, Berkshire, this week of Lady Somerset, who was widely-known in philanthropic and social work. She was born in 1851 and was the only child of the Earl Somers. She had served the whole of her married life with her husband, Lord Henry Somerset.

The Estate Market.

"THE SAMUEL ESTATES, LIMITED."

MAYFAIR FREEHOLDS.

Three or four pages of the London Gazette are occupied (June 29) with details of Mayfair freeholds which are about to be registered at the Land Registry, under the Land Transfer Acts, 1875 and 1897, as the property of "the Samuel Estates, Limited, Shell House, Hathorpe-gate."

Lord Falmouth's mansion, No. 2 St. James's-square, will be sold, with possession, next Thursday, in the City, by Messrs. Daniel Smith, Oakley, and Garrard (Charles-street) and Messrs. Osbb (Lincoln's Inn and Rochester). The former firm will also sell No. 165, New Bond-street.

A number of households on the estate of the Marquess Company at Covent-garden are to be sold next Wednesday in the City by Messrs. Henry Malcom and Co. (Mortimer-street) on behalf of executors. They are let at a total rental of £9,500 a year, and are situated in Mercer-street and Long-acre. Freeholds in York's-court, Cursitor-street, and Bloomsbury are for sale on the same occasion.

There is not much in common between Barnet and Bethnal-green, and the realisation of London properties belonging to a charity at Chipping Barnet, known as Jesus Hospital, is likely to wipe out the last association of the name of the old place with the other. Previously a contract has been entered into for the sale of nearly honest premises, known as the Priory of Wales, Barnet-green, Bethnal-green. The publichouse is subject to a lease expiring in 1924, at a ground-rent of six guineas a year. By the proposed sale the Barnet charity will receive £4,500 net, as the purchasers have to defray the costs.

DEVON AND CORNWALL ESTATES.

Part of General Sir Reginald Pole Carew's Antony estate, and pleasure and other land in Devon and Cornwall, including 400 acres on the estuary of the Lynher, belonging to Captain A. E. Pole-Carew, will be sold at Plymouth next Friday, by Mr. H. E. Holcroft and others. Body and Son (Plymouth), Messrs. Alcock, Saunders, and Son (Plymouth), and others. At the total area is 5,000 acres, in some 60 lots. Sites with fine views from Manor Head in Looe, and of Whitsand Bay, are included.

Castle-an-Dinas is a large elliptical encampment with tramroad, on the outskirts of St. Columb Major, not far from the upright stones known as "The Nine Maidens." Apparently the ancient manor has been applied to a modern residence which, with adjoining land, including a farm of 115 acres, is to be sold, by order of the executors of the late Mr. Roberts, at St. Columb Major next Tuesday. Messrs. Hancock and Sons (St. Austell) are the auctioneers. At St. Columb on July 16. Possession of the house and grounds, six acres, will be given on completion of the purchase.

COUNTRY HOUSES AT AUCTION.

Wayes Hall and 772 acres, seven miles from Chichester, are to be sold on Friday, July 14, by Messrs. Strutt and Parker (Wrexham). The park and house extend to 165 acres, and there are farms in from 40 to 130 acres.

Wyke House, Wyke Regis, Weymouth, is for sale in London next Monday by Messrs. Raymond and Graham, Limited, Oxford-street, in conjunction with Mr. J. C. Talbot, Weymouth. The tenure is supplied and the grounds have an area of seven acres. On the following day, also at Winchester House, Messrs. Bracketts and Sons, Tunbridge Wells, will offer the freehold Grateland House, in 45 acres, with pleasure gardens, six acres, with a picturesque residence about 3000; above are level, on July 15 at offices.

Lady Cholmondeley's Hurchett freehold of 10 acres, Leigh Hermes, with adjoining fields which have a building value, and Ashleigh, Collier Hall, about nine acres, are to be submitted at the Guildhall, Windsor, on July 15, by Messrs. Mordant and Bean, Slough, who are acting on behalf of the mortgagees, in conjunction with Messrs. Lofts and Warner, Mount-street.

THE COVENT GARDEN AUCTION.

At their Friday Auction Rooms on July 13 Messrs. Goddard and Smith will hold the sale, already advertised in The Times, of certain freeholds in the neighbourhood of Covent Garden. The lots include Nos. 7, 8, 9, 10, 11, and 12, Bow-street, the property of Mr. Daniel H. Pigott and others, and at £1,875 a year; Floral-street, 3, 4, 5, and 6, Henrietta-street, 14, 15, 16, 38, and 37, King-street, 85, New-street, 12 and 13, Southampton-street, 2 Tavistock-street, and 27, 28, 30, 32, and 34, Wellington-street. They comprise blocks of business premises and offices. In many cases they are let on short tenancies, or on lease, having a year or two still to run, so that a purchaser will have the benefit of early possession, or of the increased value which attaches to premises naturally to be expected on re-letting. Amongst the present occupiers are the Capital and Counties Bank, the London City and Midland Bank, Messrs. George Newnes, Limited, Messrs. E. M. Fox, Limited, theatrical costumiers, Messrs. Vincent Garden publishers, and Messrs. Duckworth and Co., publishers.

Mr. Leslie Raymond, Golders Green, is to sell a long leasehold detached house known as Heather-dene, West Heath-avenue, Hampstead, in the City on July 14. The grounds of half an acre contain a hard tennis court.

THE CHÂTEAU DE FITZ-JAMES.

In Paris on July 14 a very attractive landed estate is to be submitted at an "expert" price, according to a detailed announcement, made in the Figaro of yesterday (p. 30). It comprises the Château de Fitz-James, with pleasure gardens, a park, and several preserves in the Commune of Fitz-James, of Agnetz, near Clermont, in the Oise. The estate is situated in the Arrondissement of Clermont, Oise. The names of the lawyers concerned with the sale are stated in the announcement.

SKODER ISLAND FOR SALE.

The Scone property of Skoder Island has been designed by Mr. C. Tovar Powell, known as Raglan Hall, Caellwen, has been sold by Messrs. Dungan B. Gray and Partners (Mount-street). Skomer Island is included in the 3,600 acres of the St. Brides estate, which Messrs. Knight, Frank, and Rutley are to sell for Lord Kensington. The property extends eight miles along the Pembroke coast.

RESULTS OF AUCTION SALES.

(By Private Treaty and at Auction.)

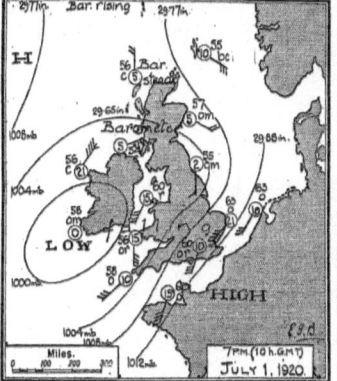

'MONTSERRAT' LIME JUICE CORDIAL & PURE LIME-FRUIT JUICE

Seafarers to the Western Indies brought us to the values that make the "Montserrat," and for the health of the seamen themselves the medicinal virtues of the Lime have rendered great service.

As a delicious cordial and a cooling drink "Montserrat" has made its way to every corner of the world.

The night before Michael Collins sent his 'Squad' out to assassinate the 'Cairo Gang', a team of undercover British agents working and living in Dublin. A series of shootings took place throughout the night, which left 14 members of the British Forces dead.

The Crown Forces, led by the Auxiliaries (and supported by the 'Black and Tans') mobilised in Dublin on the morning of the match with orders to go to Croke Park and search the crowd for known gunmen and weapons.

Throw-in for the match was scheduled for 2.45p.m. but when three I.R.A. men, Sean Russell, Tom Kilcoyne and Harry Colley, were informed (by their contacts) of the planned search of Croke Park, they came to Croke Park and pleaded with Luke O'Toole, General Secretary of the G.A.A., to cancel the match.

O'Toole took the decision not to cancel the match; the mood in Dublin, and the Stadium, was very tense. Rumours of the previous night's exploits were circulating amongst the crowd and thoughts of reprisals must have been prominent in peoples minds. O'Toole judged that any announcement to clear the stadium would lead to a panic-induced exodus amongst the 10,000 strong crowd and that a crush could develop at the turnstiles.

Mick Sammon, the Kildare referee, threw in the ball at 3.15p.m. Accounts given by eye-witnesses suggest that five minutes after the throw-in the stadium was raided by the British forces with shooting breaking out almost immediately. The British had entered the stadium at the Canal End and when the shooting began the crowd surged away from that end of the stadium hoping to make it over the wall at the railway end.

Ultimately fourteen people lost their lives as a

result of the shooting in Croke Park that day. Included among the dead were Michael Hogan, a player on the Tipperary Team (whom the Hogan Stand is named after); Thomas Ryan, shot on his knees whispering an act of contrition to Hogan; Jane Boyle, due to be married five days later and fourteen year old William Scott, so badly mutilated that it was at first thought he had been bayoneted to death.

Two military enquiries were established into the shootings and the findings of these enquiries, made public in 2003, are the main primary source for the events of that day. Strangely the main historical records of the Association, (the Central Council minute books), make no reference whatsoever to Bloody Sunday.

The findings of the enquiry and the statements released by Dublin Castle often contradict one another. In a series of 'official statements' the British Authorities offered three possible scenarios for the bloodshed; the first being that the raiding party returned fire at I.R.A. pickets placed outside Croke Park; the second was that the raiding party came under fire in the ground itself while the third explanation was that upon the raiding party's arrival three warning shots were fired by an I.R.A. man in the crowd and this caused a stampede. In all Dublin Castle scenarios however one thing is constant, the British had come under fire first.

Almost immediately serious doubts were expressed about the official version of events; the media picked glaring holes in the Dublin Castle statements; in particular their claims about I.R.A. pickets outside the ground; were these not instead unofficial ticket sellers, a common match-day feature. One claim made by Dublin Castle, that thirty revolvers had been found in the stadium, caused particular annoyance amongst the public and the media who begged the question that if thirty arms were found, why were they not

93

presented to the enquiry and why was no-one arrested when found with a gun? The purported aim of the raid was, after-all, to search for guns and gunmen.

The events of the day had a profound impact on the people of Ireland; it seemed as if the British authorities had deliberately chosen an easy target – a stadium full of innocent people- to exact revenge for a military loss suffered the night before. Bloody Sunday shocked the British public too and while it is too simple to say that it helped end the War of Independence it must certainly be considered a key factor.

Lord Lamont approved the story and felt that this event would have a lasting effect on Irish-British relations: he was right.

Lamont is a Scottish Clan name, one of the oldest clans in the country.

Legend has it that the clan is descended from the royal house of Dalriada and from the O'Neill princes of Tyrone in Ireland in the 11th century. Lamont therefore empathised with the Irish cause.

"The Observer" had written a story about the Polish Russian war. The article was favourable to the Russian stance, which followed David Lloyd George's view while Lord Lamont was more inclined to agree with Winston Churchill's opinion supporting the Poles.

Even so, Lord Lamont approved of the story with the proviso that Churchill's views were also to be expressed.

Charles was enjoying his new life and the status that he held in British society. He often had dinner parties with the elite and although his appearance could be quite off-putting, people were getting used to it. It is amazing what tremendous wealth and power can do to win over people's acceptance.

Charles held a New Year's Eve party at the town house and invited one hundred guests to join him in welcoming in 1921.

His current consort was Josephine Windsor, a rather attractive woman, five years Charles' senior; she was American but had lived in London for over ten years.

The only time Lamont had difficulty in his impersonation of his murdered brother was at functions such as these. If Oxford University friends of Charles attended, they would expect Lamont to recognize them and engage in conversation about the old days. This was of course impossible for Lamont so he relied on his old excuse:

'I am sorry. The war has taken many memories away from me.'

It seemed to work and Charles' friends were very sympathetic. Their sympathy also applied to his appearance; both Charles and Harold had been known for their good looks but now Charles wore a prosthetic mask and had scarring on his hands and neck.

This was not unusual in Britain after the war, as many soldiers were burnt by mustard gas and many more bore horrible facial scars from bullets and shellfire.

Lord Lamont had very good relations with David Lloyd George, the Prime Minister, and key members of his cabinet including Winston Churchill who was Secretary of State for the Colonies. Churchill was responsible for the reallocation of territory from the Ottoman Empire.

Lamont also had cordial relations with King George V and a strong friendship with his son and heir, Edward V111. As a result, on a regular basis Lamont would receive Royal invitations to dinners and other functions. He really was enjoying the good life.

New York, New York

Chapter 19

New York City, 1920

Emily decided she needed a credible story to explain her pregnancy when she arrived in America. The most believable tale was that her husband, a Captain in the British Army, was killed on the Western Front; he was unaware that his wife was pregnant.

Emily Scott became "Emily Brown". Ironically, that name was part of the Lamont Clan unbeknown to her.

Emily quite enjoyed living in New York with the Ashworths, whose home was magnificent and, although similar in size to her parent's house, was actually located in the city, making it convenient to shop for all the things she required to raise her baby. Of course she hid the clothes and the pram and other baby paraphernalia from the Ashworths, as they believed the child was to be adopted.

Ashworth House

Emily did not meet many people in New York prior to the birth of her baby, but she did meet one particular person who would change the rest of her life. His name was John Weatherspoon, a wealthy banker from Boston Massachusetts.

John had decided to drop in to see George and Sophie, at Ashworth House while he was in New York on business. He had known them from when he was a young boy as his parents and the Ashworths had belonged to the same tennis club.

Emily was sitting in the parlour reading "A Poor Wise Man" by Mary Roberts Rinehart, recommended to her by George. John was shown into the parlour by James, the Ashworth's butler, and after introductions, they started a polite conversation. John could not help but notice Emily's condition and asked where her husband was. Emily explained the situation and John commiserated.

The two of them got on famously and when it was time to go, John thought he would like to see her again.

He contacted George Ashworth and asked his permission to see Emily once more; George could not see anything wrong with it, although given Emily's state, he did not see much of a future in the relationship.

The young couple went walking in Central Park; they ate in small cafés rather than the famous restaurants that were prolific in New York. They fell in love.

The baby was discussed at length and John promised he would raise the child as though it was his own. Emily continued with the "war widow" story and even started to believe it herself.

She wrote to her parents in England telling them of the news and not surprisingly, they were very supportive of her engagement and imminent marriage. However they did not attend the wedding.

Emily and John settled in Boston, where John owned a beautiful three-storey house.

Emily's baby boy was born on 28th April 1921; they named him Charles, in honour of her late fictitious husband.

Life was good. Emily and John were deeply in love and little Charles Weatherspoon was an absolute delight, although having a live-in nanny made it much easier.

Business was booming for the bank, an inheritance from his father. The bank had grown substantially since John took the reins. The economy was growing as fast and the "Roaring Twenties" were in full swing.

When Charles was two years old, she received a telephone call from her parents, asking them all to visit England so that George and Sophie could meet their grandson and also finally meet John. All had been forgiven, so it seemed.

It was agreed and the young family sailed from New York on 18th May 1922.

The "Andania II" berthed at London Dock on the 25th of May where George and Sophie were there to greet them and drive them back to "Cliveden House" in Berkshire.

The grandparents were besotted with their little grandson; they took him for walks in the stroller around the estate. He was intrigued with seeing deer for the first time, not to mention the rabbits, squirrels and other wildlife. He had never got to see any animals before, apart from the family cat back in Boston.

Their idyllic holiday was about to change, however and Emily's life would never be the same.

Guess Who's Coming to Dinner

Chapter 20

George and Sophie received an invitation to attend a dinner party at Lord Lamont's Pall Mall residence. George rang Charles to see if Emily and John could attend and of course Charles was more than happy for them to come. Sophie arranged for one of the house staff to baby-sit young Charlie.

It was a Saturday night, 17th June. The men wore dinner suits and the ladies were to wear long gowns.

George's Rolls Royce pulled up at the front portico of Clivedon House and the chauffeur opened the doors for the guests; it would only be a thirty-minute drive to Pall Mall.

When they arrived, they were ushered into the great hall, where earlier arrivals had gathered. Emily immediately recognized her old friend, Sarah, so she went over and reacquainted herself. After the initial greeting, Emily asked Sarah to accompany her to a quiet part of the room.

'Darling, you need to know the situation.'

Emily told Sarah the whole story to ensure she did not blurt out what she knew at the dinner table. Sarah was delighted to know she had married and kept the baby.

'Sweetheart, you know your secret is safe with me.'

'Well, you are the only friend who knows the truth, so I'm grateful.'

'Come on, introduce me to your very handsome husband.'

'He is rather handsome, isn't he?'

Emily and Sarah walked over to the group where John was talking and, at the appropriate time Emily introduced Sarah.

The only other concern Emily had, was seeing Charles again after all these years. The fact that she and Sarah were the only ones who knew that Charles was the real father of young Charles made it even more daunting.

A bell rang, and they were all asked to be seated. Charles arranged for his butlers to show his guests their correct seating allocation.

Emily was seated directly opposite Lord Lamont.

Once they had eaten their entrée, conversation began across the table. Lord Lamont asked Emily how she was enjoying living in America.

'How did you know I am living over there, Lord Lamont?'

'Your father mentioned it to me.'

'Oh, I see. Well I am really enjoying it; having my husband and little boy with me does help, of course.'

'Of course.'

'How long have you been there'?

'Just four years, although it seems longer.'

'I haven't been over there yet; it is my intention to visit soon. I'm keen to see how they run their newspapers.

'You really must go, my Lord. I am sure you would enjoy it.'

That comprised the extent of Emily's conversation with her former lover and father of her child.

'Either Charles has no idea who I am or he has significant memory loss from his war injuries,' she thought subsequently.

She suspected the former, but was left with the question: who is he?

Born in the USA

Chapter 21

The year was 1926. The economy was still booming as was John's bank, The Bank of Boston. According to U.S President, Calvin Coolidge: "The business of America is business."

Among significant events occurring in 1926 were: Robert Goddard launched the first Liquid Fuel Rocket in the USA and Erik Rotheim invented aerosol sprays in Norway, but a more significant event was that young Charles Weatherspoon enrolled in the "Sage School" in Boston." Sage School" was limited to gifted students who scored 120 plus in the school's IQ test.

These primary school years were uneventful for Charles; he was always near the top of the class and had a healthy interest in sports. He was the pitcher in the school's baseball team and was the quarterback in the football team.

The Great Depression 1929

John Weatherspoon took the normal route to work. It was Wednesday, 30th of October. As usual, he parked his Cadillac Sport Phaeton under the building.

He had a premonition that his life was about to change irrevocably. On the previous day, which would be known evermore as "Black Tuesday", the Great Depression had begun, with a massive crash of shares on Wall Street.

He entered the bank from the car park; he could immediately sense there was something terribly wrong. There were no staff members at the tellers' counters waiting for the doors to open as usual. Instead, they were all looking out the windows at a large crowd amassing outside the bank. John knew what was happening; there was going to be a "run on the bank." People wanted to withdraw all their savings and hide them under a mattress or convert their cash to gold.

John knew that if he did not act quickly, there would be no bank remaining at the end of the day.

He rang Emily and told her to rally up all their friends and come down to the bank. They all needed to make a deposit to show the crowd that people still had faith in the bank. He instructed all his staff to do the same.

He then rang the Brinks Armoured Truck Service and ordered one hundred thousand dollars to be delivered to the front doors, so the milling crowd could see that all was well. Brinks assured him they could be there by 11am.

It was approaching 10am and the doors were expected to open. He instructed his manager to go out and inform the angry customers that everything was under control. If they wished to withdraw their savings, they could do so at 11.30am.

The fact that the bank was opening an hour and a half late did nothing to placate the customers.

John called the staff together. He instructed them to be friendly and smile as the customers withdrew all their savings; he hoped he would stem the tide before the bank ran out of cash.

The time came to open and the manager stepped outside again and addressed the mob:

'We, at the Bank of Boston, are very comfortable with our cash reserves. If you wish to withdraw your funds, so be it, but we ask you to do so in an orderly manner. I would ask if there are any customers who wish to make a deposit, please hold up your hand as we need to take care of you first.'

About fifty people indicated they wished to make a deposit and were ushered through the large revolving door.

This did seem to have some effect and several people decided that they were being overly anxious and left. Gradually, more and more departed and a sense of calm started to permeate the crowd.

Just then, a Brinks truck pulled up and the guards started to carry in bags of cash under the armed protection of their fellow guards.

The two significant actions of depositors and cash arriving saved the day for the Boston Bank; however, fifty percent of their customers did withdraw all their savings.

Many other banks did not fare so well, with many closing and their customers losing their life's savings.

John and his family were affected by the ongoing depression. They sold the Brownstone terrace and moved into a much more modest abode and instead of driving a Cadillac, John drove a Ford Model T. The bank survived the remainder of the depression and went on to be one of the most successful banks on the east coast.

One thing the Weatherspoons did not compromise was their son's education.

Charles began his high school years at Dexter School, a new private school that promised much. John Weatherspoon was on the Board of Directors, although this did not allow him any special privileges.

The school was set in thirty-six acres and despite being a new school, it had many facilities other schools did not have, including an astronomical observatory.

Charles continued to do well both in academic subjects and in sports.

In 1939, he completed his studies at Dexter and applied to Harvard, where he was accepted as a student in English and Journalism. It was at Harvard that he developed his interest in world politics and, in particular, Europe.

The world was watching what Hitler was up to and feared another world war.

The King and I

Chapter 22

Lamont's close friend, Edward, King of England, had invited Lamont to Balmoral Castle for a weekend of hunting and general relaxation. Lamont had been very close to Edward since the First World War and his subsequent elevation to Lord Lamont. He was a guest at Edward's coronation and had often enjoyed hunting weekends with him at Balmoral.

He loved Scotland and missed his estate at "Torwood", but he had extended the lease to the National Health Department, as the Second World War had produced so many soldiers with facial injuries. "Torwood" had become the pre-eminent centre in the United Kingdom for trating such injuries.

He arrived by train; the King's secretary collected him and drove to the castle.

Edward and Wallace Simpson met him at the entrance to the castle. The next day they had planned to go shooting, which was Lamont's favourite pastime; the deer were in abundance and he was hoping to get himself a stag.

After breakfast, Edward and Charles and various game staff headed out on horseback to the very rear of the estate.

They stopped near a beautiful stream and Edward produced a flask of the finest malt scotch to help warm them up.

'Charles, I would like your advice on a very private matter.'

'What is it, Edward?'

'As you know, Wallace and I are very much in love. I know you think 'just another affair' and God knows I have had enough of those over the years but Wallace is the only woman I have really loved; I want to marry her.'

'Ted, the Government will not allow you to marry Wallace; apart from being American she is a divorcee.'

'Divorce didn't stop Henry VIII. It really is hypocrisy,' complained Edward.

'The reality is, if you wish to marry Wallace, you are going to lose your crown.'

'Charles, I am prepared to abdicate, if that's what it takes. However, you have a very good relationship with the Prime Minister. Could you sound out Baldwin and ascertain what the Government's attitude would be?'

'I can contact him but I am afraid I know what his reaction will be.'

104

The two men mounted their horses and proceeded to where the game staff had erected a table and chairs in preparation for lunch.

After they had eaten, they pursued their hunting activities without much luck.

Lamont did arrange a meeting with Stanley Baldwin at Number 10 and broached the subject of marriage. Baldwin was aghast at the prospect of the King marrying an American divorcee and assured Lamont that if the King insisted on this union, he would have no alternative but to abdicate.

Lamont agreed to keep any talk of marriage and abdication out of his newspapers. He contacted the owners of the other major newspapers, who also agreed to remain silent.

After much unresolved discussion between the King and the cabinet, Edward duly signed the instruments of abdication at Fort Belvedere on 10 December 1936, in the presence of his younger brothers: Prince Albert, Duke of York, next in line for the throne; Prince Henry, Duke of Gloucester; and Prince George, Duke of Kent.

INSTRUMENT OF ABDICATION

    I, Edward the Eighth, of Great
Britain, Ireland, and the British Dominions
beyond the Seas, King, Emperor of India, do
hereby declare My irrevocable determination
to renounce the Throne for Myself and for
My descendants, and My desire that effect
should be given to this Instrument of
Abdication immediately.

    In token whereof I have hereunto set
My hand this tenth day of December, nineteen
hundred and thirty six, in the presence of
the witnesses whose signatures are subscribed.

SIGNED AT
FORT BELVEDERE
IN THE PRESENCE
OF

KING EDWARD'S REIGN

SHORTEST FOR 453 YEARS

PRINCIPAL EVENTS

The boy who was to become Prince of Wales and King Edward VIII was born on June 23, 1894, at White Lodge, Richmond Park. He was first educated at the Royal Naval College, Osborne, and later at Magdalen College, Oxford. His formal investiture as Prince of Wales took place at Carnarvon Castle in 1911. On August 7, 1914, he was gazetted to the Grenadier Guards, and served in France and Flanders till March, 1916. As staff captain he went to Egypt, and thence to Italy, afterwards returning to France.

Successive Dominion tours, after the War, enabled him to steer closely into Empire feeling. A journey through Newfoundland and Canada in 1919 was followed by visits to Australia and New Zealand, India and Burma, Ceylon, Malaya, and Hong-kong, West and South Africa. He has also travelled in the United States and South America.

The accession of King Edward on the death of King George was proclaimed at a meeting of the Privy Council on January 21. In his declaration to that body the new King referred to the irreparable loss the British Commonwealth of Nations had suffered, and stated his determination to follow in his father's footsteps in upholding constitutional government.

On the same day the oath of allegiance was taken by members of both Houses of Parliament, and next day came the public Proclamation in London and the United Kingdom. The traditional proceedings at St. James's Palace, Charing Cross, Temple Bar, and the Royal Exchange were followed by great crowds. A comparison of dates will show that 10 calendar months and 10 days have elapsed between the Proclamation and the Abdication.

The present ceremony of this short reign—the shortest for 453 years of English history—was the funeral of King George. King Edward, and his three brothers, who on the previous midnight had mounted guard over the catafalque in Westminster Hall, walked behind the coffin as it was borne through the streets of London.

AN ALARMING INCIDENT

In February the new Monarch performed at Buckingham Palace the Royal duty of investing with honours and decorations those who had been mentioned in King George's last New Year's Honours List. His Majesty himself had assumed the highest ranks in the Navy, Army, and Air Force. Early in March he quietly took a seat in the Church of All Hallows, Barking-by-the-Tower, where the Welsh Guards, with whom he had been closely identified as Prince of Wales, celebrated their coming-of-age on St. David's Day. The other Guards and other regiments were inspected on various occasions; and the culmination of such minor military formalities came on July 16, a day so brilliant in general as it was, in due sequence, unfortunate.

At an impressive martial display in Hyde Park King Edward had presented new Colours to the six battalions of the Guards, and as he was riding along Constitution Hill on his return to Buckingham Palace a man in the crowd threw a revolver at his feet. At the moment, and to the bystanders, this looked like an attempt at assassination, though it was afterwards assumed to be the foolish act of an unduly excited individual. The real importance of the incident lay in the demonstration of widespread thankfulness and relief that followed.

So recently as the middle of November the most important of the Royal visits in the Navy took place at Portland, when the Home Fleet was inspected in wild weather, and his Majesty spent part of an evening with the lower deck at a smoking concert. King Edward, the first English King to fly, was untiringly to omit the Royal Air Force from his programme, and during the summer, in the company of the Duke of York, he spent some hours at their station in Suffolk.

CONCERN FOR INDUSTRY

The concern for industry, employment, and unemployment which the Prince of Wales had consistently shown was equally apparent in King Edward. His first public engagement as King, as soon after his accession as February, was with the British Industries Fair at Olympia and the White City. Then, in March, he acquainted himself with Glasgow housing reform when in Glasgow to see the Queen Mary, which, in May, he saw again at Southampton on the eve of her maiden voyage to New York. Of those industrial visits the last was to South Wales on November 17-18. South Staffordshire and Birmingham were in town here included this week, but the tour was cancelled.

At the end of July 6,000 Cornduan ex-Service men and their relations gave his Majesty an enthusiastic reception at Vimy Ridge, where, in the presence of President Lebrun and the Prime Minister of Canada, he unveiled the Canadian National Memorial. Speaking at first in French, afterwards in English, he paid an eloquent tribute to the fallen sons of the Dominion.

During the summer there began on the Dalmatian coast a yachting cruise which, though undertaken as a private holiday, ended in several semi-official visits. It touched King Edward met Kemal Ataturk, and, continuing his trip by land, was received in Bulgaria by King Boris, and in Austria by President Miklos. Flying home from Zurich, he spent the later days of September at Balmoral.

On November 3 King Edward opened Parliament and delivered in person the Speech from the Throne.

THE NEWS AT WINDSOR

At Windsor the news was received with sorrow, for King Edward was not only King but a resident and neighbour. Now Prince of Wales he made it a hobby to read every book and guide on the castle that was issued, that he had often sat over for four fateful days, and it was a frequent masterpiece for him to bring a party over from Fort Belvedere and to conduct them around the Castle, explaining the various treasures and curiosities of the rooms to them himself. At the command of no one for 15 years.

ROYAL DUCHIES

HISTORY OF LANCASTER AND CORNWALL

King Harry IV, who was declared King in Parliament on September 30, 1399, after the abdication of King Richard II, had inherited the Duchy of Lancaster from his father, John of Gaunt, who had been created Duke in 1362. The Duchy was composed of the estates which came to John of Gaunt on his marriage with Blanche, co-heir of Henry of Grosmont, Earl of Lancaster, Leicester, Derby, and Lincoln, who had been created Duke of Lancaster in 1351.

One of the first acts of King Henry IV was to promulgate in Parliament a charter in which the lands and possessions of the Duchy of Lancaster were declared to be a separate inheritance, distinct from the lands and possessions of the Crown now known as the "Crown Lands," the revenues of which, in virtue of the customary surrender at the beginning of every reign, are paid into the Treasury. The prerogatives of the Crown were annexed to all the possessions as separated, but the rule or government of the estates was to be under an appropriate management, the distribution of the revenues by a distinct Treasury, and the ordering of all matters connected therewith was vested in an establishment called the Chancellor and Council of the Duchy. The refusal and the Sovereign became by this act one, identified in personal capacity, but separate in interests.

On November 10, 1399, the Duchy of Lancaster was granted to Henry Prince of Wales (afterwards King Henry V) to him and his heirs, disinvested from the Crown of England." In 1445 the bulk of the estates of the Duchy were vested in trustees for the support of the Household of King Henry VI, and in 1447 the pension of £333 (equivalent perhaps approximately to £10,000 nowadays) which had been charged upon the Duchy of Lancaster for the benefit of the King's uncle Humphrey, Duke of Gloucester, was transferred to Queen Margaret, then Queen Consort.

In 1461 King Henry VI was declared to have forfeited the Duchy, which was annexed in perpetuity to the Crown, although still disavowed under the terms of the Charter of 1399.

It may be added that the Duchy of Lancaster, which produced a net revenue of £4,970 in 1399, yielded in 1934 a net revenue to the Privy Purse of £83,000.

FROM THE BLACK PRINCE

The Duchy of Cornwall was first conferred on Edward Earl of Chester, afterwards Prince of Wales, who later became famous as the Black Prince, eldest son of King Edward III, in 1337. The remainder was to the eldest sons of his heirs, the Kings of England, and although, owing to changes in the succession to the Throne, there have since been Kings who were not the heirs of the original grantee, under the usual interpretation of the succession to the peerage dignity it has always been held that the Duchy of Cornwall was vested in the eldest son of the King. In the case of the eldest surviving son of King James II, his right to the Duchy of Cornwall was extinguished by an Act of Parliament in 1702 (N.S.).

The revenues of the Duchy of Cornwall, which amounted to £3,000 net in 1399 (roughly estimated as equivalent, perhaps, to £90,000 now) in May of this year was returned as £164,000, of which £25,000 was allocated by King Edward to the Duke of York, while the balance was inherited for the Privy Purse, when there was no Duke of Cornwall to share the revenues it has been the custom hitherto for the Sovereign to retain them until there should be a Duke of Cornwall.

In December, 1460, by an Act of Parliament, the revenues of the Duchy of Cornwall were assigned to Richard, Duke of York, who had been for political reasons declared heir to the Throne, although at that time Edward, Prince of Wales, only son of King Henry VI, was Duke of Cornwall. This arrangement ended a few weeks later on the death of the Duke of York on December 30, 1460. The Princess Mary, elder daughter of King Henry VIII, who, in 1525, was the Heir to the Throne, was given certain rights and revenues in Wales and later her Court at Ludlow. She may also have enjoyed part of the revenues of the Duchy of Cornwall, and was commonly styled the "Princess of Wales," though such a title was not conferred on her by Patent of her creation as such was enrolled or is known to have existed "Princess of Cornwall and Wales."

UNHAPPY AUDIENCES IN THE CINEMAS

CHEERS FOR THE DUKE OF YORK

The announcement of King Edward's abdication was made in most West End cinemas shortly after 4 o'clock and was received, especially where it took the form of a bold statement thrown upon the screen, in sympathetic and unhappy silence. The announcement of the name of his successor was welcomed with cheering and cheers.

Before 4.30 both general and more cinemas were showing special short films collected from ordinary news films, from recent public appearances of the Duke and Duchess of York, Princess Elizabeth and Princess Margaret, Queen Mary, and Mr. Baldwin. All these were received with warm applause. It was noticeable that in one or two cinemas in which no previous announcement had been made these special films were run by a hush among the audience, which for the moment was prejudicially concerned with the fact of abdication.

Principally concerned with the Abdication at the conclusion of two pictures also evoked varying responses. In some cinemas the audience spontaneously stood to attention, while in others nobody stirred and had the heart either of the national anthem.

Most of the large cinema combines including Gaumont-British, instructed their houses in all parts of the country not to show the picture of King Edward at the close of their performances last night, but to play "God Save the King" as usual.

Mr. George Black, director of the General Theatre Corporation and Moss Empires, instructed all managers of theatres on the two circuits to play "Land of Hope and Glory" instead of the National Anthem last night.

HISTORY OF THE CRISIS

RUMOUR AND FACT

THE KING'S DECISION TO ABDICATE

The first intimations of the events which led, swiftly and tragically, to the abdication of King Edward VIII have made public on the other side of the Atlantic as long ago as last May.

In that month the Court Circular noted the presence of Mr. and Mrs. Ernest Simpson at the King's first formal dinner-party after his accession. This signal honour for American citizens attracted legitimate attention. But subsequently the name of Mrs. Simpson appeared alone, and the American Press began to give prominence to the gossip which had been circulating in London. When Mrs. Simpson accompanied his Majesty on his Balkan holiday, and later when she was his guest at Balmoral, the American newspapers dropped all pretence of restraint. Neither party to what was described—sardonically, not sentimentally—as a "Royal romance" was spared; and it was not long before his Majesty's subjects in Canada became painfully aware that no matter to whom they owed their loyalty was being made the target of a campaign of publicity throughout the United States.

A SILENT PRESS

Confident in the hope that his Majesty would, by some act or announcement, put an end to a situation so damaging to his own and to his Empire's prestige, the British Press kept silence. When Mrs. Simpson divorced her second husband at Ipswich on October 27, the case was reported in this country briefly and without comment. But for some time the King's Ministers, as well as public men in almost every walk of life had been given, by correspondents all over the world, good reason to know how seriously the breath of scandal was impairing the dignity of the Throne. Unofficial advices from the Dominions and Colonies revealed how gravely the rumours about the King's conduct of his private life struck at the roots of British solidarity; and, as the susceptibilities of a section of the American Press gained currency in hinted but rapidly spreading circles over here, the most loyal subjects of an intensely popular King became uneasy. Still—such was the nation's confidence in a man who throughout his life had done everything to deserve it—no hint of criticism was made public.

On the other side of the Atlantic uninspiscific annual-mongering had now reached a crescendo: and in this country spreading rumour increased apprehension. Behind the scenes the King's advisers, as well as his truest friends, must have been of a bold statement thrown upon the date and painful subject with his Majesty himself. At last (on October 18, as Mr. Baldwin revealed yesterday) the Prime Minister informed the King of the gravity with which he viewed the situation. The tax was broken, and his Majesty freely discussed the matter with his friend and adviser. It was at their next interview—on November 16, soon after the Duke of Kent visited him at Fort Belvedere. There were two Cabinet meetings of his intention of marrying Mrs. Simpson whenever she should be free, and of his readiness to abdicate if necessary. The same night he informed the Queen of his decision, and within a few days his brothers knew of it. On November 25 another interview with the Prime Minister further clarified the position. Acute anxiety meanwhile prevailed in Ministerial circles. The Dominion Governments, informed of his Majesty's attitude, intimated that they would not be prepared to accept his choice of a queen. The King, however, remained adamant.

Finally, a few days after the King's return from a visit to South Wales, during which fresh proofs of his popularity were spontaneously vouchsafed by the least fortunate of his subjects, the King on December 3, after a further period of Bradford, speaking in public on December 1, made reference to his Majesty's attitude, intimated that they would be prepared to accept his choice of a queen. The King, however, remained adamant.

The special photograph of King Edward VIII taken by a staff photographer of *The Times* in his study at St. James's Palace.

London Press broke its self-imposed silence for the first time. There could be no mistaking the tone of editorial comment. Affection and sympathy for the King to be predicament were generally and warmly expressed ; but his duty to his Imperial heritage was respectfully pointed out, and he was urged on all sides to find, in consultation with his Ministers, some solution of his domestic problems which would prove not incompatible with the wishes and the welfare of the peoples over whose destinies he presided. On that day Mr. Baldwin informally but unambiguously acquainted the King with the bitter alternatives before him.

In some quarters it was hastily but hopefully suggested that a morganatic marriage might provide the solution. But no such instruction exists under English law, and last Friday Mr. Baldwin was obliged to make it clear that neither the British nor the Dominion Governments would give their assent to the introduction of legislation which would make a morganatic marriage possible.

The public in this country had now been apprised of the situation for three days. There was much sympathy for the King, and universal sympathy for his mother ; but, in spite of attempts in some quarters to sentimentalize the issue and to make political capital out of a wholly false picture of a conflict between King and Ministers, opinion both at home and throughout the country was not in harmony with the King's Knighthead, being for the most part staunchly on the side of the family united against the marriage. At most theatres the National Anthem was sung by the audience, not in a spirit of partisanship, but in the loyal and reverent hope that a beloved King would find in this ordeal dilemma the guidance he needed. Sporadic small-scale demonstrations before Buckingham Palace and elsewhere, though unbiased by organized bands of Fascists who were exploiting the occasion for factional ends, reflected no deep or widespread support for the King's marriage. Dismayed and anxious, the country passed a December week-end in a December mood.

Mrs. Simpson, in the meantime, had left England for a villa near Cannes on December 3, and on December 7 Lord Brownlow—the Lord-in-Waiting who had accompanied her—issued a statement on Mrs. Simpson's behalf, in which she declared herself ready, " if it would serve the problem, to withdraw from a situation that has been rendered both unhappy and untenable." On the strength of this at least one London newspaper speciously expressed the hope that, on second thoughts, the King, still set-faced all along, with the King and with the King alone. On Monday a statement by Mr. Baldwin in the House of Commons made this doubly clear.

ANXIOUS INTEREST

The country followed with an anxious interest the development of the crisis, of which the chief outward and visible sign was a steady and constant coming and going of cars and advisers between Fort Belvedere and Downing Street. Markets reacted unfavourably to the future of the British Monarchy hung, as it seemed, in the balance. Many branches of trade lost their seasonal upward impetus, and all enterprises dependent, directly or indirectly, on next year's Coronation began to suffer.

On Tuesday, December 8, Mr. Baldwin had his last interview with the King. On Wednesday the King motored through fog to Windsor and thence to Fort Belvedere. During the day the Duke of York and the Duke of Kent visited him at Fort Belvedere. There were two Cabinet meetings of his intention of marrying Mrs. Simpson whenever she should be free, and of his readiness to abdicate if necessary.

In London the day was murky and over-cast. Beyond an announcement by Mr. Baldwin that he would make a further statement on the following day the people had no news in the light of which to read the future. But by dark there seemed on all sides to be an awareness that the course of events had decided to make a final appeal to the King. There was, in fact, no last hope. The Cabinet had met that morning and had decided to make a final appeal to the King to revoke, at the eleventh hour, his decision to abdicate, which had last been communicated to them by the Prime Minister at a result of his interview the day before. The appeal proved in vain. There was, in two words, too late. The Cabinet passed its last evening and its last night deeply divided on all the issues. In this grave crisis, which followed with an intense fatality which has pursued the eldest sons of the last Kings of our own Dynasties in our history. The eldest son of King

PRECEDENTS OF HISTORY

THE KING'S STYLES AND TITLES

A STRANGE FATALITY

When the Prince of Wales, who was a Knight of the Orders of the Garter, the Thistle, and St. Patrick, Grand Master of the Orders of St. Michael and St. George and of the British Empire, a Knight Grand Commander of the Orders of the Star of India and of the Indian Empire, and Grand Cross of the Royal Victorian Order, became King in January of this year he became Sovereign of those Orders, as also of the Order of the Bath, to which he had not previously been admitted, and thereby ceased to be an ordinary member of any of them, by ceasing to be Sovereign of the Orders in virtue of his abdication the Crown it would appear that his Majesty will sever his connexion with these orders, and until, they resume should be renewed by a fresh appointment.

His Majesty's Knighthead, being for almost all throughout the country with the Sovereignty of this Realm, survives, and would be held completely with any Peerage title which might be conferred on him after his abdication. The Bill for amending the Act of Settlement provides that the provisions of the Royal Marriage Act shall not apply to King Edward or to any issue that he may have.

PRINCESS ELIZABETH

On the accession of the Duke of York as King, Princess Elizabeth and Princess Margaret advance a step in the order of the succession to the Throne and might be considered to be in the same relation to the Crown as were the Princess Mary and her half-sister, the Princess Elizabeth, to their half-brother, King Edward VI, from 1547 to 1553, were it not for the fact that various Acts of Parliament then in existence had imposed disabilities on both the daughters of King Henry VIII.

The position with regard to the immediate succession is now different, therefore, both from that which existed in the sixteenth century during the reign of King Edward VI and in the seventeenth and nineteenth centuries during the reigns of King William III and King William IV when there a single Princess in each case, the Princess Anne and the Princess Victoria, was Heir Presumptive. It has been argued that in the case of succession as between two daughters has never been laid down in England as in the case of the Crown of Scotland, where a single Princess could succeed, but this has not hitherto been determined by legislation because the case has never yet arisen. Up till now it has been the custom to assume that the principle of primogeniture prevails between males, and between females, and the matter would be settled by legislation.

IMPAIRED SOVEREIGNTY

With regard to precedents for the present development, both King Edward II and King Richard II were deposed from the Throne and King James II was held by an Act of Parliament, to have abdicated. K. King Edward II, who was held prisoner at several castles and forced after his abdication, was afterward abroad for some time, was considered thereby to have in some measure impaired his Sovereignty, became on his abdication by his grandson in 1327 so England he was crowned a second time King Edward V was never deposed. In March, 1461, and again, after a brief restoration, in April, 1471, King Edward IV was deposed by an edict of October, 1470, but recovered the Throne in April, 1471. His son, King Edward V, who was never crowned, was deposed by his uncle, King Richard III, after reigning for a minor (to only 77 days).

The popular proved a grim one, Twenty-day morning, at Fort Belvedere, the King drew up and signed an instrument of abdication. It was witnessed in his presence by his three brothers, the Duke of York, Gloucester, and Kent. Thus, in circumstances which will evoke wonder and pity so long as history continues, the British Monarchy passed in one fateful generation through a fatality which has pursued the eldest sons of the last Kings of our own Dynasties in our history. The eldest son of King

William I, Robert Duke of Normandy, was twice supplanted on the Throne of England by his brothers, lost his Duchy and died in prison. The eldest son of King Stephen, and of the House of Blois, died before his father. The eldest son of King Henry II, of the House of Anjou, also died before his father. The eldest son of King Edward IV, of the House of York, was deposed before he was crowned. The eldest son of King Henry VII, of the House of Tudor, Arthur Prince of Wales, did not live to succeed to the Throne. The eldest son of. King James I, of the House of Stuart, also died before his father. The eldest son of Queen Anne, to her Consort of the House of Denmark, died before he came to the Throne. The elder son of King Edward VII, the first Monarch of the House of Saxony, the Duke of Clarence, predeceased his father, and now the first son of the first Sovereign of the House of Windsor is abdicating before his Coronation.

EFFECT OF SUSPENSE ON TRADE

"NO HEART FOR BUYING PRESENTS"

Business decreased in the shops during the past week. Christmas buying in many of the more important business houses became desultory. The managing director of one firm whose figures were considerably down on those of last year said : " People have lost heart and are too disturbed to buy Christmas presents."

But while the usual Christmas trade fell off, except for the children's side, there were no contestations of orders for restoration robes or gowns. A house which supplies many of the Court dressmakers with materials and has orders ahead for the coronation velvets for delivery in January had no cancellations. The jewelry firms have been the chief sufferers in loss of business. There has been very little doing during this week of anxiety.

The news of the King's abdication was received very quietly in the shopping districts, and the gossip which had been widespread previously died down. The hope was expressed generally that the date of the Coronation would not be altered and that business might resume its course, which up to Thursday of last week was on the upgrade. As far as could be ascertained yesterday the hotel bookings for Coronation week have not been cancelled, and if the date is not changed the business community feel that they can proceed with their resuming of placing orders ahead.

LORD ZETLAND ON THE NEW KING'S TASKS

Lord Zetland, Secretary of State for India, submitted the toast of "The King" at the dinner of the National Trust for Places of Historic Interest or Natural Beauty, held at the May Fair Hotel last night.

They could not forget, he said, indeed that most not forget, that while the occupant of the Throne might pass, the Throne remained. The thought in the form of events of the last few days was, he confessed, one of peculiar pathos. He wished that it had not fallen to his lot to address an audience on such an occasion as this on such a night, but it was not necessary formalities had been introduced which should be remembered by a fresh appointment.

SHIPPING AND THE CORONATION

FROM A SHIPPING CORRESPONDENT

The reactions of a postponement of the Coronation ceremony next year would in no industry be greater than in shipping, where bookings from overseas have been exceptionally heavy for the event to which every one was looking without apprehension only a few weeks ago. So far as some of the outports of Empire are concerned the time had almost arrived when those who intended to be present should think at least of packing even if not, just yet, departing. Wholesale cancellations of berths would leave gaps which the various shipping managements could not hope to fill, not, indeed, could they be expected hurriedly to transfer the voyagers to later dates when in other respects ordinary seasonal bookings would be pressing their full demands on accommodation.

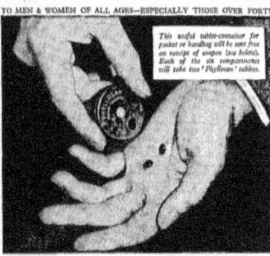
GOOD EFFECT ON MARKETS

FROM OUR CITY EDITOR

To the City the announcement that a decision had at last been reached was received with great relief, though with profound regret at the cause events had taken. Members of the Stock Exchange listened in business silence to the broad-cast of the King's statement, the authorities of the Stock Exchange having for the first time installed loudspeakers in order that members might be able to receive the news with the shortest possible delay. Even after the statement was finished the silence continued for a few moments, and this subdued atmosphere was eloquent of the regret felt by every one in the City at the nature of the decision. The reception given to the statement by the Stock Exchange was typical of that given by other markets.

At the opening of business yesterday the tension was still unrelieved, and with dealings aiming at a standstill the Stock markets sagged away further. Gradually a calmer and more confident air began to pervade the "House," which felt insufficient to operate, and under the lead of Gilt-edged securities all markets made a recovery which persisted to the end, the closing prices being about the highest of the day. In many cases the recovery wiped out the losses that had been sustained since the development of the crisis.

There were signs yesterday that the tension was easing some of the foreign institutions to be less true lenders of funds in the short loan market, but with the end of the crisis such manifestations of nervousness may be expected to disappear. A moderate recovery occurred in sterling in the foreign exchange market following the announcement of abdication, and there were indications of increased demands for sterling on Paris account. The commodity markets also passed a more satisfactory session with rises in prices recorded in many cases.

The better tone of the London markets seemed to spread to markets abroad, and the New York Stock Exchange found its own strength fortified by the fact that events in Throgmorton Street showed that England had once more passed calmly and successfully a momentous crisis.

Albert, or 'Bertie' as he was known, became King George V1, who had the onerous task of restoring credibility to the Royal Family despite his obvious stammer and initial reluctance to be King; he did a wonderful job including "being there" for the British people during the Blitz.

His relationship with Lord Lamont was cordial but nowhere near the level Lamont had enjoyed with Edward.

We're Back

Germany's Revenge

Chapter 22

On March 15th 1939 Germany invaded Czechoslovakia. In September 1939, the situation worsened when Germany invaded Poland. Both Britain and France warned Germany to move all soldiers out of Poland or there would be war. Germany did not comply. So the two countries declared war on Germany.

Charles waited along with the rest of the world but not much happened. It certainly was not yet a full scale war. Britain dropped pamphlets over Berlin which was the limit of their aggression. Then on May 10th, Germany invaded Belgium, France, Luxembourg and the Netherlands.

Now there was a full scale war!

Winston Churchill became Prime Minister of the United Kingdom and things really intensified.

May 1940, was a very significant month; the allies evacuated three hundred thousand troops back to Britain.

Charles Weatherspoon followed every development in the war from a journalistic point of view.

Things became even more intense on December 7th 1941 when Japan attacked Pearl Harbour. Now the USA was in this war and they were going to need every available able-bodied man.

Charles Weatherspoon was required to register for the draft and even though millions of men were drafted, Charles was not one of them.

He made the decision that if the war was still in progress by the time he completed his degree, he would enlist.

German Army Marching into Prague

AT WAR WITH GERMANY

BRITAIN AND FRANCE TAKE UP THE CHALLENGE

THE KING'S MESSAGE TO HIS PEOPLES

CABINET RECONSTRUCTED

Since 11 o'clock yesterday morning Great Britain has been at war with Germany.

A final British Note presented in Berlin at 9 a.m. gave the German Government two hours in which to give an undertaking that they would at once withdraw their troops from Poland. At 11.15 the Prime Minister broadcast to the nation the news "that no such undertaking has been received and that consequently this country is at war with Germany."

A French ultimatum presented in Berlin at 12.30 p.m. expired at 5 p.m. and at that hour France, too, was at war.

In a message broadcast last evening the King called upon "my people at home and my peoples across the seas" to stand "calm, firm, and united." The King afterwards received the Prime Minister at Buckingham Palace.

After an anxious Session of the House of Commons on Saturday, when members showed their uneasiness that definite action had not been taken, they were reassured yesterday, and heard with calm and resolution the Prime Minister's statement on the declaration of war.

A War Cabinet of nine members has been created, including two new Ministers—Mr. Churchill as First Lord of the Admiralty and Lord Hankey as Minister Without Portfolio.

In Poland the Germans have continued to bomb towns and villages, only some of which are of strategic importance. Heavy fighting continues in Polish Silesia, near Katowice, and in the north.

FIRST NEWS OF THE DECISION

PRIME MINISTER'S BROADCAST

The fact that Great Britain had been at war with Germany from 11 o'clock yesterday morning was made known by the Prime Minister in a broadcast message a quarter of an hour later.

Mr. CHAMBERLAIN said:—

I am speaking to you from the Cabinet Room at 10, Downing Street.

This morning the British Ambassador in Berlin handed the German Government a final Note stating that, unless we heard from them by 11 o'clock that they were prepared at once to withdraw their troops from Poland, a state of war would exist between us.

I have to tell you now that no such undertaking has been received, and that consequently this country is at war with Germany.

You can imagine what a bitter blow it is to me that all my long struggle to win peace has failed. Yet I cannot believe that there is anything more or anything different that I could have done and that would have been more successful.

HITLER'S FORCE POLICY

Up to the very last it would have been quite possible to have arranged a peaceful and honourable settlement between Germany and Poland, but Hitler would not have it. He had evidently made up his mind to attack Poland whatever happened, and although he now says he put forward reasonable proposals which were rejected by the Poles, that is not a true statement. The proposals were never shown to the Poles, nor to us, and, though they were announced in a German broadcast on Thursday night, Hitler did not wait to hear comments on them, but ordered his troops to cross the Polish frontier. His action shows convincingly that there is no chance of expecting that this man will ever give up his practice of using force to gain his will. He can only be stopped by force.

We and France are to-day, in fulfilment of our obligations, going to the aid of Poland, who is so bravely resisting this wicked and unprovoked attack on her people. We have a clear conscience. We have done all that any country could do to establish peace. The situation in which no word given by Germany's ruler could be trusted and no people or country could feel themselves safe has become intolerable. And now that we have resolved to finish it, I know that you will all play your part with calmness and courage.

At such a moment as this the assurances of support that we have received from the Empire are a source of profound encouragement to us.

"RIGHT WILL PREVAIL"

When I have finished speaking certain detailed announcements will be made on behalf of the Government. Give those your closest attention. The Government have made plans under which it will be possible to carry on the work of the nation in the days of stress and strain that may be ahead. But these plans need your help.

You may be taking your part in the fighting services or as a volunteer in one of the branches of Civil Defence. If so you will report for duty in accordance with the instructions you have received. You may be engaged in work contributing to the prosecution of war for the maintenance of the life of the people—in factories, in transport, in public utility concerns, or in the supply of other necessities of life. If so, it is of vital importance that you should carry on with your jobs.

Now may God bless you all. May He defend the right. It is the evil things that we shall be fighting against—brute force, bad faith, injustice, oppression and persecution—and against them I am certain that the right will prevail.

CONFIDENCE IN THE COMMONS

MR. CHAMBERLAIN'S ANNOUNCEMENT

WESTMINSTER, SUNDAY

The House of Commons met on occasion—it might easily have become an act of solemnity—sitting yesterday afternoon because of suspicions that the Government (who could not help themselves) were being dilatory in fulfilling the British pledge to Poland. It transmuted to-day with confidence fully restored and a resolution that had never shaken.

Yesterday the House, expecting a statement at any time from the Prime Minister, applied itself, with a dispatch that clashings could not have excelled, to a string of emergency measures, the more important of which made military service compulsory between the ages of 18 and 41. It was nearly 8 o'clock when Mr. Chamberlain entered to the accompaniment of a rousing cheer.

The PRIME MINISTER told a tense and anxious House that no reply had been received to the warning message which the British Ambassador had been instructed to deliver at Berlin. Possibly the delay was due to a proposal by the Italian Government that hostilities should cease and that a Five-Power Conference should be held. There was a rider of cheers when Mr. Chamberlain declared that Great Britain could not participate in a conference while Poland was threatened. Germany, he went on, should agree to withdraw her forces from Poland that the attainment would safeguard the vital interests of the latter and be secured by international guarantee.

The House was obviously disturbed, and when Mr. Greenwood, the Acting Leader of the Opposition, rose, there were cries by some Ministerial members of 'Speak for Britain.' He admitted that there might be reasons for delay in fulfilling our obligations to Poland and that "we must march with France. But," he said, "I wonder how long we are prepared to vacillate at a time when Britain and all that Britain stands for and civilization are in peril. Every hour's delay now imperilled by an AMERICAN SINCLAIR, and the greater part of the House obviously shared it. Mr. Chamberlain intervened to say that he would be horrified if the House thought that his statement implied any intention to weaken our resolve. The whole House realized that as long as there was any hope that Germany would withdraw her troops the Government must act.

VANISHED DOUBTS

To-day any lurking doubts were vanished. Members, who were crowded in the Chamber, knew how events had moved, and their knowledge must have been shared by the great array of the Diplomatic Corps in the Distinguished Strangers' Gallery.

In a few brief sentences Mr. CHAMBERLAIN announced the termination of the House of the presentation of the final note to Germany. The immediately regarding Poland which the Government asked for had not been received in the time stipulated, and consequently the country was at war with Germany. The French Ambassador making a similar démarche, had been accompanied also by a definite time limit. Mr. Chamberlain's closing words, in which the House listened sympathetically and which members cheered warmly, were:—

This is a sad day for all of us, and to none is it sadder than to me. Everything that I have worked for, everything that I have hoped for, everything that I have believed in during my public life has crashed into ruins. There is only one thing left for me to do—that is, to devote what strength and powers I have to forwarding the victory of the cause for which we have to sacrifice so much. I cannot tell what part I may be allowed to play myself; I trust I may live to see the day when Hitlerism has been destroyed and a liberated Europe has been re-established.

POLAND'S GRATITUDE

During the Ministerial discussions on Saturday Count Raczynski, the Polish Ambassador, anxious for information, was a frequent caller at No. 10, Downing Street. In conversation with him yesterday last night he expressed in moving words his country's gratitude to the British people for their response to Poland's appeal and for their determination in taking up arms against aggression. A fuller report of what he said is given on page 5.

As soon as it became clear that Great Britain and Germany were enemy countries, Sir Nevile Henderson, the British Ambassador, prepared to leave Germany with the Embassy staff, entrusting their interests to the United States Ambassador in Berlin, London the German Chargé d'Affaires, Dr. Kordt, went yesterday to the Swiss Legation to ask them to take over any interest which the German Government is likely to have remaining in this country, and it is reported that before long Europe has taken its leave.

The British Government are keeping in the closest touch with all national countries, and have assured Holland that they will respect her neutrality.

THE KING TO HIS PEOPLES

"CALM, FIRM, AND UNITED"

MEETING CHALLENGE OF FORCE

The King broadcast a message to his peoples from his study at Buckingham Palace yesterday evening. He wore the undress uniform of an Admiral of the Fleet. The Queen listened to the broadcast from another room in the Palace.

The King said:—

In this grave hour, perhaps the most fateful in our history, I send to every household of my peoples, both at home and overseas, this message, spoken with the same depth of feeling for each one of you as if I were able to cross your threshold and speak to you myself.

For the second time in the lives of most of us we are at war. Over and over again we have tried to find a peaceful way out of the differences between ourselves and those who are now our enemies. But it has been in vain. We have been forced into a conflict. For we are called, with our allies, to meet the challenge of a principle which, if it were to prevail, would be fatal to any civilized order in the world.

THE ULTIMATE ISSUE

It is the principle which permits a State, in the selfish pursuit of power, to disregard its treaties and its solemn pledges; which sanctions the use of force, or threat of force, against the sovereignty and independence of other States. Such a principle, stripped of all disguise, is surely the mere primitive doctrine that might is right; and if this principle were established throughout the world, the freedom of our own country and of the whole British Commonwealth of Nations would be in danger. But far more than this—the peoples of the world would be kept in the bondage of fear, and all hopes of settled peace and of the security of justice and liberty among nations would be ended.

This is the ultimate issue which confronts us. For the sake of all that we ourselves hold dear, and of the world's order and peace, it is unthinkable that we should refuse to meet the challenge.

It is to this high purpose that I now call my people at home and my peoples across the Seas, who will make our cause their own. I ask them to stand calm, firm, and united in this time of trial. The task will be hard. There may be dark days ahead, and war can no longer be confined to the battlefield. But we can only do the right as we see the right, and reverently commit our cause to God. If one and all we keep resolutely faithful to it, ready for whatever service or sacrifice it may demand, then, with God's help, we shall prevail.

May He bless and keep us all.

A COPY FOR EVERY HOUSEHOLD

THE KING'S SIGNATURE

The Ministry of Information made the following announcement last night:—

"The King has graciously consented that a copy of the message which he broadcast at 6 o'clock this evening shall be sent to every household in the country so that all may be able to keep it as a permanent record. Each copy will bear his Majesty's own signature in facsimile.

"In present circumstances it is inevitable that the preparation in a suitable form of more than 15,000,000 copies of his Majesty's message will take some time, but steps will be delivered as soon as they are ready."

REASONS FOR ALLIES' DELAY

COMPLETING FRENCH PLANS

FROM OUR DIPLOMATIC CORRESPONDENT

The formal declaration of war against Germany was made by Mr. R. Dunbar, head of the Treaty Department at the Foreign Office.

About 11.15 a.m. yesterday—a quarter of an hour after the British time limit had expired—he called on Dr. Kordt, the German Chargé d'Affaires, at the Embassy in Carlton House Terrace, and handed him a notification that a state of war existed between the two countries. The week-end that brought Great Britain and France into the war had long hours of waiting during which not even the two Governments knew at what hour precisely they would take up arms. On Saturday the only certain thing was that the two Governments would fulfil their pledge to Poland at the earliest possible moment. Both in London and in Paris there were frequent Cabinet meetings during the day, which ended with a midnight meeting of the British Cabinet at 10, Downing Street. Mr. Chamberlain and Lord Halifax were often telephoning to Paris during the day, and gradually it became known that it was strictly technical reasons the French Government and their General Staff wished to delay the opening until later day—simply in order to complete their plans.

That was the sole reason for the delay at this end.

OPPOSITION LEADERS

The Prime Minister conveyed through Mr. Arthur Greenwood last week an invitation to the Parliamentary Labour Party to permit some of the Opposition leaders to join the Government. This matter was considered at a joint meeting of the Executive of the Labour Party and the Parliamentary Labour Party and the decision reached was that, for the present at least, the invitation should not to be accepted. The Parliamentary Labour Party decided to give no support to the Government than the most complete support in the effective prosecution of the War, but they feel that it is very important to maintain in the House of Commons an independent and vigilant Opposition.

On Saturday the Prime Minister also invited Sir Archibald Sinclair, leader of the Opposition Liberals, to accept a Cabinet office, but after consulting his colleagues Sir Archibald Sinclair replied that he and his friends considered that "in the present circumstances they could render better service to the nation and the Government by supporting all necessary war measures from an independent position."

Parliament will meet again to-day to continue the passage of war emergency measures.

INVALIDS

Lord PORTSEA, who underwent an operation for appendicitis on August 26, was last night stated to be going on satisfactorily.

WAR CABINET OF NINE

TWO NEW-COMERS

MR. CHURCHILL AND LORD HANKEY

FROM OUR PARLIAMENTARY CORRESPONDENT

It was officially announced last night that the Prime Minister had decided to reconstitute the Government and set up a War Cabinet on the lines of the War Cabinet established in December, 1916. Mr. Chamberlain invited his colleagues in the Ministry to place their resignations collectively in his hands to enable the new arrangements to be put into effect.

The King has approved the following appointments, and the War Cabinet consists of:—

Prime Minister and First Lord of the Treasury
  MR. NEVILLE CHAMBERLAIN
Chancellor of the Exchequer
  SIR JOHN SIMON
Secretary of State for Foreign Affairs
  LORD HALIFAX
Minister for Coordination of Defence
  LORD CHATFIELD
First Lord of the Admiralty
  MR. WINSTON CHURCHILL
Secretary of State for War
  MR. LESLIE HORE-BELISHA
Secretary of State for Air
  SIR KINGSLEY WOOD
Lord Privy Seal
  SIR SAMUEL HOARE
Minister without Portfolio
  LORD HANKEY

It was announced later last night that the King had also approved the following appointments of Ministers not in the War Cabinet:—

Lord President of the Council
  LORD STANHOPE
Lord Chancellor
  SIR THOMAS INSKIP
Home Secretary and Minister of Home Security
  SIR JOHN ANDERSON
Secretary of State for Dominion Affairs
  MR. ANTHONY EDEN

Further Ministerial appointments will be announced in due course.

PREVIOUS EXPERIENCE

New members of the Ministry, who are also members of the War Cabinet, are Mr. Churchill and Lord Hankey. Mr. Churchill, who is 64, has previously held most of the great offices of State. He now succeeds Lord Stanhope as First Lord of the Admiralty and thus returns to the post which he held at the outbreak of the last War.

Lord Hankey, who is 62, has never held Ministerial office before, but he belongs to the War Cabinet as experience and knowledge of public affairs in many ways are expected. Throughout the last War he was Secretary of the Committee of Imperial Defence, and he was also Secretary of the War Cabinet set up by Mr. Lloyd George in 1916 and the Imperial War Cabinet which was established later. After the War and until just before he held jointly the three offices of Secretary to the Cabinet, Secretary to the Committee of Imperial Defence, and Clerk of the Privy Council.

Sir Samuel Hoare, who is also a member of the War Cabinet, has vacated the office of Home Secretary, which he has held since 1937, to become Lord Privy Seal. In this post he succeeds Sir John Anderson, who had been appointed Lord Privy Seal and Minister for Civil Defence.

MR. EDEN'S RETURN

Mr. Eden's return to the Government is another notable feature of the Government reconstruction. From 1935 until February of last year Mr. Eden was Secretary for Foreign Affairs; he resigned that office because of his disagreement with Mr. Chamberlain about the Government's decision in the circumstances then existing to enter upon negotiations for an Anglo-Italian Agreement. Mr. Eden now succeeds Mr. Thomas Inskip as Dominions Secretary, in order that he may be in the best position to maintain contact between the War Cabinet and the Dominions. He will have special access to the War Cabinet. Lord Runciman as Lord President of the Council; and Sir Thomas Inskip gives up the House of Lords as Lord Chancellor in succession to Lord Maugham. Sir John Anderson succeeds Sir Samuel Hoare as Home Secretary, with the additional office of Minister of Home Security. He will continue to be in charge of A.R.P. administration.

FOREIGN ENVOYS CHEERED

The declaration of war by Great Britain and France was received in Warsaw with delirious enthusiasm and demonstrations which went on all day. The news arrived soon after 11, and spontaneously the crowds which had been wailing nervously in the streets all yesterday and to-day, rushed towards the British Embassy cheering, singing, shouting, and waving flags. They surged through the gateways and gave an ovation to the Ambassador, Sir Howard Kennard, who came out to the balcony with Colonel Beck, the Foreign Minister. "Long live Great Britain, long live the fight for liberty!"

The crowd then surged on to the French Embassy, in the Nowy Swiat, and again there were cheers while Colonel Beck, having with difficulty obtained silence, read the French Ambassador the shoulders of the enthusiastic crowds. The next stage of the crowd's march was to the British Consulate-General, where Mr. Savery, the Consul-General, appeared on the balcony and addressed the people in English-speaking spokesmen among the demonstrators shouted in reply, "Long live King George," "Long live England," "Long live British democracy and twentieth-century civilization."

WARSAW, Sept. 3.—An official communiqué to-night reported that Warsaw was among the towns raided by German aircraft to-day. It also announced this the German aircraft had been shot down during the day, while the Poles had lost three machines and crews.

An official Polish communiqué says that Polish troops have been unable to abandon Czestochowa, about 17 miles from the frontier of Upper Silesia.—Reuter.

POLAND'S STOUT DEFENCE

INCESSANT AIR RAIDS

ANGLO-FRENCH DECISION CHEERED

FROM OUR CORRESPONDENT

WARSAW, SEPT. 3

The German invasion, as far as can be observed at present—reports are scanty and hard to confirm—seems to have two aims, apart from terror. Towns and villages of strategic importance for communications are being bombed, and military offensives are being directed so as to pinch off certain salient connexions with areas.

A communiqué issued on Saturday night states:—

The German Government with the Dutch Legation in Warsaw as intermediary protested to the Government of Poland that air bombing should be restricted to military objectives. The Poles accepted, and yet on Saturday the Germans bombed the following "open towns": Lublin, Radom, Tomaszów, Radzymin, Ostrowiec, Grojec, Siedlce, Torun, Puck, Kutno, Gdynia, Poznan, Czeladz, Katowice, Grudzic, Pszow, Chelmno, Andrychów, Radom, Lodz, Pszczyna, and Sosnowiec. Several of these places were bombed on Saturday many times—Lublin six times; Radom twice; and some towns were attacked. The total casualties on Friday and Saturday are known to be 1,500 killed and wounded, including women and children.

Other key cities which have been bombed and where the damage is still uncertain are Gdynia, Dziadkowo, Kutno, Wielun, Czestochowa, Jaslo, Krosno, Lwow, Biala Podlaska, Brest Litovsk, Kalwyn, and Zambrów. The strategic importance of Poznan, Lodz, Torun, and Grodno, which have been bombed, is obvious.

MILITARY SITUATION

Five main sectors are at present distinguishable in the general military offensive. Torun is apparently the objective of attacks from the Pomeranian front; attacks launched from the North, a few miles east of Grudziadz, and from the West slightly north of Chelmno. Poznan seems threatened by drives from two parts of the Pomeranian front approaching by way of Pleszen and Leszno. Leszno seems to be the objective of an offensive launched near Kepno. On the Upper Silesian front Czestochowa is threatened along a route via Lubliniec, which has fallen. Katowice, on the same front, which has been under heavy artillery and air bombardment since 4.30 on Friday morning, is threatened by advances from Bytom, Hybrik, Olsa, and Frystat. Cracow, which is threatened by the advance towards Katowice, is reported to be facing an offensive from Slovakia via Zakopane.

Offensives have now also been launched along the East Prussian frontier and round Gdynia, neither of which has been reported hitherto. It is also clear that the offensive against Czestochowa must be most intensive, and probably on a similar scale to the fighting round Katowice and Krakow.

The range of air bombardments is very wide. Bombers from East Prussia attacked states as far east as Grodno, Kobryn, Brest Litovsk (Brest Litewsk), and Tomaszów. Aeroplanes from Slovakia have bombed Lwow.

RAIDS ON WARSAW

It is noteworthy that there has been no bombardment so far of Poland's industrial triangle, while the effect of the raids on Warsaw—there were nine on Saturday, but they did little damage—must be to wear down the nerves of the population with constant alarms by day and night.

Communication with Katowice after being cut off was re-established later. It was then stated that bands of local Nazis, reinforced by a Freikorps from Germany which had crossed the frontier, had attempted things. The Poles, however, have the situation well in hand there. One band of 50 young men was taken out from Katowice and shot. Two other bands were driven through the streets by the guns of the crowds with bayonets pointed at them as an example. The Nazis had sought to stampede the revolt of the civil electrical manufacturing works.

The villa at Konstancin of the American Ambassador, Mr. A. J. Drexel Biddle, was bombed this morning. Five windows were smashed, but the Ambassador and his family were unhurt.

TOKYO CABINET'S DECISION

VIRTUAL NEUTRALITY

FROM OUR OWN CORRESPONDENT

TOKYO, SEPT. 3.

The Cabinet, at a meeting held this afternoon, decided to watch European developments and preserve freedom of action. The Press interprets this as "an attitude of complete neutrality," and points out that Germany's violation of the Anti-Comintern Pact had been a position of complete freedom. Mr. Suwada, the Vice-Foreign Minister, outlined the situation to the Cabinet, explaining how the former Cabinet's plans to strengthen the Anti-Comintern Pact had been abandoned as the result of Germany's agreement with the Soviets. Then he described the present position in Europe from the latest disposition of Japanese Ambassadors.

On the basis of this information the Cabinet decided its policy, which, though qualified for the time being by the intention to wait and see, is almost certain to become complete neutrality. The Japanese people's feeling that they have been betrayed by Hitler is so strong that their neutrality is not likely to be friendly to Germany.

WAR SUPPLIES

Having virtually decided on neutrality, the Cabinet next considered the economic effects a European war is likely to have on Japan's industrial expansion and "mobilization of materials policies," both of which are vital to the "new order" she is attempting to create in China. The Cabinet's views are not divulged, which is a pity, since this aspect of the situation is more important to Japan than her relations with the European combatants. All Japan's military supplies from Europe will cease and Europe will absorb America's surplus. The puzzle of how she will keep reconstructing in China will be slowed down as machines and raw materials are diverted to Europe. The China war has handicapped their power to acquire raw materials at a moment when Japanese industry might make another vast leap forward while European nations are cutting each other's throats. To a great extent Japan's immediate future is in the hands of the United States.

GERMAN REPLY TO BRITISH NOTE

RECRIMINATION AND REFUSAL

A German reply to the British Note of Friday night demanding the withdrawal of German troops from Poland has been handed to the British Ambassador in Berlin. Points from it are as follows:—

The Reich Government and the German nation refuse to accept or even to satisfy the demands in the form of an ultimatum from the British Government.

It was at the intervention of the British Government that the alleged willingness of Poland a month ago to enter into direct negotiations between Germany and Poland.

The German Government would resolutely put and the British Government refused Signor Mussolini's peace proposal, although the German Government had been ready to accept.

British politicians have for years been preaching the extermination and elimination of the German nation.

The German Government are determined to defend their freedom and independence, and will oppose British aggression with force and in a like way.

The Note went on: In the event of the German reply not receiving acceptance by Herr Hitler's appeals to the public, and the Army will be found on p. 7.

THE ARMY COMMAND

LORD GORT APPOINTED C.-IN-C

The King, on the advice of the Government, has approved the following appointments:—

Commander-in-Chief of the British Field Force—General Lord GORT, V.C., G.C.B., C.B.E., D.S.O., M.V.O., M.C.
Chief of the Imperial General Staff—General Sir Edmund Ironside, G.C.B., C.M.G., D.S.O.
Commander-in-Chief of the Home Forces—General Sir Walter Kirke, G.C.B., C.M.G., D.S.O.
Commander-in-Chief of the Aldershot Command—Lieutenant-General Sir John Dill.

Lord Gort, who is 53, has been Chief of the Imperial General Staff since December, 1937. He won the Victoria Cross during the last War.

General Sir Edmund Ironside has been Inspector-General of Overseas Forces since June. He is 59. He has served in many campaigns, including the Boer War and the last War.

General Sir Walter Kirke, who is 62, has been Director-General of the Territorial Army.

THE DUKE OF KENT

The Admiralty announces that Rear-Admiral the Duke of Kent has taken up war appointment.

FISHING VESSELS TOLD TO RETURN

The following navigational warning was broadcast by the B.B.C. last night:—" All British fishing vessels off the East Coast of England south of latitude 55deg. north are to return to harbour."

OBITUARY

We announce with regret the deaths of Sir ALEXANDER LAWRENCE, puisne Judge of the High Court; Mr. ALFRED TURTON, second baronet; and Mr. TREVELYAN CLARK, portrait painter. Memoirs will be found on page 10.

ON OTHER PAGES

AUSTRALIA TAKES UP ARMS

AT ONE WITH GREAT BRITAIN

MR. MENZIES' BROADCAST

FROM OUR OWN CORRESPONDENT

MELBOURNE, SEPT. 3

Mr. Menzies, the Australian Prime Minister, announced this evening that Australia was at war with Germany. Lord Gowrie, the Governor-General, signed the proclamation declaring Australia to be in a state of war, at an urgent meeting of the Executive Council.

Brigadier Street, Minister for Defence, announced that the Navy and Air Force would be fully mobilized on a war basis and that a number of militia units would be called up for special duty, but that no immediate call would be made for recruits. The Ministers, who are on their way to Canberra to-morrow for the meeting of Parliament on Wednesday, immediately set in motion the last phase of the Commonwealth's war plans.

Speaking over 125 national and commercial stations at 9.15 p.m., Mr. Menzies said:—

It is my melancholy duty to announce officially that in consequence of Germany's persistence in her invasion of Poland, Great Britain has declared war, and that as a result Australia is also at war. Great Britain and France, with the cooperation of the Dominions, have wrought to avert this tragedy. They have patiently kept the door for negotiation open, and given no cause for aggression: but their efforts have failed. We therefore, as a great family of nations, are involved in the struggle; we are at war as one with all, and we believe in our hearts that we will prevail.

Mr. Menzies described the course of recent events in Europe, declaring that it would exhibit to history some of the most remarkable instances of bad faith and indifference to common humanity for which the darkest records of European history could scarcely provide a parallel. It demonstrated that Hitler was equally prepared deliberately designed to produce either war or the subjugation of one country after another by the threat of war.

Bitter as we all feel about this wanton crime, Mr. Menzies concluded, this moment is not the minute but for quiet thinking—that calm fortitude which rests on the incomparable sense of man controlled by God. In this image I ask you all to stand in the knowledge that such stark truth must win. In the bitter months ahead calmness, resoluteness, confidence and hard work will be required as never before. Our staying power, and particularly the staying power of the mother country, will be best assisted by our keeping production going as fully and uninterruptedly as possible, and by our not allowing ourselves to be stampeded into panic or undue depression. We shall maintain an unbroken line of unity that the world may know that strength, calm and firm.

OPPOSITION SUPPORT

Mr. Menzies earlier conferred with Mr. Curtin, Leader of the Opposition, who pledged the support of Labour in war-time. Mr. Menzies will meet Mr. Earle Page, the Leader of the Country Party, at Canberra on Tuesday, when the possibility that the Country Party would like to join in war ministry may be discussed. It is unlikely that the Labour Party will join, as the Party platform forbids this.

Stock exchanges throughout Australia were closed on Saturday; they will review the situation to-morrow. Newspapers emphasize the Commonwealth's determination to give Great Britain all possible assistance to Australia's economic strength; since 1914 the capacity of factories has multiplied by two, thirds and is still capable of great expansion; finance is now under the tight control of a strong central bank.

"ONE KING, ONE FLAG, ONE CAUSE"

The Australian Prime Minister, in a statement on Saturday (says Reuter) declared:—

The British Cabinet has made a momentous decision. Unless Germany withdraws her attack on Poland Great Britain will be at war, and it will be necessary to set procedures in motion and bring upon ourselves the burden of war. Great Britain would be at war and if so the whole Empire must be brought in, for Britain will take the first hostility and lead to ourselves.

We are too, the whole world over, one people in time of deadly peril. The price in service and sacrifice must become known immediately to maintain a united front while the world is at one. There is unity in the Empire-loving world of to-day. There is only one King, one flag, one cause.

FULL SUPPORT FROM NEW ZEALAND

GOVERNMENT'S MESSAGE

The following telegram was received yesterday from the Government of New Zealand:—

With reference to the intimation just received that a state of war exists between the United Kingdom and Germany, his Majesty's Government in New Zealand hereby associate themselves without qualification with the action taken, which involves a state of war with Germany. His Majesty's Government in the United Kingdom assume that this message carries with the action taken, which involves a state of war. This reply cannot be too warmly appreciated, since it was received in the clearest possible terms that the British Commonwealth of the kindred British peoples of the world are at one. There is unity in the Empire-loving world of to-day. There is only one King, one flag, one cause.

From Boston to Normandy

Chapter 23

Boston, U.S.A. 1942

Charles felt very proud to be wearing his graduation robes; he and another twelve hundred students would end the day as Harvard graduates in a myriad of disciplines.

John and Emily, his parents, were there, as was his latest girlfriend, Jane. She was also graduating in Business Studies. The ceremony went off without a hitch apart from some students who were objecting about America's involvement in the war.

Charles chose not to have a graduation party. Instead, he requested that he and Jane and his parents dine in his favourite restaurant, Marliave, in downtown Boston; it was established in 1875 and was popular with Bostonians of all age groups.

Charles wanted a more intimate spot to break his news, rather than a party.

The group was seated by the waiter, who asked if they would all care for a glass of Dom Perignon Champagne.

'Oh my goodness' exclaimed Jane, 'I have never had French champagne before. How exciting!'

'Well, it is not every day that your favourite son graduates from Harvard.' John was radiant with pride.

'I am your *only* son, Dad.'

Laughter came easily.

Conversation eventually turned to the war and what was happening in the Pacific and in Europe.

'Well, that brings me to an announcement, everybody. I applied for, and have been accepted by West Point Military Academy, for an officer's training course.'

'My God, that means you will be going to war,' his mother exclaimed.

'That's right, Mum, I think it is my duty to fight for my country and try to help bring this war to its natural conclusion.'

'Well, son, worried as I am, I applaud your decision.'

Jane just sat there, trying to come to terms with what she had heard.

Charles travelled to New York for a couple of days with Jane and then made the forty-mile drive to the academy to start his six-month course.

At the end of the six months, Charles graduated as a second Lieutenant and was immediately assigned to the second Ranger Battalion. He was shipped off to England in July 1943 and joined the millions of Allied troops waiting to combat the Nazis and win back Europe.

Charles Weatherspoon

The Blitz

Chapter 24

Correspondent Ernie Pyle

It was a night when London was ringed and stabbed with fire.

They came just after dark, and somehow you could sense from the quick, bitter firing of the guns that there was to be no monkey business this night.

Shortly after the sirens wailed you could hear the Germans grinding overhead. In my room, with its black curtains drawn across the windows, you could feel the shake from the guns. You could hear the boom, crump, crump, crump, of heavy bombs at their work of tearing buildings apart. They were not too far away.

Half an hour after the firing started I gathered a couple of friends and went to a high, darkened balcony that gave us a view of a third of the entire circle of London. As we stepped out onto the balcony a vast inner excitement came over all of us - an excitement that had neither fear nor horror in it, because it was too full of awe.

You have all seen big fires, but I doubt if you have ever seen the whole horizon of a city lined with great fires – scores of them, perhaps hundreds. There was something inspiring just in the awful savagery of it.

The closest fires were near enough for us to hear the crackling flames and the yells of firemen. Little fires grew into big ones even as we watched. Big ones died down under the firemen's valor, only to break out again later.

About every two minutes a new wave of planes would be over. The motors seemed to grind rather than roar, and to have an angry pulsation, like a bee buzzing in blind fury.

Children sit among the rubble

of their home September 1940

The guns did not make a constant overwhelming din as in those terrible days of September. They were intermittent – sometimes a few seconds apart, sometimes a minute or more. Their sound was sharp, nearby; and soft and muffled, far away. They were everywhere over London.

Into the dark shadowed spaces below us, while we watched, whole batches of incendiary bombs fell. We saw two dozen go off in two seconds. They flashed terrifically, then quickly simmered down to pin points of dazzling white, burning ferociously. These white pin points would go out one by one, as the unseen heroes of the moment smothered them with sand. But also, while we watched, other pin points would burn on, and soon a yellow flame would leap up from the white center. They had done their work - another building was on fire.

The greatest of all the fires was directly in front of us. Flames seemed to whip hundreds of feet into the air. Pinkish-white smoke ballooned upward in a great cloud, and out of this cloud there gradually took shape - so faintly at first that we weren't sure we saw correctly - the gigantic dome of St. Paul's Cathedral.

St. Paul's was surrounded by fire, but it came through. It stood there in its enormous proportions - growing slowly clearer and clearer, the way objects take shape at dawn. It was like a picture of some miraculous figure that appears before peace-hungry soldiers on a battlefield.

The streets below us were semi-illuminated from the glow. Immediately above the fires the sky was red and angry, and overhead, making a ceiling in the vast heavens, there was a cloud of smoke all in pink. Up in that pink shrouding there were tiny, brilliant specks of flashing light- antiaircraft shells bursting. After the flash you could hear the sound.

Up there, too, the barrage balloons were standing out as clearly as if it were daytime, but now they were pink instead of silver. And now and then through a hole in that pink shroud there twinkled incongruously a permanent, genuine star - the old - fashioned kind that has always been there.

Below us the Thames grew lighter, and all around below were the shadows - the dark shadows of buildings and bridges that formed the base of this dreadful masterpiece.

116

Later on I borrowed a tin hat and went out among the fires. That was exciting too; but the thing I shall always remember above all the other things in my life is the monstrous loveliness of that one single view of London on a holiday night – London stabbed with great fires, shaken by explosions, its dark regions along the Thames sparkling with the pin points of white-hot bombs, all of it roofed over with a ceiling of pink that held bursting shells, balloons, flares and the grind of vicious engines. And in yourself the excitement and anticipation and wonder in your soul that this could be happening at all.

These things all went together to make the most hateful, most beautiful single scene I have ever known."

The Bombing of London

London, September 4[th,] 1940

Lord Lamont was sitting at his desk having just spoken to Winston Churchill on the telephone. It would seem that Churchill was still worried about an invasion and couldn't understand why Hitler had not attempted one. Naturally, he was relieved that Hitler had not attempted the crossing, but he had a feeling something big was on the horizon.

Lamont had just asked his secretary to come into his office to take some dictation, when he heard the drone of aircraft overhead. He went out onto his balcony and was horrified to see German planes blotting out the sky. The Luftwaffe bombed London for two hours and the London Blitz had begun.

At 8 pm, Lamont was eating his dinner alone when the second wave started to drop their deadly cargo. He could hear loud explosions all around his house and prayed that he would survive this night. He ventured out into Pall Mall to see if any buildings had been damaged, but the Mall was spared. Hitler obviously didn't want to damage any valuable real estate, or was it purely luck?

Lamont decided to walk towards the flames he could see towering into the London sky. When he arrived at the site, he was horrified: the building alight was a children's hospital. Firemen were doing their best to control the flames to try to gain entry to save any children, but it was futile. One hundred children lost their lives on that terrible night.

Lamont walked back to his town house with a heavy heart. How frustrated he felt that he had so much wealth and exercised so much power, yet he could do nothing about ending this war.

The next day, The Luftwaffe bombed London again and wreaked as much damage as the first day and so it continued for fifty-seven consecutive days, bombs delivering death and destruction on London as well as on many other British cities, including Liverpool, Coventry, Belfast, Bristol and Manchester.

On May 8th 1941, a retaliatory raid against Bremen and Hamburg was made in an effort to raise morale. Four hundred British bombers raided both ports. The German cities suffered significant damage and the death toll was high. Hitler was furious and ordered a bombing raid more immense than any other previous raid. This was to be the last raid of the Blitz and it killed over fifteen hundred people. Shortly after this, Hitler switched his attention to the Soviet Union. London was free from attack until the summer of 1941.

Londoners Seeking Shelter in the Underground

22,000 dead and London Almost Destroyed

MONDAY SEPTEMBER 9 1940

TO-DAY'S ARRANGEMENTS

TO-DAY'S NEWS

THE WAR

HOME

IMPERIAL AND FOREIGN

THE ASSAULT ON LONDON

Munitions from the Empire

Cockney Welsh

Earnings in Coventry

"NAZISM A DESTRUCTIVE FORCE"

A DISCOVERY OF NEED

HOP-PICKING

AIR BATTLES

NIGHTLY BULLETINS FOR CANADA

A RECORD OF COURAGE AND CALM

TO THE EDITOR OF THE TIMES

JAPANESE ANGLICAN CHURCH

TO THE EDITOR OF THE TIMES

THE POWER OF THE CHURCH

INTERNMENT OFFICERS

TO THE EDITOR OF THE TIMES

SALT AND HEAT

PERUVIAN EXPERIENCE

SEED POTATOES

AXIS ACTIVITY IN LATIN AMERICA

I—PSYCHOLOGICAL PREY FOR THE NAZI AGITATOR

TURNING FROM MARX TO SCHACHT

By Rosita Forbes

A CATTLE FOREMAN

REHABILITATION

A NATIONAL BOARD

TO THE EDITOR OF THE TIMES

Hitler's Secret Weapon

Chapter 25

Lamont had lived through the First World War; his newspapers were now reporting that the Battle of London had finally drawn to a close, albeit with twenty two thousand Londoners dead.

He firmly believed that the D Day invasion and the entry of the USA into the war would bring an end to this horrific conflict very soon. He had survived yet another war, this time as a citizen, not a front line soldier.

The blitz had devastated London and much of it had been destroyed but Lamont knew the resilience of the British and that when the war finally ended they would build a bigger and better London.

He was having lunch with his good friend, Lord Woolton who was Minister of Reconstruction, responsible for rebuilding London and the other cities that had been bombed by the Nazis. It was a new position and could have been called premature, but Winston Churchill felt they should be ready to reconstruct immediately the war ended. Lord Lamont felt much more at ease when in public now that he had undergone several more plastic surgery treatments and no longer needed his tin mask.

The two peers were discussing life after Hitler, when an enormous blast rocked the building. There was no structural damage but many a plate had been broken.

Both men rushed out from the club, wondering if the Germans had resumed aerial bombing. There were no German planes in the sky and there had only been a single almighty explosion rather than the blanket bombing as before. They soon discovered that Hitler had sent England his secret weapon, the V1, a flying bomb, the world's first cruise missile, an unmanned gyro-guided plane that delivered a tonne of high explosive each time one hurtled into the ground.

The distinctive noise became well-known over London between June 1944 and March 1945, when two thousand four hundred and nineteen Doodle Bugs (as they were nick- named) exploded into London's homes and commercial buildings. The toll of human suffering was six thousand, one hundred and eighty four people killed and seventeen thousand, nine hundred and eighty one seriously injured and maimed. Tens of thousands of others received lesser injuries. Countless more would suffer the pain of bereavement or loss of their home and treasured possessions.

Sarah Armstrong was ten years old. She was a beautiful girl in both looks and nature. Her beautiful red hair came half way down her back in tight ringlets. Her best girlfriend was Rosie Baker three months older than Sarah, and just as pretty.

Both girls loved playing skippy outside their neighbouring homes in Stavely Street, Chiswick, London.

During the blitz they were banned from playing in the street, as their parents knew it was far too dangerous. It now seemed the bombs had stopped falling.

On September 8th 1944 both girls were permitted by their mothers to play in the street directly outside their homes. There was no longer the fear of Nazi bombs wreaking havoc in their neighbourhood.

They were playing skippy and enjoying themselves as little girls do.

The local constable, Constable Adams strolled by and gave the girls a wave.

At that instant, Constable Adams heard a sound he had never heard before, not the sound of a Doodle Bug; he looked up to see a huge flying bomb heading straight for them.

'Oh my God, girls, run for your lives!'

It was too late!

They never found a trace of the three, not a skipping rope nor clothing, nor even the Bobbie's badge: all had been vaporised.

Home News

THE KING'S TOUR IN LONDON

AIR RAID DAMAGE INSPECTED

SYMPATHY WITH VICTIMS

The King yesterday spent the morning touring various districts in East and South-East London where air raid damage has been caused. He sympathized with many of the victims and he expressed his appreciation of the valuable work of the civil defence organizations.

At the scenes of the greatest damage he was received with demonstrations of loyalty, in which many people rendered homeless by the raids joined. On several occasions he expressed his admiration for the spirit and determination of the people amid their suffering.

The King was accompanied by Captain Euan Wallace, Commissioner for the London Region, Sir Alexander Maxwell, and Colonel Plan Leigh. At the first place he visited in East London he watched firemen still playing their hoses on a partly burned factory. At the second he witnessed the rescue by firemen of women and children buried in the debris, and he expressed his deep sympathy with one woman who had lost most of her children.

At a place where several houses had been destroyed the King examined a large crater, climbing a pile of debris to see the interior.

Visiting next a dock the King saw the embers of the warehouse fire of Saturday, and learned from the firemen how they had dealt with it. Next the docks a number of people were occupying temporary quarters after their homes had been destroyed.

FEEDING THE PEOPLE

FROM OUR SPECIAL CORRESPONDENT

Lord Woolton, the Minister of Food, visited several centres in East London yesterday afternoon to satisfy himself that the people are being fed. Food is provided by the L.C.C.

Lord Woolton told me that he was proud of the morale of the people he had visited. "It is astounding," he said, "and I saw that cheerful these folk who were through terrific big times, and had borrowed everything, still are. One man I talked to was injured, but he saw the spirit was wonderful."

The Minister called at a rest centre, and a conference with local food officers. "Don't be sticky about rules and regulations," he urged. "Cut out forms and ceremonies and red ministries. The immediate aim is to keep the people fed.

"I was his officers in the area he toured that food distribution is being tackled, and although some retailers had lost their businesses, satisfactory emergency arrangements had already been made to ensure that the people continued to get their supplies of food. They must be the public were cooperating splendidly."

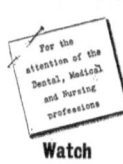

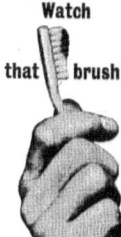

Watch that brush!

The first sign of pyorrhoea and gingivitis is soreness of the gums. But a far more eloquent warning is the toothbrush stained with blood. This danger signal means that immediate action is necessary. Unless these diseases lead to prematurely lost teeth. The use of Sodium Ricinoleate to clear up gum diseases is widely known. Sodium Ricinoleate arrests the bacterial poisons present, but encourages the stimulation of natural resistance in the tissues—as valuable a point for the healthy mouth as for the infected. The wide marketing of a toothpaste—Gibbs S.R. in 6d. and 1/3 sizes—which contains Sodium Ricinoleate means that there is available to all clients of the public a form of both preventive and curative oral hygiene which is complimentary to the dentist's treatment.

S.R.
TOOTHPASTE

"BLIND SAVAGERY" OF NIGHT ATTACKS

OFFICIAL REPORTS

The following joint Ministry and Ministry of Home Security communiqué was issued yesterday morning:—

On Sunday night enemy attacks on London were renewed soon after darkness fell, and continued throughout the night. In this offensive the enemy employed successive relays of aircraft, which, often arriving singly, dropped bombs over a widespread area of London. At no time during the night was an intensive attack delivered by a large force.

Our principal defence have been in continuous action against the enemy.

The main objective of the enemy's attacks were again made on the Thames-side districts. Here a number of fires were caused. Elsewhere in several parts of London some bombing attacks resulted in many fires, temporary interruption of public services, and considerable damage to private houses and to some public and inevitable buildings. A further comment will be made in due course.

HEAVY DAMAGE

This further communiqué was issued in the afternoon:—

Reports of the damage caused in the attacks on London on Sunday night are not yet complete, but some particulars can now be given. The attacks were severe and continued throughout the hours of darkness. Bombing was widespread over the London area, and considerable damage was caused, but indiscriminate. The damage was heavy and comprised many casualties among the dead and injured, including women, and many residential flats and commercial buildings.

The number of casualties cannot at present be assessed, though, so far as information is available, it is not anticipated that the numbers will exceed those of Saturday.

The figures of casualties given for the attacks on this day are now found to be rather lower than was estimated. According to present information, 306 people were killed and 1,337 seriously injured.

Docks, too, both old and the river were again subjected to heavy and repeated bombardment with high explosive and incendiary bombs, and a number of fires broke out. Many of these fires have been extinguished and all the others are now at work. London has once more seen the main objective of the enemy, and its citizens bore the blind savagery of these latest night attacks with admirable courage and resolution.

BOMBING WITHOUT AIM

ATTEMPTS TO LOWER THE PEOPLE'S SPIRIT

FROM OUR AERONAUTICAL CORRESPONDENT

Beginning at twilight on Sunday and continuing, with hardly a break of a minute, until just before dawn yesterday, the Germans made their biggest night raid of the war on London. It lasted nearly 10 hours and was the worst case of concentrated indiscriminate bombing this country has known.

Hardly a district of the Metropolitan area escaped damage and casualties. Usually the bombers did not even trouble to take aim; they simply unloaded their bombs from above the clouds.

There could not have been a night when high-altitude bombing had less chance, for there were no tearing in the deepened district gave the readers an ideal guide instead of using huge formations of bombers, the Germans sent over small numbers at short intervals. Not more than 150 aircraft in all came over London the whole night.

A CRITICAL MONTH

We must expect more of these night raids during the weather breaks. September will probably prove the most critical month of the war. There are indications that the enemy is willing to lose a great many of his aircraft in going all-out on this kind of attack, provided this costs him its intended objectives.

By day, raiders are being made on our facilities organization in all classes of our air. Yesterday there was another bout of slight heavy raids all being developed on our communications, as dealt with the idea of hindering land airfares.

The night raids have the further object of trying to undermine the spirit of the people. But with the good sleep and determination, and in spite of the deprivation suffered in the ground and at elsewhere.

The German population have been harried their nerves tested the time and a half months by the nightly raids of our bombers. To some extent the London raids were an attempt to repay us in our own coin, and it is a small price to save London, in a few weeks perhaps, now time will come. But by far the more particularly the inhabitants of London, object is to stop of his warning formation, to create an impression of London, which they will regard as a reprisal for our regular raids on Germany.

The population are quite satisfied with the available chances of higher gales and greater security. When we see the old raids not only aircraft guns, but what we have are adequate, and to destruction have a very small proportion of the enemy's night raids, the problem of night interception, which, up to now, has baffled both sides in nearly unexplained.

IMPROVISED HEATING IN SHELTERS

BRAZIER FUMES DANGEROUS

At an inquest at Birmingham yesterday on the body of William Warren Stanton, aged 61, who was found dead outside a public air raid shelter which contained a volunteer's brazier, the Coroner, Dr. W. H. Davison, warned the public of the danger of improvising heating in shelters without proper precaution. A woman who was in the shelter said that she was almost suffocated by the fumes from the brazier. Other deaths who had been in the shelter were overcome by the fumes. Dr. J. M. Webster, director of the West Midland Forensic Science Laboratory, said the man's death was due to heart failure and to the condition of the arteries and congestion in some measure to his condition. The jury found a verdict of "Death from natural causes." the Coroner said there was no doubt that a brazier or a means of heating could be installed in a shelter, but should be away from the occupants, and the brazier fire must have a free escape of fumes.

SOCIAL PROBLEMS OF THE WAR

L.C.C. NEW YOUTH SERVICE SCHEME

Three recreational evening institutes of a new type are about to be opened by the London County Council. They are designed as part of the council's consideration of the campaign of youth service to prevent the appearance of those "social disease problems" which arose in the last War.

The following are the schools concerned:—Oxford, Brecknock Road, Gospel Lane, N.W.1; St. John's and St. Barnabas, Little Ormond Street, Bloomsbury; Chalk Farm, Princeton, E.C.16, for youth; and Holiday Street, Rushmere, S.W.8, for girls.

A fee of Rs. a session will be charged.

SELF-HELP PLANS FOR COLLIERS

Mr. D. R. Grenfell, Minister for Mines, said at Cardiff yesterday that unemployment in Durham, Wales, and other highly exposed regions in the coalfields, was not exempt from those problems of peace-time. On the south Wales coalfields there were three times as many men out of work as there were before the war. Already the output for the first time this year had dropped to about 120,000 tons of coal short, since the start of the war.

END OF THE TRAINING SHIP WARSPITE

The training ship Warspite, which has been out thousands of boys in the Royal Navy and the Merchant Service, has been sold by the Marine Society for breaking up at Grays. The Warspite, a three-decker of 1,127 tons, 4,260 tons gross register, was built in 1881 and used her last voyage in 1918. Her site was adapted for use at Woolwich and named. At the outbreak of the present war she was closed, being in a naval station upon which it was not possible to avoid more boys.

Legal Notices will be found on page 2

AERIAL TORPEDO

50 KILLED IN BLOCK OF FLATS

HOSPITALS, CHURCH, AND MUSEUM HIT

It is feared that over 50 people were killed when an aerial torpedo partially demolished a block of flats in East London on Sunday night. Twelve families were sheltering in a buttressed ground floor.

A warden said: "We heard a terrific crash, and when we saw what had happened we stared standing away with our bare hands at the rubble." A rescue party took out 20 bodies. Outside the flats was a brick and concrete shelter, which was empty and undamaged. The occupants of the flats had thought that their shelter was more strongly built than it really was.

Seven people, including a mother and father, daughter and her child, are believed to have been killed when a high explosive bomb fell on a garden shelter in South-east London. Only one member of the family, who was out in the shelter, escaped.

A bomb killed 15 inmates of an institution in East London. The bomb crashed through one of the wards to the main kitchen and demolished a whole section of a new building. Two bombs which fell in a store area damaged a church 200 years old, in which many thousands worshippers have been buried. One end of the church was cordoned from its interiors, and it is feared that this end will have to be pulled down. An official said that the bomb which did all the damage was a third bomb. Two others, which failed to explode, had to be removed. All the windows in one building and those adjoining were broken, but no casualties were caused.

A London museum was hit by two incendiary bombs, which struck the roof's fire and balcony platform and were extinguished by the hose of a foreign Legation. All the windows in this building were shattered and furnishings were damaged, but the only damage caused was in a part of it. An incendiary bomb which fell on another building, set the contents of the museum on fire by members of the staff. An official stated that a collection of pictures had been damaged, but the galleries containing the valuable exhibits were untouched except by water. The treasures had been moved.

YOUNG WOMAN TRAPPED

There was considerable damage to hospital buildings. At one hospital hit by a bomb it was reported that five young women were missing. When the raid subsided there were two nurses and four musicians in that part of the building which was a separate theatre, but though buried under wreckage, was able to make her rescue signal. She is feared missing, but there were several missing whose bodies had not been recovered. Her occupation apparently was used to carry through a telephone point. When they had got through a wall 20 feet thick, they rescued the young woman who was lying with a door and marble wreckage. She was only able to cut a small passage into a small corridor of the building and a marble staircase and stared for nearly an hour, until a wall of the basement wards at once. She had given a traumatic laboratory. The search parties then worked through the night to free the woman.

At another hospital, one wing was completely wrecked. Fortunately it was empty, having been moved some months ago for possible air raid casualties.

SHIP SUNK IN FOG

ALL ON BOARD RESCUED BY DESTROYER

A steamer lost towards of the 72 passengers and 24 crew of a sinking steamer off the West Coast of Scotland. It was fishing in thick fog. They have been landed at a Scottish port.

The steamer was the Burns and Laird steamer Lairdscastle (1,945 tons), which sank within three hours after being in collision in darkness and fog with the Vernon City, a cargo steamer of 4,748 tons belonging to the Reardon Smith Line, Limited. The order of abandon the Lairdscastle was given. There was no panic among the passengers and crew, who abandoned ship in perfect order. The destroyer standing by picked up everybody, all of whom were assembled and brought to port.

When a steamer arrived after dinner, was seen all away, but the crew of the destroyer working for just remained the crew that came on board the last ship and they their nerves steeled.

CIVIL DEFENCE OF LONDON

WOMEN'S DEVOTED HELP IN GRIM TASK

FROM OUR PARLIAMENTARY CORRESPONDENT

When the Prime Minister visited the heavily bombed districts of East London on Sunday evening he was deeply impressed both by the resilient spirit of the civil population in a grim ordeal and by all that he saw and heard of the splendid work of the civil defence services. Mr. Churchill was candidly granted while he was making his tour of damaged streets.

All the evidence goes to show that London's defensive scheme of passive defence against air attacks is functioning smoothly and well. Its success in action is due, not merely to the thoroughness of the organization, but also to the leading and devoted work of all branches of the civil defence corps. The raiding are at the test of experience, and none of the organization either worked well. The fire brigade—in which special pride in the work of the professional service, alone had the personnel of which surpasses all others. The rescue parties and that doing their hazardous work with great efficiency and devotion. For the morgue who are rescued from collapsed buildings, including many of London's population remained adequately staffed to deal with all emergencies, but most especially to the very anxious which were completed to the civilian population of the defence services.

GIFTS FOR AIRCRAFT

SOLDIERS' TRIBUTE TO R.A.F. EXPLOITS

In appreciation of the exploits of their comrades in the R.A.F. the men of The North Staffordshire Regiment have sent a first cheque for £50 towards the purchase of a Spitfire.

Mr. John A. Fielden, of Hollywood, Hollow Green, has sent £100 to the Minister for Aircraft Production.

Other sums received by Lord Beaverbrook yesterday:—Collector's Comfort Club, £100; Cardiff, £61; W. H. Holwell, £100; and the staff of D. G. Robertson, Limited, and Wine Industries, Limited, £100; and Allied Bakers, London.

Mrs. M. Harwood has given a special sum of £1,000 to be spent on a fourteenth of a fighter Greek Swift Brewing from Weston Brewery, Lower; from £200. At an aircraft production fund established at the beginning of the war by the directors and staff of the Commercial Gas Company, £100 has already been subscribed by the Waterside, Becom End, and £100.

UNIFORM THEATRE

NON-STOP VARIETY

Sir Seymour Hicks began yesterday at the Garrick Theatre his scheme of non-stop variety at prices and the war privileges which recognize that the armed forces deserve every consideration as theatre-goers.

Sir Seymour Hicks himself appears in a sketch by M. Sacha Curmi, Mr. Mark Hambourg plays the piano, and there already is a programme, but number 16 items are about to be made on show.

When the curtain fell, the numbers have become a permanent institution at the Garrick. Lunch and as many children are admitted as possible at all ages. Clive Sands is a child of eight. Other successful were produced—a notable achievement in accordance with arresting deeds of Sir Seymour Hicks, Mr. Hicks had a fresh change which enabled bombed war Romans on a very curious and ill-conceived. In addition, we recommend Sir Seymour Hicks and some other players. There was nothing in the Garrick Gallery to go at an old impression in the week, and no programme was made—but is a piece of acting completely fitted and controlled. Liberation, styling, and wholly highly praised. The portables were just bit funny.

RED CROSS AND ST. JOHN FUND

FURTHER £2,000 RECEIVED

The Lord Mayor's Red Cross and St. John Fund for the Sick and Wounded in the War now stands at £3,103,000.

Gifts included £800 from the Northern Rhodesia Central War Charities Fund (making in all £12,157); £500 from the Lord Mayor of Perth; £300 from the London children's special section. Newbolt, Knight, Brewers General Law, £350; and Mrs. Hicks, £100. Sundries.

Mr. Francis Gervaise, of Exmouth, has sent a beautiful gold necklace with many diamonds for the Red Cross Sale. Gifts of gold and silver should be sent in the treasurer's office at our confusion, 17 Old Bond Street, W.1.

LONDON CHILDREN IN DEVON

FOOD PRODUCTION AND RED CROSS WORK

Mr. A. And Doyle, chairman of the London County Council, with evacuee about 55 London children evacuated in South Devon, near Plymouth. In almost every case he found the children in very good health, and obviously happy. He was told that evacuated mothers, their schools and schools, were working actively.

In a memorandum submitted to the committee he wrote of his pleasure in seeing the practical results of a scheme prepared for the care of refugee camps, in which work with children, were also being given. Pits at present the children keep the 100 up to which was continued by a lady club. Here the children help school work with enthusiasm. The children's spirits are high, and the work of rebuilding can be continued when times return. At the outbreak of the present war the Warspite, under pressure of evacuation from which it was proposed on vulnerable estuary, now unemployed at too many districts or mentioned estuary trade are good. There engaged in some of the permanent or mentioned help in munitions and other industries.

Law Report, Sept. 9

HIGH COURT OF JUSTICE

KING'S BENCH DIVISION

DEFENCE REGULATIONS: HABEAS CORPUS REFUSED

IN RE LEES

Before Mr. Justice Humphreys, Mr. Justice Oliver, and Mr. Justice Croom-Johnson

The Court delivered judgment giving their reasons for refusing, on August 23, the application for a writ of habeas corpus by Mr. Aubrey Trevor Oswald Lees, now in St. Mamet's Prison, Brixton.

It was stated on August 23 to counsel for the applicants when applying to prove for the writ that Mr. Lees had been detained by the Executive without charge or trial and therefore it appeared to be contrary to the liberty of the subject guaranteed by the Great Charter and the Bill of Rights.

When the matter was again argued could not afterwards by Mr. Lees in which he maintained that the reasons for which he believe that he had been detained were mostly wholly untrue, or he had very little confidence in the performance of the solicitors of, on supplication to consider the decision of this Court, he was detained by the Home Secretary local assurances the Home Secretary had given being such that the reason able that Mr. Lees would be detained.

He said that the order stated that whereas the Home Secretary had reasonable cause to believe that he, Mr. Lees had been of too hostile associations, or that he had been recently concerned in the preparation of the commission of, on organization was a subject.

Mr. Justice Humphreys, in giving the judgment of the Court, said that the application for a writ of habeas corpus could not be granted, and as a reason it must be granted or refused upon some principle of law. Unless the applicant could show some ground for interference with the order made by the Home Secretary for his detention, the Court had no option but to refuse the application.

JUDGMENT

Mr. Justice Humphreys, in giving the judgment of the Court, said that it was at the instance of one of our Judges that Mr. Lees was brought before them for his detention. It was a reasonable order made under the Defence (General) Regulations, 1939, the Home Secretary stated that the applicant should be detained.

The particulars given in him (Mr. Lees) in a document from the advisory committee of the Home Office appointed under the Defence Regulations alleged that he had expressed pro-Fascist views. Mr. Lees said that he was satisfied.

The fact then in support of the contention had failed, both in the evidence in respect of documents which they felt about him, in the security of the State but further reasonable suspicion in them, and had enough to call a person who had been stated was satisfied.

Only if the applicant could show that there was no evidence on which the Home Secretary could form the opinion that there was reasonable ground would the Court interfere. No such ground existed here, and the application was refused.

Solicitors—Messrs. Oswald Hickson, Collier and Co.; Treasury Solicitor.

RACING

MAHMOUD SOLD

FROM OUR RACING CORRESPONDENT

The Aga Khan has sold his million Mahmoud (by export) to the United States of America. The sale was arranged by the British Bloodstock Agency, who also sold for export to the same country the Aga Khan's other good sires Blenheim and Bahram.

Mahmoud, by Blenheim out of Mah Mahal, who won by Eiderdownmah out of that remarkable racing machine Mumtaz Mahal, till he is a useful stallion potentially, in winning and good fortune to the Turf industry. Besides his sire of successful stallions his sons, a short time ago there was a good chance that this would be one of those bloodstock breeds in this country clears is now a rare, another that there will be a shortage.

Mahmoud was a very good racehorse. He was the wonderful two-year-old of his time of his first season was placed second in the Two Thousand Guineas and won the Derby, which he did not run in by a head yet there was a little delay, he seemed to find his Aga Khan by Lord Astor's Pay On. Out that running many faced difficulties of stable, and won this small race, but about the which the Derby is run. The Aga Khan also has the American horse Bahram and beat at the present year, winning every important race. At the outbreak of the present war Bahram was brought to an end. It is feared that the Aga Khan's stud will be wind up.

News in Brief

The Spitalfields Market Tenants' Association has issued £12,100 from tonight for all services, to the Government for the duration of the war.

The Nissler legal Corporation's Prudence has brought about a prize buildings as is shown by a last Master's orders, over the compilation will be unusual for the whole war.

Alarm was caused in West Somerset early yesterday by the ringing of church bells in about five towns. The Somerset Command stated that that had been no attempt to invade the areas in which bells may be rung.

Hundreds of thousands of signatures are being collected for a memorial to be submitted to Mr. Churchill as possible evidence that the British people join in the nation's determination and vigour in prosecuting the war. The memorial may be found at the Kinema.

The L.C.C. Education Committee has reviewed, subject to competition by the Board of Education, recommendations of the Standing Joint Committee on the Salaries of Teachers, relating to the payment, from April 1, for a consolidated bonus of a week to teachers in establishments receiving £1 a week or less.

From THE TIMES of 1840

THURSDAY, SEPTEMBER 10, 1840. Price 5d.

The more we inquire the more thoroughly we are convinced that in the arrangement made by the railway companies for the conveyance of the public, convenience and the comfort of the passenger are very insufficiently consulted, and attention is paid very little to their safety. ...

U.S. LAWN TENNIS

...

186 DECREES MADE ABSOLUTE

Mr. Justice Hope-Colville yesterday made absolute the decrees nisi in 186 matrimonial causes.

AUCTIONS TO-DAY

...

Every newspaper reported the incident:

```
8th September 1944.

A   huge   explosion   occurred   in   Chiswick   in
southwest London.

There  was  no  siren,  no  warning.  This  was  the
first  ballistic  missile,  Hitler's  much  vaunted  V2
Rocket.  It  weighed  thirteen  tons  and  had  arrived
via  the  stratosphere  at  3,000  miles  per  hour.

Three  people  died  and  seventeen  were  seriously
injured  in  the  first  attack,  which  reduced  rows
of  houses  to  the  appearance  of  a  battlefield.
```

No mention of Sarah, Rosie or Constable Adams, who each became just another civilian death statistic.

Londoners would have heard for the first time, the distinctive sound of the V2 Rocket.

The V2 Attacks went on until the 18th September by which time five hundred had fallen on the London area and nine thousand British had died, but then they stopped abruptly because of the Allied Operation "Market Garden" at Arnem, which forced the Rocket batteries to withdraw.

VI Flying Bomb

V2 Heading for the Target

V2 Ready to Launch

D Day

What a Day

Chapter 26

"They came, rank after relentless rank, ten lanes wide, twenty miles across, five thousand ships of every description. There were fast new attack transports, slow rust-scarred freighters, small ocean liners, Channel steamers, hospital ships, weather-beaten tankers, coasters and swarms of fussing tugs. There were endless columns of shallow-draft landing ships-great wallowing vessels, some of them almost 350 feet long. ... Ahead of the convoys were processions of mine sweepers, Coast Guard cutters, buoy-layers and motor launches. Barrage balloons flew above the ships. Squadrons of fighter planes weaved below the clouds. And surrounding this fantastic cavalcade of ships packed with men, guns, tanks, motor vehicles and supplies, ... was a formidable array 702 warships."

(Cornelius Ryan: "The Longest Day")

Photo # 26-G-2343   Army troops wade ashore on "Omaha" Beach, 6 June 1944

Rope Ladders Scaling the Cliff

The landing craft made slow headway through the rough sea and approached the beach. The Germans were well prepared; they fired their deadly artillery with great accuracy, sinking many of the flotilla. Shrapnel from the shellfire littered the beach. The enemy's machine gun fire ricocheted off the landing craft as their ramps were lowered. The Allied troops disembarked, but anti-personnel mines greeted them as they struggled onto the beach. Those first few minutes turned Normandy's pristine beaches into a killing field. The shoreline was covered with dead and wounded men screaming in agony and the sands turned red.

Charles Weatherspoon was a platoon leader and the senior officer in his landing group since Captain Slater and Lieutenant McBride both drowned trying to get to shore.

'OK, men, we're close to the beach. I'm going to fire off our rockets, so stay back and cover your eyes!' Charles yelled.

Where the rockets landed, nobody knew, it was so bloody hard to aim them as the launchers were attached to the deck.

'Lower the ramp and run like hell!' Charles screamed.

The men jumped into chest-deep water and started wading ashore. Bullets were cutting a swathe through the landing troops. The sea had turned red and soldiers were floating face-down like dead fish, some shot, some killed by shrapnel, others drowned in the deep water with the weight of their packs pulling them down.

Charles led his men to the base of a steep cliff, instructing them to grab any rope available and get up as fast as they could. Soon he stumbled across his good ex-Harvard friend, Captain Bailey,who was slumped against a rock at the top of the cliff with most of his left hand blown off.

'Take it easy, Captain, we'll send a medic back to take care of you', Charles reassured him.

Charles knew he couldn't have his platoon wait; they had a job to do and speed was essential as the Huns were defending their positions relentlessly with machine guns and mortar.

'Our men were dropping like flies,' muttered Captain Bailey. 'My Platoon Sergeant, Richard Edwards, jumped into a shell crater to protect himself from the hail of bullets but landed on one of his own men's bayonets, skewering him through the stomach. He didn't take long to die, thank God."

Charles led his remaining men from one shell crater to another, constantly dodging bullets. He paused, until he figured it was safe to run to the next crater, edging closer and closer to the German machine gun position.

'Listen, men. I want someone to volunteer to come with me to blow up these bastards.'

Several men volunteered. He chose Private Riley, for no particular reason.

Charles and Riley ran to the next crater, only twenty yards from the nest.

'Riley, fire as much lead at them as you can. I'm going to run around their flank and throw these grenades, OK?

'Yes, Sir.'

'Right, let get the bastards!'

Riley started firing his Browning machine gun and Charles went for the mad dash making it to the position he felt was best to hurl the grenades. In quick succession, he threw them and each one exploded in the nest. When the smoke had lifted, he edged his way to the machine gun nest. Four German soldiers were killed.

The rest of the platoon joined him and Riley.

'Right men, we move on.'

Just as they started off, an enormous tirade hit them. An anti-aircraft gun was firing at them and they lost ten more men in less than a minute.

One of their own big guns had its position and blasted the German position.

Charles' orders were to proceed to the coast road and establish a roadblock.

His platoon was the first to reach the road and they manned the road block on guard for any vehicles that may approach.

'Quick, get low now,' yelled on of his men, Frankie Vailes.

Charles looked up the road and saw a convoy of German trucks laden with troops and pulling abundant artillery behind them.

'Fucking hell! We'll be slaughtered if they see us!'

He ordered his men into the ditch beside the road, reminding them to keep their heads low.

When the boys were in the ditch, Charles discovered what seemed to be a sunken road; obviously it had taken some pretty heavy equipment recently.

The acting platoon Sergeant, Jack Scrimshaw, destroyed the communications along the coastal road by blowing up the telephone poles.

Charles and Private Gary Winters explored the sunken road which was leading them inland, when they came across a little trench covered in camouflage.

Charles lifted a piece of it.

' Bloody hell, Gazza, take a look at this. Take a look at these guns,' Charles whispered.

Sitting in the correct firing position, with ammunition piled neatly beside them, they were ready for business.

'It seems they're pointing at Utah Beach, not Omaha,' observed Gary.

'OK, Gary, we need to make sure there are no Krauts around, then we can blow these babies up.'

Examining the cache, they were convinced there were no Germans waiting to rip them apart.

'You cover me, Gaz. I'm going to blow these fuckers up with some thermite grenades.'

Charles placed the grenades in the guns' traversing mechanisms and pulled the pin before running back. The incredible heat melted the guns at a temperature of 4000 degrees.

Charles silently destroyed all the guns; thermite grenades make no sound.

Charles's platoon saw plenty of action from that first day. One significant battle was the taking of Cherbourg.

Cherbourg was a strategic objective for the Allies. The success of the Overlord plan depended on its capture, as the port was to be used by ships coming straight from the United States, laden with the soldiers and the equipment needed to regain Europe.

Charles and his replenished platoon were advancing to Cherbourg; Charles had been promoted to Captain and had a number of platoons under his command. He had also received "The Medal of Honour" for his bravery in taking out the German machine gun nest on the first day of the invasion.

The platoon was moving towards the village of Montebourg and receiving very little resistance from the Germans.

On the outskirts of the village, they discovered a large warehouse. Charles decided to investigate, thinking it may have been a weapons stock.

'I want you, Wilson, and you, Jones, to follow me in. Make sure you're prepared to shoot. You don't know what we might encounter. The rest of you, encircle the building and if anything moves, shoot it!'

Charles and the two privates slid open the very large doors and peered in; all they could see were some very large crates.

Charles used his bayonet to pry open one of the crates, and ordered his companions to help him.

'Holy hell, it's a rocket! It must be one of those V2s I've heard about. My God! There must be fifty crates here.'

As it turned out, there was a mixture of V2s and V1s, a significant find.

V2 Rocket in the Warehouse

Two days later, Charlie's battalion and a significant contingent of men and machinery from other Divisions, were on the outskirts of Cherbourg.

Major General Lawton Collins was in charge of the operation. He was confident they would be able to take Cherbourg in the next twenty-four hours. However, Lieutenant General Karl-Wilhelm von Schlieben, the German Garrison Commander defending the port city, thought otherwise. He had 21,000 men at his disposal but they were either inexperienced or totally exhausted, as well as disorganised. Food, fuel and ammunition were short.

'I know that Hitler will send us reinforcements any day now. We just have to hold out until then,' Von Schlieben assured his second-in-command.

'What are our exact orders, General Von Schlieben?'

'Hitler has demanded that we fight to the death.'

Later that day, as the U.S. troops were progressing towards the city, German planes were seen overhead.

General Von Schlieben stepped outside his command centre to see what was happening. The Germans started dropping supplies into the city. He ordered his second-in-command, Lieutenant Schmidt, to ascertain the extent of the provisions dropped. He reported back that there was very little food and water, no ammunition to speak of, but they did drop one hundred Iron Crosses, to be awarded as General Von Schlieben saw fit.

'Iron Crosses! They should guarantee our successful defence of the city,' scowled the General. 'Fight to the last man. I think we'll have to.'

Major General Collins issued a demand to the Germans to surrender the city and save many German and U.S. lives but General Von Schlieben refused, based on orders from Hitler.

Collins subsequently launched a general assault on 22nd June. Resistance was stiff at first, but the Americans slowly cleared the Germans from their bunkers and concrete pillboxes. On 26th June, the 79th Division captured Fort du Roule, which dominated the city and its defences. This finished any organised defence. Von Schlieben was captured. The harbour fortifications and the Arsenal surrendered a few days later, after a token resistance. Some German troops, cut off outside the defences, held out until July 1st.

Captain Charles Weatherspoon and his troops marched into Cherbourg, along with twenty five thousand other U.S Troops.

Hitler was devastated and held Von Schlieben responsible as a very poor role model and leader.

Photo # SC 191143   MGen. J. Lawton Collins tells LtGen. Omar Bradley how Cherbourg was taken, June 1944

M Gen Collins and Lt Gen Bradley at Cherbourg

Hitler's Last Stand

Chapter 27

Hitler and his generals knew they had to do something significant to halt the Allied forces broaching the German border and taking Berlin.

They met in the infamous "Wolf's Lair" in East Prussia to plan their attack.

Hitler and His Trusted Generals Planning the Battle

On December 16, 1944, the German army launched its last great counter-offensive of World War II. 'The Battle of the Bulge' was meant to be Hitler's "last stand" in order to break apart and defeat the Allied forces. Hitler believed the relationship was fragile between the British, the US, and Russians. He anticipated he had enough troops left to launch a surprise attack on the Western Front through the thinly held line in the Belgian Ardennes Forest.

He was relying on bad weather, difficult terrain and the Allied troops celebrating Christmas. Hitler and his generals were hoping to catch the Allies by surprise. The Allies regarded the Ardennes as an unlikely location for an attack, although four years earlier, the German Blitzkrieg had shattered the Allied front, which led to France's surrender.

Hitler's plan was to divide the Allied forces by reducing their superior air power. The Germans planned to take Antwerp, in Belgium; this would cut off a major Allied supply base servicing the Western Front. He would then be able to surround Canada's 1st army, Britain's 2nd army, and, in addition, the US's 1st and 9th armies. Hitler thought this would result in the northern forces being surrounded and cut off from their supplies. The southern forces would then be pushed out of Germany.

Hitler underestimated the strength of the Allied forces and the speed at which Eisenhower could mobilise his troops.

On the eve of the battle, Hitler sent in troops to infiltrate the front. Some were dropped by parachute, while others came in driving captured American jeeps. These men spoke perfect English and wore U.S. uniforms. They managed to spread confusion by cutting off telephone lines, giving false directions, and changing road signs.

The battle began at dawn on 16th December. After a two-hour bombardment, Hitler managed to push back American forces. The Allies were totally unprepared, the attack was a complete surprise. The allies' lack of communication and the fact their troops were outnumbered, led to Hitler's initial success. In spite of this, after two days of fighting, the Germans had made very little progress. Hitler managed to attack two American southern divisions that were in front of Elsenborn Ridge, and surrounded only the least experienced division of the US VIII Corps.

On December 17, 72 American POW's were captured outside the town of Malmedy, which is just south of Ardennes. An S.S. unit commanded by Lieutenant-Colonel Joachim Peiper, massacred these POWs. He simply brought them out to an open field, and machine-gunned them. Their bodies were then buried beneath the deep snow.

Much of the battle depended on the weather. At the start, it was foggy and the ground was unfrozen, but not muddy. For Hitler, these conditions were ideal because the Allied air power could not intervene. A little snow had fallen around the Schnee Eifel, a group of low-ranging hills to the east where the heaviest German concentration had been assembled. According to one soldier, "the rest of the Ardennes lay bare and ugly". The Allies desperately needed fair weather to begin their air attack. However, a great snowstorm fell upon them during the first week.

On December 22, Hitler sent a message to American Major-General Anthony Mcauliffe, at the Bartongre Garrison, telling him to surrender. His response to Hitler's request was simply "Nuts!" On this same day, skies cleared, and reinforcements were sent by airdrop to the Bartongre Garrison; Allied airplanes began their attack on German tanks. Then, on December 23, Americans began their first counterattack on the southern flank of the Ardennes "Bulge".

At midday on December 24, sixteen German jet aircraft attacked a ball-bearing factory and tool-die warehouse in Ciege. They then proceeded to attack railway yards supplying the Allies. This was the first jet bomber attack in history. However, by evening, the German offensive had been halted. Their advance was less than sixty miles at its furthest point. This was nowhere close to the objective of the assault.

The fighting grew more intense on Christmas Day, and for some weeks thereafter. The period of surprise was now gone, and the panzer armies were simply trying to blast their way through the front. Instead of beginning a retreat, more and more guns were sent forward to the Bulge. This was done in an attempt to hold what had been gained, and to expand the front, if possible.

Losses from exposure to the cold grew as large as the losses from fighting. The Germans began attacking in white suits, in order to blend in with the snow. Men were fighting for shelter and warmth, as well as fighting the enemy. Some of the people of Ardennes opened their homes to the American soldiers. They shared food, blankets, and fuel. In addition, these people helped the wounded and the ill.

The Germans were plagued by lack of supplies. Tanks simply ran out of fuel and could go no further. Allied forces eventually surrounded Lieutenant-Colonel Jochen Peiper, commander of the 1st SS Panzer Division.

Peiper's battle group, surrounded and out of fuel, began to make their way back to Germany on foot. Therefore, tanks and other vehicles were abandoned.

The struggle between the Allies and Germany ended in January, after the Allies' original line in Ardennes was restored. It turned out to be the largest land battle of WWII. The Americans suffered 81,000 casualties, 23,554 captured, and 19,000 killed. Germany's casualties were 100, 000 killed, wounded, or captured.

Hitler's faith in the theory "an attack is the best defence" proved to be totally misguided.

His immediate future looked grim.

Tanks in the Battle of the Bulge

ENEMY TIDE IN ARDENNES EBBING FAST

AMERICANS ENTER ST. HUBERT

BRITISH AND THIRD ARMY FORCES LINK UP

CONVERGING THRUSTS ALONG LATERAL ROADS

The enemy's withdrawal from the western bulge of the Ardennes salient is increasing in speed, though he is resisting strongly the First Army's attempted movement southward from Bihain.

The Americans have entered the important centre of St. Hubert. British patrols have also reached the town, thus linking up with the Third Army.

HEAD OF SALIENT RINGED

GROWING FRONTAL PRESSURE

From Our Special Correspondent
PARIS, Jan. 12

Whatever Rundstedt may have achieved in delaying and to some extent disrupting the allied winter campaign, his armies in the Ardennes are now possibly faced with a major disaster. Snow and rain, fog and daunting cold inevitably retard the rate of our progress, but they are in no way diminishing the pressure along the flanks of the salient, which is now taking on a forbore look compared with the menacing bulge that, nearly a month ago, stretched to within four miles of Dinant.

The fall of Laroche and St. Hubert removes the main rivets from the enemy's western position, and he would seem to be left with no alternative but a swift withdrawal before the growing frontal pressure being exerted against the head of the salient by British forces, who have completely ringed it off in the area by linking their right flank with General Patton's Third Army in the region of St. Hubert. There are indications that the enemy has already pulled back to the branch of the River Ourthe that flows into the main stream from the south-west, and he is faced with the danger of converging thrusts along two lateral highways running across the salient, one from Bastogne to Liège by way of the vital communications centre of Houffalize.

THREAT TO HOUFFALIZE

The heavy fighting around Rhain and Petite Langlir clearly holds a decisive menace to Houffalize. It will be overlooked by the American advance, but although the northern shoulder of the salient has been retained by active since Field-Marshal Montgomery's attack began, American losses in the south of Malmedy are no more than eight miles from St. Vith, the most vital road junction of them all, and that the bridgehead established on the River Salm by crossings from the west to the vicinity of Vielsalm is more secure than might be expected. All these indications for the enemy to the south of his line are that the enemy has been reserved at the head of his line that the country that has to be reversed at the height of a ragged order.

It will be recalled that Rundstedt's element was launched with three armies—the Seventh and Fifth and Sixth panzer armies commanded by Manteuffel and Kurt Dietrich. Apart from the cutting blow struck from the pit during the five days in the attack General Hodges' First Army has gone on the offensive. From January 11 he deployed 30,000 troops, though the armoured strength of four German armoured divisions at their present establishment: 620 transport vehicles, and nearly 60 guns of various types.

No considerable losses are available from the American Third Army, but as the enemy deployed most of his armour in holding actions along the southern front, presumably it may be inferred that German losses in general are considerable. The vicinity of Bastogne is away to the north. Allied losses cannot be inferred even in respect of St. Vith, the most vital local function of the whole area. In continuation of its usual policy, nothing is said to have Headquarters about allied losses, but they are on nothing like this scale.

GAINS IN BITCHE AREA

It would be at a moment like this, when the tide appears to have turned decisively in the Ardennes, that Rundstedt would be expected to try to create a major diversion aimed elsewhere along the Alsatian plain generally. No marked developments in the situation in this theatre are reported in American Headquarters this evening, though thrusts of General Patch's Seventh Army continue to make small headway in the Bitche area, north of the Wissembourg corridor another fairly heavy attack by infantry with 25 tanks came to grief American machines in Hatten, a little to the north-east of Haguenau itself. Another attack was finally beaten off, at least six of the tanks being knocked out. The American Seventh Army, on the other hand, still continues to press General Devers's positions in the region of the Colmar pocket. The enemy threw some 35,000 troops in this area yesterday, attacks by infantry with 25 tanks came to grief American machines in Hatten, a little to the north-east, east of Colmar, with loss of eight of their armour. They suffered very heavy casualties, and the only withdrawal from the salient south of Strasbourg, which began in December, is proceeding normally.

FROM OUR SPECIAL CORRESPONDENT
ARDENNES FRONT, Jan. 12

American troops thrusting into the Bastogne bulge from three directions this afternoon met at Bras, four miles south-east of Bastogne. The escape for the remaining Germans was cut off until the bulge has now been eliminated.

ALTERED SHAPE OF SALIENT

THE NEXT STAND

WILTZ-VIELSALM LINE POSSIBLE

From Our Military Correspondent

It is reported that no German troops remain west of the Laroche-St. Hubert road. In view of the limited road space at the disposal of the enemy and the effect of snow and alternate frost and thaw upon the roads in hilly country, his withdrawal has been relatively rapid.

While the chief obstacle to the allied advance at the western end of the salient has been materially in many instances compounded of major congestion items of mud on these dreadful roads—the situation has been bad from the first and more. The main difficulty which the allied troops face along the front will lie in the forming it in the German official report in unusually sober terms. It admits a "break-through" application of powerfully fused reckoned American attacks. "It admits a "break-through" application of Bastogne, and underpinning also limiting concentric pressure recoil that the enemy, then of thinking that the bombardment has been avoided, the object of which will be remain is not too imported to let our front round would be attainable. If it turns out that the enemy has been beaten on the north-western edge of the salient, and will be mindful at remaining a pivot in the region of Houffalize.

For several days now it has been clear that the German was aware at the end of their attack on the salient. It is now equally clear that the enemy, after day midnight, but this delay is made more difficult to resist until, now, then, these parts of Greece most difficult to reach, can be given the news well in advance of the appointed time, thus avoiding misunderstanding. Actually, according to all reports so far received, the news spread fast and fighting ceased forthwith wherever it was heard. E.L.A.S. units are already withdrawing in Peloponnesus and Laurin in accordance with the terms of the truce.

NOT A PEACE TREATY

The text of the agreement was issued in London at the same time as it was published in Athens. It is not a peace treaty, although in Athens the truce with this agreement is in force even on a peace treaty, is it the words of its first clause, we agree not including hostilities "it is stated from "unilateral" action, to infer that the reverse is dated. Senator Vandenberg said today that he "must stand" it is alleged to be completely posted in real action during both and for the President and the Department of State, "and Today the declaration has highly impressed the Senator's speech, nevertheless, points out that he however acknowledged the passing and he had himself made a proposal which would regularize the situation in which we find ourselves and he would never offer a take-it-or-leave-it fashion yet can only suggest it as a basis for negotiations and give plenty it in working the real of the mutual present positions out of those on "take it or leave it" China. The present aim is a light resolve of the Kutari class and specific proposals, destroyer escorts and greying convoys. The Third Fleet, which is undersupplied, is continuing its relationship to the aircraft-have destroyed 39 Japanese aeroplanes over bases reached between Saison and Quinhon Harbour.

The many convoys were attacked between Saison and Camrath Bay. Enemy small craft were sunk, a torpedo boat was set ablaze. Heavy units of Japan's fleet on the mainland of Asia, and some of the war self-defence harbour. It is probable that a considerable effort was made to camouflage positions for the defence of the Polish question to counter up the been retained ashore or in base waters at Saison. The enemy troops at the engagement were not made to the last beginning in get their aeroplanes airborne, and then with his chance the last Japanese efforts in the Japanese chaos.

"CEASE FIRE" IN GREECE

E.L.A.S. HOSTAGES STILL HELD

REGENT'S OFFER OF DISCUSSIONS

From Our Diplomatic Correspondent

More than five weeks of bitter fighting in Greece were brought to an end yesterday morning when General Scobie, British Commander-in-Chief in Greece, announced that he had arranged a truce

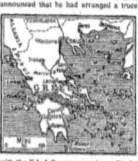

with the E.L.A.S. representatives. By the terms of the truce the precise time for ceasing fire is set for a remote part from day midnight, but this delay is made more difficult to reach certain in some of these most difficult parts of Greece most difficult to reach, can be given the news well in advance of the appointed time, thus avoiding misunderstanding.

FURTHER UNDERTAKINGS

It is true that more or sense on the roads affects the movement of the defenders and attackers equally. Yet such obstacles have generally been far more hindrance to the side attempting a extending force because very slender circumstances a backing into sharp defence of a supremely difficult to give a real finish, while the zones behind them will fill. The bombs in it is therefore to be expected that more of the German forces will be withdrawn to whatever positions they can take up. The line of the River Ourthe, for it has probably been sited that a logistic position in the Ardennes which will be subtly a primitive if it should possibly be cleared. Those who assess the facts, it may be, may take time to realise that the enemy finds it difficult anyway, and that the danger may be best of the check he has suffered. And he is capable of another blow, and could the allies urging him from southern if he wishes, which it called "the initiative," every hostile will be dangerous. It is possible this assessment will now shortly present themselves.

12,000-LB. BOMBS ON U-BOAT PENS

SHIPPING ATTACKED AT BERGEN

Two squadrons of R.A.F. Lancasters attacked by Mustangs of R.A.F. Fighter Command, attacked with 12,000lb. bombs the U-boat shelters at Bergen and enemy shipping in and near the harbour yesterday afternoon.

Bergen is now one of the main bases from which the Germans can handle U-boat offensive. The weather was clear, but there was only a little anti-aircraft fire. Crews reported that the bombing was well concentrated on the shelters, and that also on one enemy vessel seen after being hit. Near the entrance to the harbour a merchant ship of some 8,000 tons was left lying on her side. Crews returning that the bombing was well concentrated on the shelters, and that also on one enemy vessel seen after being hit. Two direct hits on the U-boat shelters were claimed.

Three craft operating on reconnaissance off Norway yesterday shot down a German Ju 52.

THE GIANT-KILLER

AN ATLANTIC NAVAL INCIDENT

FROM OUR OWN CORRESPONDENT
OTTAWA, Jan. 12

Records available here of Canadian participation in naval warfare indicate that the Royal Canadian Navy is giving excellent account of itself, not only in the anti-U-boat challenge but also in encounters with enemy surface craft. The only case which affords a little pleasant reading is that of the corvette Mayflower, when she and three other craft made prisoners of the crew of a German submarine in the Atlantic.

In 1940, one day at dawn, the Mayflower sighted what appeared to be a large and powerful enemy vessel. The corvette stood by its guns to signal the enemy. No reply was received. The craft then made to close, and three revolvers, this was the signal of its objective by the enemy. The Mayflower immediately opened fire on the stranger, and with a lucky shot hit a depth-charge near the water-line. This sank the enemy's vessel, and the survivors abandoned ship in a British manner. Three quarters of an hour later, the crew of the U-boat surrendered under the orders of the Mayflower to enable him to be subsequently identified as H.M.S. Rothay.

A FOREIGN POLICY FOR U.S.

LEAD BY SENATOR VANDENBERG

BROADCAST OF SPEECH

From Our Own Correspondent
WASHINGTON, Jan. 12

Senator Vandenberg made known today that his speech on the subject of foreign policy will be broadcast by the Office of War Information in condensed form to the outer world. Whether it will stimulate further debate in the Senate or anywhere outside the statement of the Prime is uncertain. Senator Connally, chairman of the Senate Foreign Relations Committee, certainly speaks the mind of the Administration when he attempts to discourage Congressional discussion in advance of President Roosevelt's meeting with Mr. Churchill and Marshal Stalin, but since, as inescapably appears, Senator Vandenberg's utterance has not made all things easier for everybody it is evident that complete restraint will be exercised.

One thing is to should be clear—that Senator Vandenberg is no longer the isolationist or narrow internationalist he once was. "I do not believe," he said, "that any nation henceforth can retain its certain that the shape of action," to which may be added his admission that "our minds have changed" to the minds which communicate proved over ourselves." Without such an advanced speech, brown-day nations his proposal could never have been made that the United States should throw itself wide open to the outer front, when there may he some provided in this direction as one-third threatened the choice concerns which of one thousand and when the possible value of these threats is to be exploited. In America's expansion that he is too important attracted by what used to be called "Intelligent spheres national art."

LIMITED ACTION

Senator Vandenberg stands for collective security and as a condition precedent for the formation of an alliance—against whom again? Germany and Japan? This is a ready dismissal of the basic approach. The address also any Congressional restrictions upon the President's right to act for his country. It is worth noting that it is no certain which we could have within limited to action against Germany and Japan, but it remains doubtful in many result concerning the objections of a resolution thereby, that the "actual issue" is all the aforesaid a Presidential resolution has been provided for the President and the Department of State, and Today the declaration has highly impressed the Senator's speech, nevertheless, points out that he however acknowledged the passing and he had himself made a proposal which would regularize the situation in which we find ourselves and he would never offer a take-it-or-leave-it fashion yet can only suggest it as a basis for negotiations and give plenty it in working the real of the mutual present positions out of those on "take it or leave it" China.

"WORKABLE POLICY"

The New York Herald Tribune commends Senator Vandenberg highly for his contribution towards the "universally workable" international policy which our position—and which, in American policy, but it has neither the policy of isolationist or narrow internationalist he once was. An attempt to recognise the unsatisfactory status of nations of which is making wider of all our ends absolutely we can recognise the ever-shelling of importance of establishing a stable world order in others he seems to drive the diverse generalizations of the Atlantic Charter, or the outcome of the Polish question to counter up the been retained ashore or in base waters at Saison. Vandenberg has perceived "I am in earnest." The fundamental verities, and that with his speech "we are in fact beginning to get down to business."

JAPANESE LOSE 25 SHIPS OFF INDO-CHINA

FOUR CONVOYS ATTACKED BY U.S. CARRIER-AIRCRAFT

AMERICANS 10 MILES INLAND ON LUZON

American carrier-borne aircraft of the Third Fleet have sunk 25 Japanese ships and damaged 13 in an attack on four convoys off Indo-China. Early this morning the Americans, who had suffered no damage, were reported to be continuing their assault.

On Luzon, in the Philippines, General MacArthur's forces have made advances inland of 12 miles on a wide front, and have overrun at their northern end four main roads leading to Manila.

FLEET KEEPS UP ASSAULT

ENEMY WARSHIPS SUNK

From Our Own Correspondent
NEW YORK, Jan. 12

Admiral Nimitz, Commander-in-Chief, Pacific, reports that 25 Japanese ships have been sunk and 13 others heavily damaged by American carrier aeroplanes of the

46 ENEMY SHIPS SUNK OR DAMAGED

A report from General MacArthur's Headquarters accounts for 46 enemy vessels lost night stated:—

Americans troops on Luzon Island are continuing their advance inland virtually unchecked. They have penetrated 12 miles inland along the coast and have edged over 10 miles of the only railway link to the Lingayen Gulf with Manila. Japanese resistance is increasing all along the front.

On the eastern sector there is sharp fighting along the Manan-Pangu-Futa road.

A Japanese communication at the merchant marine and coastal vessels scattered to second of San Fernando, North of the capital of San Fernando, North of the Lingayen Gulf yesterday. Naval forces singled that concentrations of sank or bombed naval of 46 ships without loss.

JAPANESE WAR COUNCIL SUMMONED

General Koiso, the Japanese Prime Minister, has summoned a supreme war council of the general staffs from all branches of war to make defence decisions related by the tide of the Lingayen action before it is too badly that Japanese troops from the Lingayen northern withdrew from the mainland to positions in the Japanese areas.

COMMONWEALTH AIR TRANSPORT

COMING CONFERENCE

FROM OUR AERONAUTICAL CORRESPONDENT

The first full meeting of the Commonwealth Air Transport Council will be held in London later in the year. Final arrangements are now being discussed.

The council was set up at Ottawa last October during the Empire talks which preceded the international civil aviation conference in Chicago. Its purpose is to ensure, by co-ordination of policy, that Commonwealth interests in the various technical developments in the field of radio and radar navigational aids are used for the main benefit of all.

ENEMY PLIGHT IN BUDAPEST

RUSSIANS TIGHTENING THEIR GRIP

The Russians are tightening their hold round the enemy groups in Budapest, and are quickening their advance into Pest. The German garrison is reported to be short of ammunition, and to have little chance of receiving further supplies by air.

Y The Russian High Command's report of y message from the Moscow radio quarters spoke on page 1.

AMERICANS ON ROADS TO MANILA

PATROLS ACROSS AGNO

FROM OUR OWN CORRESPONDENT
NEW YORK, Jan. 12

American forces on Luzon have widened their beach-head on Lingayen Gulf to 25 miles by the occupation of Labrador, on their right flank. They have penetrated inland on a wide

In later editions the following appeared:—

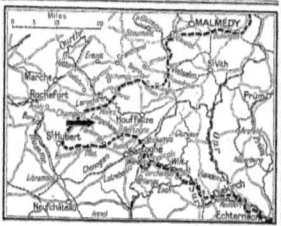

Liberation of Paris

Chapter 28

General Eisenhower was at his command post, drawing up plans to move forward into Germany and eventually Berlin. He had been under some pressure to liberate Paris and then proceed to Germany but to him and his command team, it did not make sense. By taking Germany and Berlin, all the territory held by the Nazis would be liberated, including Paris.

The French capital learned that more Allied troops had landed in the south of France. The French citizens rejoiced and the Germans thought they had better evacuate the city before the Allies arrived.

The Parisians went on strike as the Germans began to depart. The Metro workers, police, postal workers and many more put down their tools of trade and picked up arms to attack their German oppressors. Barricades were erected in the streets, which caused total disruption to the city.

General de Gaulle contacted General Eisenhower and insisted that Paris should be liberated at once.

'General Eisenhower, I insist that the Free French Forces march into Paris with your help and take back our magnificent city,' General de Gaulle demanded.

'General, I understand your impatience, however I am not sure we are ready to do that.'

'General, if you do not help us, we will do it on our own. We cannot wait, we will not wait.'

General Eisenhower agreed reluctantly.

Back in Berlin, Hitler ordered his commander in Paris, General Dietrich von Choltitz to destroy the city before he left. He mined the bridges and monuments but could not bring himself to carry out these ludicrous orders.

General Jacques Leclerc, leading some of de Gaulle's forces, finally reached the city. By the next day, more Free French soldiers arrived. Despite areas of intense German fighting, the liberators of Paris reached von Choltitz's headquarters. Without resisting, the erstwhile commander of Paris signed a surrender document.

Paris had been liberated after four tumultuous years of German occupation.

Allied Troops Marching down the Champs-Élysées

Captain Charles Weatherspoon was one of the soldiers proudly marching into Paris. He would remain in Paris as part of the liberation forces until the end of the war.

The Parisians welcomed the U.S troops into their homes and their hearts. Charles learnt French and had a relationship with a beautiful French woman called Françoise.

He had been assigned a position in General de Gaulle's command centre responsible for writing press releases and other propaganda. It was not what Charles really wanted; he would have preferred to be marching to Berlin with his comrades but it was a good life with plenty of spare time to get to know Paris and be with Françoise. She was a very attractive woman with an infectious laugh and a wicked sense of humour. They spent time together visiting Paris's famous museums including the Louvre. They had a favourite meeting place in the Marais district, Saint-Jacques Tower, a small park where they would feed the birds and enjoy a simple lunch, a prelude to long afternoons of love-making. Life was good in Paris.

Paris, Free at Last

Vive la France!

Peace

At Last

Chapter 29

Lamont was sitting at his enormous desk in his office in Fleet Street, reading all the day's newspapers; some he owned, some he didn't. It didn't matter; the headline was the same: Hitler was dead. What a glorious moment for the free world!

'It would only be a matter of time before Germany would surrender and this wretched war in Europe would come to an end,' he thought.

He was right. Germany officially surrendered on 7th May 1945 and the free world celebrated.

Celebrations in London

VE Day, Trafalgar Square.

Charles was just as happy and elated as every other person in Paris on V.E. Day. Many a Parisian girl came up and gave him a kiss some more passionate than others; he was enjoying the moment.

Thousands of people crowded into iconic Paris landmarks including the Eiffel Tower and the Champs Elysees.

V.E. Celebrations Paris

Charles lived in Paris for a further three months before being shipped back home. He would miss this beautiful city with its cafes and wine and of course, his beautiful Françoise.

Mistaken Identity

Chapter 30

Captain Weatherspoon sailed out of Marseilles on 21st August bound for New York City and was discharged from the army on arrival. He was looking forward to seeing his parents again after an absence of two years.

He boarded the train for Boston, arriving at Central Station four hours later to be met by his mother and father. They were all very emotional and tears flowed from the entire family group.

Charles enjoyed being home, although this was not the Brownstone he grew up in. After the Great Depression, the world economy started to recover, Boston Bank had started to grow again and become profitable and John's wealth also grew .

The family moved out of their modest home and purchased a magnificent home in Back Bay, one of the more exclusive areas.

John was a very influential banker amongst the business community of Boston and New York. He used his influence to secure a position for Charles as a journalist at "The New York Times".

Charles moved to Manhattan where he rented a one-bedroom apartment and started at "The Times" under the mentorship of Meyer Berger, a senior journalist and a Pulitzer Prize winner.

Berger taught Charles the importance of a diligent work ethic and relentless investigation. Charles excelled under Berger and soon established himself as one of the shining stars at "The New York Times".

On 21st August 1952, John Weatherspoon suffered a massive heart attack and died in the ambulance on the way to hospital: he was fifty-six.

This was a huge shock to both Charles and his mother, Emily. John had been the true patriarch of the family and was loved by all who knew him well.

The funeral was held at the Old North Church circa 1723.

The church could accommodate three hundred people, the police had to cordon off the street to allow another four hundred mourners to show their respect. After the service, family and friends joined Emily and Charles for a wake at the family home.

It had been a very big day and emotionally tiring. Emily and her son were sitting in the formal lounge room after the last of the guests had gone. Emily offered Charles a glass of John's fifty-year-old Malt Scotch, which he duly accepted. She poured one for herself and asked Charles to listen to her without interruption.

'Charles, I have something very important to tell you, I promised your father I would not tell you until he was deceased.

'My God, mother what could be so important?'

'I said no interruptions.'

'Sorry.'

'When I was twenty and living in England I fell in love with a very dashing young man. I had actually known him from a much earlier age but it was only when I saw him again at Oxford University did we become much closer. When he graduated from Oxford, he enlisted in the army with his identical twin, Harold. They both completed officer training and became Second Lieutenants. They were due to leave for France to fight in The Great War very soon after they both graduated.

'The night of their graduation, a party was held at Charles and Harold's parents' house. I was Charles' partner; one thing led to another. For the first time, we made love. The result of that magic night was you, my love. You were conceived.'

'What! You can't be serious Mother! Are you saying my Dad was not my father? Some bloody Englishman had his way with you and here I am? I don't believe you, this is some sort of a joke surely?'

'Charles, I can understand how upset you are and how hurt you must feel, but you must never forget that your father married me, knowing that I was with child and he raised you and cared for you better than most fathers could or would.'

'I know that, but I am in shock! I don't know what to think. Who then is my real father?'

'I wish I knew.'

'What do you mean by that?'

'Charles, what I am about to tell you must remain our secret; is that clear?'

'Sorry, yes of course.'

'Your biological father is Charles Lamont.'

146

'Not Lord Charles Lamont, the newspaper Baron?'

'Well, this is where it gets strange. My lover was Charles Lamont and as I said earlier, we knew each other as children. I would say we were not friends but acquaintances. Your father and I travelled to England when you were four so your grandparents could see you for the first time. You were probably too young to remember.'

'No, I do remember bits and pieces of that trip.'

'OK, well your father and I were invited to Lord Lamont's London home along with my parents who were part of his social circle.'

'That must have been uncomfortable for you?'

'What was uncomfortable is that Lord Lamont did not know who I was! I am certain he had never laid eyes on me before, nor I on him!'

'How can that be?'

My suspicion is that 'Lord Lamont', is not Charles. He is Harold, the younger of the twins whom I have never met.'

'So, what happened to Charles?'

'Harold was reported "Missing in Action" presumed dead, during the First World War.'

'Are you suggesting that it was Charles who was killed'?

'I am. That's exactly what I am suggesting.'

'Then that would mean my real father is dead.'

'That's right, Charles, and if I am correct, that makes you Lord Lamont with all the riches and power it brings.'

'My God! This is all too much for one day, Mother. I am going to bed. Let's talk about it more tomorrow.'

'Goodnight, son. I am sorry I had to bring it up today of all days but that was your father's wish.'

'You mean he knew the whole story and your suspicions?'

'No, just the fact that you were not his real son. He believed my story that I was married to a British officer who was killed in the war.'

'This really is too much. Goodnight.'

Emily stayed up for another two hours thinking about the wonderful life she had spent with John and how she might convince her son to travel to England and France and uncover the truth about the Lamont twins.

147

Private Investigations

Chapter 31

When Charles came down for breakfast he looked just as bemused as he had when he retired the night before. Emily was already seated at the breakfast table sipping a cup of coffee. Dorothy, their maid, was preparing pancakes and maple syrup, Charles' favourite.

He joined his mother at the table.

'How did you sleep, darling?' asked his mother, knowing what the answer would be.

'Not very well. Intermittently…'

'I can understand that. You had a lot to think about.'

'Mom, why did you come to America when you were pregnant?'

'My parents wanted to hide the fact that their nineteen-year old daughter was having a baby out of wedlock. It would have caused them great embarrassment.'

'Yeah, I see what you mean.'

'A penny for your thoughts.'

'Well, to be perfectly frank, I don't know what to think. Let's examine the facts, as we know them. Charles Lamont, known as Lord Lamont, lives in London, England and owns several influential newspapers. He had an identical twin brother called Harold, who was very slightly the younger of the brothers. I assume the younger brother missed out on the title and most of the wealth?'

'Correct.'

'Both brothers go to war and Charles, the elder, gets killed. He is classified as "Missing in Action." If Charles was killed in action, the younger brother, i.e. Harold, would inherit the family fortune and the title. On the other hand, if Harold had been killed, it would be status quo. Did Charles have anything else that Harold would want, Mother?'

'I have delved into it a little bit. I discovered Charles was promoted to Captain, Harry reported to him. Charles also won a Victoria Cross, the highest British medal for bravery in the field. I am sure Harry would have coveted both.'

'Do you know of anything that would distinguish Charles from Harry? Maybe a mole on his back or something?'

'Well, this is a little embarrassing but there *was* something.'

'Well, what was it?'

'Charles had a port-wine birthmark on his buttock.'

'You are kidding me! Really?'

'It was in the shape of Tasmania, or so Charles boasted.'

'Tasmania, in Australia?' 'What side was it'?

'Oh dear, let me try and picture it; it was the left side. Yes, definitely the left side.'

'I won't ask why you remember, let's just leave it at that. Anyway, that is certainly something definite we have in order to identify Harold. No Tasmania, no fortune and a murder conviction we hope! I need to think about all of this and see if I can formulate a plan. I will call you tomorrow, Mom.'

Charles left the family home and was driven to the station by his father's chauffeur.

'I imagine this could be the last time I drive for the Weatherspoons, Sir?'

'Not at all, Joseph. I want you to continue driving my mother.'

'Excellent,Sir. That would be my pleasure.'

Charles started back at "The New York Times" two days after he returned to Manhattan. His colleagues were very understanding and offered their sympathies. Meyer Berger, in particular, was concerned for his young protégé. When out on assignment, he suggested they have lunch at Delmonico's and enjoy one of their world – renowned steaks.

The two journalists were seated towards the rear of the restaurant where they started to discuss the frailty of life. Meyer had lost his father just nine months before and was still having trouble coping with it.

Eventually, Charles asked if it would be possible to take twelve months' leave of absence to pursue some writing in England and on the Continent. Meyer believed it could be possible and offered to speak to the paper's Chief Editor on Charle's behalf.

Charles did not divulge his true purpose as he felt it premature.

He rang his mother and told her of his plan. She was very supportive and offered to help him in anyway, including financially.

Leave of Absence was approved and Charles left for England on BOAC Flight 451, 13th October 1952.

Charles approached the editor of "The Daily Telegraph" a paper that Lord Lamont had recently acquired, to ascertain if it was possible to write articles for the paper on a freelance basis. The Editor, George Shearer, agreed, on the provision that the stories submitted met with the paper's standards and editorial principles.

Charles was on his way to unravelling the mystery of the Lamont brothers.

The first thing he did was to contact their old school, Eton College, under the pretext of researching for a story on the Lamont Family.

He discovered there were still masters teaching who had taught the twins. The Head Master arranged for Charles to meet with some of them.

'Mr Weatherspoon, I would like you to meet Mr Pitt, who was the Lamont twins' Maths teacher.'

Introductions over, Charles started to delve into the twins' history at the renowned boys' school. He asked Mr Pitt what memories of the brothers he had.

'The most vivid memory I have is their competitive spirit, particularly young Harold. He was always trying his utmost to beat his brother at anything he could. Of course Charles was just as competitive, so quite often the jousting would end in tears, if you know what I mean.'

'Do you think it was just the normal thing with brothers, or a bit more than that?'

'No, it was very intense, not the normal behaviour I would expect from brothers and God knows, I have taught a few over the years.'

'Thank you, you have been most helpful, I appreciate your time.'

Charles interviewed three other masters and the story was pretty much the same: extreme competition between the twins. However, one master, Mr Collins, remembered Harold fighting a much older and bigger boy, defending his brother's honour on the rugby field, so there was a deep brotherly love between the two as well.

Although Charles was beginning to get a feel for the twins' psyche, it was not really leading him in the direction he thought he should be heading. If Harold had murdered Charles, the relationship between the two brothers had obviously deteriorated since their school days.

The next step was to visit Oxford University and The Royal Agricultural College and speak with their lecturers and also try and track down some of their friends.

He drove from London to the Cotswolds and booked into "The Fleece" at Cirencester, a beautiful three hundred year-old hotel in the centre of Cirencester, just a few kilometres from the RAC.

He checked into his room, which was delightful. It had a large bay window overlooking magnificent gardens and a large four-poster bed a bit of a waste, he thought.

He had telephoned the Vice Chancellor a few days before and arranged to meet him at the college at three in the afternoon that day.

John Foley was not your typical V.C. He looked more like a farmer than anything, well over six feet tall and when he shook hands with Charles, his hand totally enveloped Charles.

After the introductions were over, John invited Charles to take a walk in the gardens, which surrounded the college.

'So, what is that you would like to know about our star rugby player, Charles?'

'Yes, I had heard Harold was quite a player. Was he captain of the side?'

'No, but he was a magnificent winger. I remember when we played Oxford, I think it was 1915 and he virtually won the game for us. That really aggravated his brother who was his opposite for Oxford.'

'So you were aware Harold had a twin brother?'

'God, yes. When I saw his twin on the field I couldn't tell them apart, a spitting image, quite amazing!'

'Apart from the normal rivalry, do you think the twins were; what should I say, overly competitive?'

'Well, I only saw them together once at the rugby match and they certainly were fierce competitors on the field.'

'Any thing else you can tell me about Harry?'

'He was very bright and a very popular young man with his fellow students. He was also quite a ladies' man from what I hear.'

'Well, thank you ,Vice Chancellor, I appreciate your time.'

'My pleasure and if there is anymore I can do, please contact me directly.'

'I certainly will.'

The next stop on Charles itinerary was Oxford, where he intended to drive the next day.

He arrived in the famous university town about lunchtime and decided to have lunch at "The Rose" on the High Street which had been recommended to him by one of his fellow reporters at "The Daily Telegraph".

His appointment was for three o'clock, and he was seeing a senior professor in English who had taught Charles.

Charles met the Professor, Mr Whitecross-Jones, in the staff lounge and began the conversation in a jovial manner, however it was clear the professor had no time for light conversation and asked Charles to come to the point.

'Sir, I am researching a story I intend to write on Lord Lamont and his family. I understand Lord Lamont attended this university?'

'Yes, that is correct, as I intimated on the telephone, I taught Charles in English Expression and Literature.'

'Was he a good student, Sir?'

'He was an excellent student, Mr Weatherspoon, one of the finest I have ever taught.'

'Have you seen him since he became Lord Lamont?'

'On one occasion fairly recently, I was invited to a book launch in London, where Lord Lamont launched the book, why, I don't know. There were drinks and canapés afterwards and I took the opportunity of reintroducing myself to him. It was quite strange. He had no idea who I was! I was quite taken aback. I have since read somewhere that he has partial memory loss, due to his injuries sustained in the First World War. Damned shame!'

Charles thanked the Professor, walked to his hire car and drove to his hotel, "The Old Bank Hotel" in High Street. He checked in and went down to the lounge bar where he ordered a Macallan malt scotch and sat near the open fire. He contemplated what he had learned about the Lamont twins over the last few days.

He knew they were highly competitive.

He knew they were both highly intelligent.

Nothing really groundbreaking, although the fact that Charles was promoted to Captain could have been the fuse for Harold to act. Surely not. It had to be a more significant event than that.

The thing that really interested Charles was the story the Professor from Oxford told him about the book launch. It was very similar to his mother's experience at the London dinner party.

Lord Lamont didn't recognize them because he had no idea who they were. Why? He had never met either of them, of course! Charles knew it was time to submit a story to the paper or they wouldn't keep him on the freelance list. He would have to go back to London and cover the coronation of Elizabeth.

Once that was out of the way, he would travel to Flanders and Paris to see if he could uncover any damning evidence there.

Queen of Hearts

Chapter 32

1953: Queen Elizabeth takes coronation oath

by Charles Weatherspoon.

Queen Elizabeth II has been crowned at a coronation ceremony in Westminster Abbey in London.

In front of more than eight thousand guests, including prime ministers and heads of state from around the Commonwealth, she took the Coronation Oath and is now bound to serve her people and to maintain the laws of God.

After being handed the four symbols of authority by the Archbishop of Canterbury – the orb, the sceptre, the rod of mercy and the royal ring of sapphire and rubies – the Archbishop of Canterbury, Dr Geoffrey Fisher, placed St Edward's Crown on her head to complete the ceremony.

A shout of "God Save the Queen" was heard and gun salutes were fired as crowds cheered.

The Archbishop and fellow bishops then paid homage to Queen Elizabeth II.

In a radio broadcast the Queen said: "Throughout all my life and with all my heart I shall strive to be worthy of your trust".

An estimated three million people lined the streets of London to catch a glimpse of the new monarch as she made her way to and from Buckingham Palace in the golden state coach.

The ceremony was watched by millions more around the world as the BBC set up their biggest ever outside broadcast to provide live coverage of the event on radio and television. Street parties were held throughout the UK as people crowded round television sets to watch the ceremony.

The crowds, some of whom had camped out overnight to ensure a prime position, were rewarded when the Queen and other members of her family, including the Queen Mother, appeared on the balcony at Buckingham Palace.

Despite the overcast weather conditions, the RAF marked the occasion with a fly past down the Mall.

A fireworks display then lit up the skies above Victoria Embankment.

The Queen replaced her father, King George VI, as monarch following his death on 6 February 1952. After sixteen years on the throne he passed away in his sleep and his twenty-five year old daughter Elizabeth immediately became Queen.

The princess had formally proclaimed herself Queen and Head of the Commonwealth and Defender of the Faith in February 1952 The amount of planning and a wish for a sunny day for the occasion led to the long but excited wait for this special coronation day.

THE QUEEN CROWNED AT WESTMINSTER

VAST CROWDS SEE PROCESSION IN RAIN

DAY OF REJOICING THROUGHOUT THE COMMONWEALTH

Queen Elizabeth II was crowned in Westminster Abbey yesterday, with traditional ceremony, in the presence of a great congregation that included many representatives of the Commonwealth.

Vast crowds had gathered on the route of the procession, and the Queen was acclaimed with enthusiasm as she drove to the Abbey with the Duke of Edinburgh and again when she returned by a longer route. The crowds were drenched in the afternoon by intermittent showers which at times were heavy.

The R.A.F. fly-past took place half an hour after the arranged time and in a modified form because of unfavourable weather. It was watched from the balcony of the Palace by the Queen and the Duke of Edinburgh, with whom were the Duke of Cornwall and Princess Anne.

Television gave some millions of people a close picture of the scene in the Abbey and along the route, and broadcasting again allowed the Queen to speak to her peoples at home and overseas.

In a broadcast address last night her Majesty emphasized the inspiration she had received from the loyalty and affection of her peoples. "Throughout all my life and with all my heart I shall strive to be worthy of your trust," she said.

The day was celebrated with rejoicing throughout the country and the Commonwealth, although the weather marred the festivities in many places at home.

The Queen wearing St. Edward's Crown and holding the Sceptre with the Cross and the Rod with the Dove after her crowning.

CEREMONY SEEN FAR AND WIDE

OVATION FROM GREAT THRONG

A lustre which no cloudin could dim and no torrent could ravish glowed at the heart of yesterday's tremendous events. It was not the splendour of sovereignty so much as its high solemnity which enriched the long and lovely pageantry of the day and set the mood which held the multitude in thrall. That was the reward and fulfilment of the vigil gladly endured through many comfortless hours, a bastion which all could share with the young Queen who came to her searing so richly dowered with the prayers she had herself invoked from her people.

Seldom, surely, has a nation been made so deeply aware of the religious reality which gives all the magnificence its meaning. The glitter of the gold, the glow of scarlet, the trappings and embellishments of martial pride and pallantry were but the setting of the mystery enacted within the Abbey walls.

For the first time television brought many millions into the heart of that mystery, with consequences no one can measure, in this country and far beyond its shores. They were denied the glory of colour which blazed within the Confessor's great church, but they shared with the 7,000 privileged members of that glittering congregation the enormous significance of all that was done. Much of it indeed was more apparent in its detail and fullness to the viewers in their homes than to the guests of high dignity in state and Empire and from foreign lands who thronged the scarse galleries of the Abbey.

INTO HUMBLEST HOMES

The great ceremonies which moved to their climax with such ineffable perfection in the golden spaces of the Coronation theatre spread their spell over a myriad modest villas. The great liturgy of the Church within which were set the hallowing, investing, and crowning claimed possession of the humblest home.

From the moment when the great procession—as majestic in this manner—in its infinitely slow progress from the west door to the Sanctuary until the last ceremonial act had been fulfilled television held it all within its compass—or nearly all. The great mystery of the Anointing was veiled from sight beneath the silken canopy and the greater solemnity of the reception of the Blessed Sacrament by the Queen and her Consort was a moment too sacred for intrusion.

But millions saw the culmination of the tremendous drama when St. Edward's Crown was uplifted in a majestic gesture by the Archbishop of Canterbury and descended gently in all the flashing splendour of sovereignty on the youthful brow, bowed to receive it. The stillness and composure of that slight, graceful figure, lustrous in the stiff habiliments of monarchy, endowed the moment with an enormous sense of historic import.

The hush was soon to be expelled in acclaim, but the effect was unforgettable. Prince Charles was there to see it, in the protective presence of his royal grandmother. A few moments later his father came to perform that humble, tender act of homage, to swear as liege man of life and limb and to salute with a kiss his Queen and his wife. It was an husband and consort, also, that he knelt beside her to one of the most moving episodes of the great ceremony—to say a single blessing from the Archbishop.

DIGNITY AND MODESTY

Nothing was more memorable in the long solemnities than the manner in which her Majesty bore her part in them. Not only at the Crowning but in every movement and gesture there was a deep sense of recollection. Dignity went hand in hand with modesty, simplicity with majesty, gravity with a charm which frame like crystal within all that glitter of imperial and ecclesiastical effulgence.

When the last ceremony was completed to its perfect and shapely end, and the last echo of the great Te Deum had died, when the slow recession had withdrawn the splendid tide of pomp and colour from the shining Sanctuary, the multitude outside prepared to receive their Queen. They had shared wholeheartedly in the singing of the "Old Hundredth," which by a nice touch of imaginative foresight had joined the nation in the vocal offering of the service.

And now was the moment of acclaim for their newly anointed and crowned Sovereign. To those who had borne her

on her way to the Abbey with thunderous cheers were added thousands more who thronged the ribboned miles of the long return procession.

The capital had drawn to its heart a great concourse which left to a submit cairn nearly every street outside the processional way. Rain beat heavily on the stalwarts who had braved the rigours of the waiting hours and it was still pouring from leaden skies when the first royal processions left the Abbey. But when that state coach began to move off in the wake of the endless ranks of service men and women already in position far along the route the sun struggled through its veils. Colour leapt into splendour, and metal shone like silver.

Silvery also rang the Abbey bells, mingling with the great cheer which thundered round the Queen. Framed in the golden elaboration of the coach she bowed her diademed head tirelessly, her smile as gay and brilliant as the sun. The dignity of sovereignty was lightened and gladdened now with the affection which responded to that which she drew to her. All along that coloured river of the processional way, from stands and pavements and windows, from trees and housetops the happy tumult swept her to her palace.

SURGE TO THE PALACE

The rain came again before the coach had carried her and her consort to their home, but nothing dimmed the loyal fervour of her welcome. When the gates of the Palace were closed and the troops of her realm, her dominions, and colonies had passed on their proud way out of sight the crowds swept in a great surge towards the Palace. A great cheer swelled to the sky—it could have been heard a mile away—when the Queen, in her crown, with the Duke and their two children, came from the tall windows on to the balcony to see the R.A.F. fly-past. As the aircraft swept overhead the Queen and the Duke, surrounded by their royal group had withdrawn.

On the balcony they were joined by Queen Elizabeth the Queen Mother, Princess Margaret, the Duke and Duchess of Gloucester, the Princess Royal, the Duchess of Kent with her children, and Princess Alice, Countess of Athlone. The Duke of Cornwall and his sister joined enthusiastically in the salutation to the crowd. The royal appearance on the balcony lasted for 10 minutes, five bouts of a great and sustained outburst of loyalty, which continued long after the royal group had withdrawn.

"WE WANT THE QUEEN"

The tightly packed mass of people set up a recurrent chant, "We want the Queen," and there was great excitement when Prince Charles and Princess Anne appeared—tiny figures in white—at one of the Palace windows. The royal children appeared on the balcony several times, and each time was greeted with the greatest fervour.

While all this rejoicing filled the precincts of the Palace and the gay central streets of the capital, the Coronation had been celebrated with characteristic fervour by her Majesty's lieges in east London. The weather doomed the traditional street tea parties but this was not the end of the affair. Shelter was found for them elsewhere, some in halls, others crammed into small sitting-rooms, and welcomed with television and the many millions more—indebted to the B.B.C. for a notable achievement—who had heard her voice taking the oath during the service, listened to her again last night in a Coronation broadcast.

PERMANENT RECORD OF CORONATION

"THE TIMES" SUPPLEMENT

A Coronation Supplement of The Times is published to-day separately from the paper.

This is designed as a permanent record and presents a detailed and fully illustrated biography of the Queen from her birth to the Coronation. Drawn from the and of The Times during those years, it describes not only the Queen's part in great events but also those everyday circumstances of her childhood and youth, when the slow recession had withdrawn the splendid tide of pomp and colour from the shining Sanctuary, the multitude outside prepared to receive their Queen.

Most of the young people were coloured rosettes or flaunted gay, common hats, and many of them joined together to sing songs and dance on the wet pavements. British service men and women in all parts in the procession joined men of foreign forces in revelry.

As this day draws to its close, I know that my abiding memory of it will be only the solemnity and beauty of the ceremony, but the inspiration of your loyalty and affection. I thank you all from a full heart. God bless you all.

APPEARANCES ON BALCONY

EVENING CROWDS TOUR PROCESSION ROUTE

Demonstrations of fervour and affection by cheering crowds totalling many thousands continued outside Buckingham Palace until a late hour. By 11.30 p.m. the Queen and the Duke of Edinburgh had made five appearances on the balcony.

Soon after their return the Queen and the Duke of Edinburgh, with whom were Prince Charles and Princess Anne and other members of the Royal Family, appeared on the balcony to watch the fly-past. The fly-past had been delayed and modified because of unfavourable weather.

Many of those who had watched the processions at the Palace stayed till newcomers to join in the chants of "We want the Queen" which were raised periodically for no reason at all or because a Palace official had come on to the balcony to remove a chair. In front of the Palace railings and as far back as the Victoria Memorial the people were packed in a dense mass by 7 p.m. Seats in the stands which commanded a view of the balcony were nearly all filled by that hour. For a few minutes at this time the scene was brightened by a burst of sunshine, but afterwards the cold wind persisted and there was more than a hint of rain in the air.

There was another burst of cheering when Prince Charles was again seen to come to the window and wave. When renewed demands for the Queen became more insistent the balcony doors were opened again and her Majesty and the Duke of Edinburgh, all in their royal garb, came outside and waved to the delighted and cheering thousands below. They stood for several minutes, the Queen smiling happily.

PATRIOTIC SONGS

It was sung around over the loud-speakers that the Queen would not appear again on the balcony before 8.40 p.m., and the crowd settled down to wait for the broadcast of her Majesty's speech. The Prime Minister spoke of introduction were heard clearly, and the crowd, which too reached into the Mall and St. James's Park, sang the National Anthem.

Only the sound of the wind as it rustled decorations and billowed out hanging pennants like ships' sails was heard when the Queen delivered her speech. At the end a great cheer was followed by the singing of the National Anthem and various patriotic songs.

At 8.40 p.m. the Palace balcony was floodlit and a few minutes later the Queen appeared with the Duke of Edinburgh. After waving to the crowds for about two minutes the Queen moved slightly forward and pressed a switch which gave the signal for the first group of illuminations in London to be turned on.

In their fourth appearance at 10.40 p.m. the Queen and the Duke of Edinburgh remained for three minutes waving to the crowd.

Early in the evening the streets were thronged with people walking along the Coronation route to see the decorations, but it was evident that the cold wind was driving many would-be sightseers to seek the warmth and comfort of their homes.

On the steps beneath the shining statue of Eros in the gilded "cage," groups of young people from all parts of the Commonwealth sat eating sandwiches and watching the crowds. Many foreign visitors were taking photographs and watching the fleeting moments of sunshine.

LATE REVELRY

Later, thousands of people thronged the streets in the West End, under the flashing lights of the advertising signs, to end the day with crests of their own making. The showers continued after dark, but they did nothing to damp the enthusiasm of this cosmopolitan crowd.

THE QUEEN'S THANKS

The Queen sent the following reply to a telegram from the Lord Mayor: "I send my sincere thanks, my Lord Mayor, to the citizens of London for the kind message which you have sent to me on their behalf on the day of my Coronation. To them on the day of my Coronation. I thank you for your appreciation of their loyal greetings."

BROADCAST BY THE QUEEN

INSPIRATION OF LOYALTY

"I SHALL STRIVE TO BE WORTHY"

The Queen, in a broadcast over the B.B.C. Home and Overseas services last night, said: "As this day draws to its close, I know that my abiding memory of it will be, not only the solemnity and beauty of the ceremony, but the inspiration of your loyalty and affection."

Her Majesty said: When I spoke to you last, at Christmas, I asked you all, whatever your religion, to pray for me on the day of my Coronation—to pray that God would give me wisdom and strength to carry out the promises that I should then be making.

Throughout this memorable day I have been uplifted and sustained by the knowledge that your thoughts and prayers were with me. I have been aware all the time that my peoples, spread far and wide throughout every continent and across the world, were united to support me in the task to which I have now been dedicated with such solemnity.

"HARD TO FIND WORDS"

Many thousands of you came to London from all parts of the Commonwealth and Empire to join in the ceremony, but I have been conscious, too, of the millions of others who have shared in it by means of wireless or television in their homes. All of you, near or far, have been united in one purpose. It is hard for me to find words in which to tell you of the strength which this knowledge has given me.

The ceremonies you have seen to-day are ancient, and some of their origins are veiled in the mists of the past. But their spirit and their meaning shine through the ages, never, perhaps, more brightly than now.

I have no sincerity pledged myself to your service, as so many of you are pledged to mine. Throughout all my life and with all my heart I shall strive to be worthy of your trust.

In this resolve I have myself to support me. He shares all my ideals and all my affection for you. Then, although my experience is so short and my task so new, I have in my parents and grandparents an example which I can follow with certainty and with confidence.

LIVING STRENGTH

There is also this. I have behind me, not only the splendid traditions and the annals of more than a thousand years, but the living strength and majesty of the Commonwealth and Empire, of societies old and new, of lands and races different in history and origins but all, by God's will, united in spirit and in aim.

Therefore I am sure that this, my Coronation, is not the symbol of a power and a splendour that are gone but a declaration of our hopes for the future and for the years I may, by God's grace and mercy, be given to reign and serve you as your Queen.

I have been speaking of the vast regions and varied peoples to whom I owe my duty, but there has also sprung from our island home a theme of untold and individual thought which constitutes our message to the world and through the changing generations has found acceptance both within and far beyond my realms.

Parliamentary institutions, with their free speech and respect for the rights of minorities, and the inspiration of a broad tolerance in thought and its expression—all this we conceive to be a precious part of our way of life and culture.

During recent centuries this message has been sustained and invigorated by the immense contribution, in language, literature, and action, of the nations of our Commonwealth overseas. It grows express, too, as I pray it always will, to living principles as sacred to the Crown and monarchy as to its many parliaments and peoples. I ask you now to cherish them—and practise them too: then we can confidently the future is secure, and there will be, above all else, the unshakeable faith and the benediction of Almighty God.

HEAVY ALPINE SNOWSTORMS

VILLAGE THREATENED WITH DESTRUCTION

FROM OUR CORRESPONDENT
GENEVA, JUNE 2

Abundant snowfalls have been recorded in Switzerland down to the 3,000ft. level, with the result that nearly all the Alpine passes, as well as many roads in the Engadine, have been closed to traffic.

Heavy rain caused a landslide in the Haute Savoie mountains 15 miles south of Lake Geneva, where rocks have been continuously falling on the village of Nicolas (1,800ft.). The authorities have undertaken the evacuation of the village, while a menaced with complete destruction.

Snowfalls caused the death of a Swiss skier who fell 1,500ft. on Mount Bernina south of Vicoraggia, in the Grisons. The cold spell and storms have intensified the disturbances which over snow for the two North climbers Piget Piet and Arthur Reyder, who are missing in the Bernina region. Three men reused on the foot of Wyreene's guides in hope of finding them. Two other parties are reported to have set out and have never been since the disaster.

RICHMOND TOWPATH MURDER

SECOND GIRL STILL MISSING

Police dragging the Thames yesterday recovered the bicycle of the missing girl whose friend, Barbara Songhurst, was found stabbed to death in the river at Richmond on Monday.

The two girls—16-year-old Christine Reed, aged 18, of Roy Grove, Hampton Hill, and the discovery of her body—had missed two nights out. The girl has not been murdered.

Bones worn by the girls were found on Monday. A very thorough examination of the river bank was also being made. The two girls passing over to Sunbury, on the Thames towpath near here, has been reported missing.

MR. RHEE LESS OBDURATE

U.S. ASKED FOR A DEFENCE PACT

4-POINT PROGRAMME

FROM OUR OWN CORRESPONDENT
WASHINGTON, JUNE 2

The Administration is believed to have received a request from President Rhee, of South Korea, asking for an American provision of a mutual defence pact and additional military and economic aid in exchange for South Korean support of the present allied truce proposals. These conditions were submitted to be part of a four-point programme outlined in a letter to President Eisenhower from President Rhee.

It is not clear whether President Eisenhower's letter to Mr. Rhee—as a result of which he later is reported to have withdrawn his opposition to the truce proposals—was in reply to President Rhee's request. The South Korean request for a mutual defence pact and economic aid appears to be part of the way of South Korea to efforts to untie the affairs at some future time.

President Rhee is now in a more outspoken frame of mind than he has been for the last two days.

HITHERTO RESISTED

Hitherto, however, the State Department has taken the view that the United States is not a member of the United Nations and the further questioning which Mr. Rhee has appealed, which he appears to be convinced is the only course open to him.

President Rhee's appeal to the United States cannot be regarded as a request to make bargains only firing him, clearly that the only fruits would not stand in the way of South Korea in efforts to untie the country at some future time.

President Rhee is not the only outspoken critic of the latest United Nations truce proposals. Senator Knowland, chairman of the Senate Republican majority, has expressed the view that the United States should not ratify an armistice which would leave the Communists with a foothold in Korea.

DEMOCRAT'S DOUBTS

Senator Knowland's views on Far Eastern policy are not held in high estimation in the high proposals stated here more cautiously by the Democratic Senator Sparkman, however, agreed observers today that by saying that the Korean armistice would jump the United States into a war that is a war in defence of the only real freedom. Mr. Sparkman's statement would appear to indicate that, because shortly the Communists were proposed down the Communists' demands, that he expected to have the President's pledge in spite of his doubts.

MILITARY AID ON A BIG SCALE

TERMS OF REQUEST

FROM OUR OWN CORRESPONDENT
TOKYO, JUNE 2

The situation in South Korea remained obscure to-day. Mr. Rhee is known to have received a personal message from President Eisenhower yesterday, and is reported to have sent a reply asking for certain assurances, some of which are difficult to grant. The text of the United States reply is not yet known.

Other points in the message, as reported by the Associated Press, include a request for a mutual defence pact between the United States and South Korea, military aid on a big scale, and American military and economic aid.

"DIFFICULT POSITION"

Mr. Clark, who is dreaded of continuing Commission Day possible as the Communists, he was questioned to foreign correspondents and said that he was "in a difficult position." He agreed that he had received a letter from President Eisenhower yesterday, but declined to say whether he had sent a reply. The General then drew into wait to appear at a window.

DRIVE AGAINST MAU MAU

54 KILLED IN 24 HOURS

FROM OUR OWN CORRESPONDENT
NAIROBI, JUNE 2

Security forces had their biggest day in numbers. In the intensified campaign against Mau Mau. Up to this morning 54 terrorists had been killed, 14 wounded and 17 captured during the previous 24 hours.

Three figures outside the terrorists killed during the day were responsible for the deaths of six Europeans in a recent attack at Naivasha. All of a column of European police and military in the Naivasha district, and

W. GERMAN VISIT TO WASHINGTON

BERMUDA MEETING TALKS

FROM OUR OWN CORRESPONDENT
BONN, JUNE 2

The Cabinet approved under the action of Dr. Adenauer, the Chancellor, in accepting President Eisenhower's invitation to visit Washington. The Chancellor expects to leave on June 7.

Officially it is explained that he will take up again matters already discussed between President Eisenhower and Dr. Adenauer, and the agreement between Germany and the western Powers, as well as German rearmament.

SULTAN'S REPLY TO HIS PASHAS

DISPUTED STATEMENT

FROM OUR OWN CORRESPONDENT
PARIS, JUNE 2

Some confusion remains about the issue by the French Resident-General at Rabat on the reply of the Sultan of Morocco to the demands of El Glaoui, the Pasha of Marrakesh, and the other pashas and caids who petitioned the Sultan for reform of the Moroccan State. The reply said that the pashas and caids should exercise greater care in their conduct of affairs and that the Sultan would take whatever decisions were necessary in the interest of the country.

CONFERENCE POSTPONEMENT

FROM OUR OWN CORRESPONDENT
PARIS, JUNE 2

It was learned here to-day that the Western Coronation conference proposed to be held at Bermuda between Sir Winston Churchill, President Eisenhower, and the French Premier, M. Joseph Laniel, had been postponed. It was hoped that the Bermuda conference might be held in the second half of June, but the date is to be fixed later. It is reported to-day that the conference would not be held before the end of June.

COL. HUNT'S AIM

A SECOND EVEREST FEAT POSSIBLE

MESSAGE FROM THE QUEEN

The summit of Mount Everest may by now have been reached a second time. A message (given below) from our Special Correspondent with the British expedition confirms that Colonel Hunt, leader of the expedition, and Gregory were the accompanied the first two successful climbers, Hillary and the Sherpa Tensing, as a support party to the South Col; and it is known that Colonel Hunt had every intention, if the weather and other factors were favourable, of sealing the second successful ascent with a comparative member of the expedition.

On learning of the successful ascent of the mountain, the Queen sent the following message to the British Ambassador in Kathmandu:

Please convey to Colonel Hunt and all members of the British expedition my warmest congratulations on their great achievement in reaching the summit of Mount Everest.

ELIZABETH R.

MR. SHIPTON'S VIEWS

Mr. Eric Shipton, who led the 1951 expedition to the discovery of the southern ascent, and who has taken part in more mountaineering expeditions to Everest than any other man, yesterday expressed the view yesterday that the climbers succeeded by a route of their own selection which enabled them to avoid the obstacles of the high ice-fall immediately below the final slopes.

Referring to the Queen's message he said: "I am delighted that this news has come, although I was not expecting it until the weather broke. Congratulations to you all."

CULMINATION OF EFFORT

The following message was sent yesterday by Colonel Hunt to the President of the Royal Geographical Society:

On behalf of our respective councils and members who have participated in this venture I wish to express our deep appreciation of all the encouragement we have received. Messages have been received in The Times from all over the world, as well as congratulations radio.

USE OF OPEN-CIRCUIT OXYGEN

PLANNING THE ASSAULT

The following delayed dispatch from our Special Correspondent at Everest was written yesterday by James Morris:

FROM OUR SPECIAL CORRESPONDENT
BASE CAMP, EVEREST, MAY 26

Reports from higher on the mountain say that yesterday, as planned, Bourdillon and Evans launched the initial attempt on the summit. They were using the closed-circuit oxygen apparatus, which has been relatively little tested but has particular advantages at high altitudes. The distances are too great for progress to be followed except by wireless, or by a series of prearranged time-signals transmitted by light-flashing, and telephones are not carried.

As we watched it now, the expedition's first serious assault, it is perhaps shortly to be a historical day. It will depend chiefly on the way the expedition's first attempt fares. If the two men return safely, Colonel Hunt and Gregory will then attempt a second assault, together with Hillary and Tensing.

N.Z. PRIDE IN HILLARY'S ACHIEVEMENT

OFFICIAL CONGRATULATIONS

FROM OUR OWN CORRESPONDENT
WELLINGTON (N.Z.), JUNE 2

News of the conquest of Mount Everest by E. P. Hillary, a New Zealander, and the Sherpa Tensing brought immense pleasure here. Mr. Holland, the Prime Minister, in a message of congratulation, said: "This is a result of Everest's fall of which New Zealand is justly proud."

OBITUARY

We announce with regret the death of Mr. R. P. Winnington-Ingram, and M.A.S.P. Winnington-Ingram at the Royal College of Music and one of the most experienced examiners of the Associated Board.

Reunited

Love is a Many Splendoured Thing

Chapter 33

Charles booked his ticket to fly from London's Heathrow airport to Orly airport in Paris immediately after the coronation celebrations.

The Marais district is where he chose to stay, as it was central to all the places he wished to visit. He booked himself into the "Hotel du Jeu de Paume" and went for a stroll around his old hunting ground. He still remembered the streets and boulevards; it was like coming home. Despite the war, he remembered the period he lived in Paris as one of the most happy and enjoyable times of his life.

He was walking down Rue de Rivoli, the main shopping boulevard in the Marais, intending to purchase a bottle of wine, some cheese and bread to have for his lunch at a beautiful small park close to the Seine and La Tour Saint Jacques. Suddenly he heard his name being called and when he looked around, to his astonishment, it was Françoise, his girlfriend from his time in Paris after the war.

'Charles, I cannot believe it is you; how are you?'

'Françoise, who would have thought I would run into you? This is amazing. I am well, all the better for seeing you after all this time; it must be eight or nine years.'

'What are you doing in Paris, Charles?'

'It's a long story; why don't we have lunch and catch up?'

'I would love to, but I am on my break. I am due back soon.'

OK, what about dinner?'

'Dinner would be fine.'

Françoise gave Charles her telephone number so he could call her to arrange a rendezvous. They bade each other farewell with a kiss on each cheek, and then continued on their way.

Charles was elated. In a large city like Paris, the odds were a million to one.

He bought his cheese, bread and wine and headed for the park, where he enjoyed his lunch thinking about all the wonderful times he had shared with Françoise.

He booked a table at their favourite restaurant in the Marais, "Brasserie

Bofinger". It had been a popular eating-place for Parisians since 1864. It was here, where Charles and Françoise ate their last meal before Charles was shipped back to the U.S.A.

He rang her and arranged to pick her up at 7pm; he didn't say where they would be eating.

When the taxi pulled up outside "Brasserie Bofinger" she was delighted, and even more so when they entered the restaurant and were shown to the table where they had last eaten before Charles left for the States.

'Charles, darling, you have thought of everything. Thank you. And now you must tell me what has been happening in your life since we last met.'

Charles gave her a chronological run-down of life in New York, working in the newspaper business. He also talked of his father's death.

She was sad for Charles; he had often talked about his father with great admiration.

So, Charlie, what brings you to Paris?'

'I moved to London for a year or so as a freelance writer. I am here researching a story about Paris after the war. Enough about me, what's been happening in your life?'

'When you left for America, I was very sad, Charlie, I did not go out for quite a while, then, I met an American Lieutenant Colonel. He was a sweet man, and although my love for him was nowhere as intense as the love I had for you, I married him.'

'So, you are a married woman?'

'No. I am a widow. He died in a car accident when he was driving from Boston to New York.'

'I am so sorry, Françoise.'

'It seems strange, I lived in Boston for three years and didn't bump into you. I return to Paris and there you are.'

'You lived in Boston? When?

'We moved there when Fred was posted back in 1949.'

'That's amazing. Did you like Boston?'

'I loved it. I was in two minds whether to stay on after Fred died, but in the end, I decided Paris was my real home.'

They ate their seafood platter accompanied by an excellent white wine; they talked all evening until it was time to pay the bill and go.

Charles dropped her back to her apartment and asked if he could see her again.

'Of course. When?'

'I will call you.' he leaned over and gave her a gentle kiss on the lips.

Returning to his hotel room, he lay on the bed thinking about Françoise.

He knew that he was very much in love with her; he had been since he first met her in 1945.

Tattoo You

Chapter 34

Charles realised that the task before him was tantamount to finding a needle in a haystack. He was aware that Charles Lamont had travelled to Paris in 1920. This he had discovered, with some simple research back in London. He looked up the shipping records and found Lord Lamont's name on the passenger list of a ferry that crossed the channel arriving in Calais. He believed Lamont made the journey for the express purpose of replicating the tattoo on Charles Lamont's left buttock. Once this strange task was completed, there would be no way to dispute his identity.

Charles Weatherspoon therefore needed to find the tattoo parlour in Paris that tattooed the illustrious Lord Lamont's buttock. There were approximately three hundred tattoo parlours in the greater Paris region, so it was going to be a difficult assignment.

He had asked his mother to sketch a copy of the tattoo from memory; it really was a map of the island of Tasmania!

With the sketch in hand and a reasonable map of Paris identifying where the parlours were located, he started his journey of discovery.

The first parlour he visited was Abraxas, which was very close to his hotel. It was located at street level in an old stone building.

He introduced himself to the proprietor and asked if he had ever tattooed anyone with the "map of Tasmania" design and with solid port wine colour pigmentation.

'Mais non Monsieur! We tattoo beautiful designs of dragons and roses. Why would anybody tattoo this silly thing on their arm?'

'Well, it was actually on his buttock.'

'This is too stupid for words. Now, if you will excuse me, I 'ave customers waiting.'

Charles approached ten more parlours, all with the same result, before calling it a day. He was due to meet Françoise at 7.30pm for dinner.

He decided that, as he loved Françoise, during dinner, he should divulge the real reason for his trip.

She met him at the little restaurant "Le Dôme," having walked from the Vavin Metro Station.

After the normal small talk she asked him what he had done during the day.

'Françoise, I have a confession to make.'

'Oh?'

'The reason I am in Paris, is to discover whether my "biological father" was murdered by his identical twin brother.'

'Charles! No!'

'It may have happened on The Western Front during the First World War.'

'When?'

It was in 1918. The Germans had launched the "Spring Offensive" and both the Lamont twins were in the thick of it.'

'So, what makes you think your father was murdered?'

Charles explained all that he had discovered and all that was told to him by his mother.

'So, that's why I walked the streets of Paris today trying to find the tattoo parlour that tattooed Harold so that he could steal his brother Charles' identity.'

'I think you are looking in the wrong areas. You should go to Montmartre.'

'Why Montmartre?'

'This is where the old parlours are located; some have been in operation for over one hundred years.'

'OK, I'll go there tomorrow.'

Charles was pleased he had told Françoise the whole story as he knew it, so that he could now discuss things openly.

The next day he took the Metro to Montmartre and walked around the cobbled streets and little laneways. He had only observed the Basilica of Sacre-Coeur from a distance and decided he would climb the three hundred odd steps. During the Second World War, the Germans dropped thirteen bombs on the basilica's dome without inflicting any damage. Some say it was the "Hand of God" protecting it. Most say it was inaccurate bombing!

'Well, I'd better get on with my research,' he decided.

He had just about given up hope when he noticed a tiny laneway and in the distance he saw a tattoo sign above a shop. Soon he was standing outside "Tatouage". Inside he saw a very small reception area with one sofa and a counter.

Sitting on the sofa reading "Le Monde" was an old man, possibly in his seventies, maybe even his eighties.

'Bonjour, Monsieur.'

The old man looked up.

'Bonjour, Monsieur.

Are you looking to be tattooed? We are the best in Paris.'

'Monsieur, I would like this tattoo on my buttock.'

Charles showed the old man the image his mother had drawn.

'Strange tattoo. I remember somebody getting the same tattoo on his buttock many years ago.'

'Are you sure, Monsieur?'

'Monsieur, how would I forget such a strange tattoo in such a strange place?'

'Do you keep records of all the people you tattoo, Monsieur?'

'The authorities require us to. It's a real nuisance but, nevertheless...'

'If you can find who it was, and in what year, I will give you ten thousand francs.'

'What! Ten thousand francs.'

'You need to testify in an English court. I will pay you at the completion of the proceedings.'

'Cela vaut la peine! You better follow me out the back, where I have all the old records in boxes. Now, how long ago are we talking?'

'I believe it would be between 1919 and 1925.'

'Eh bien, let's start with 1919.'

'Do you have a copy of the tattoo each customer received?'

'I do. It's not required by the authorities, but I 'ave always done it for my own records.'

'Fantastic.'

After about twenty five minutes, they had gone through all the records for 1919 without any luck. Charles was hoping it wasn't 1925, or they would be looking all night!'

'Let's look at 1920.'

They were halfway through the box when the old fellow looked up at Charles with a wry grin.

'Ca y est! I think this is it!'

He opened the manila folder and displayed "The Map of Tasmania" tattoo sketch.

```
Name: Charles Lamont
Address: Lamont Hall Pall Mall London.
Age: 24
Tattoo Location: Right Buttock
```

Up until that point, Charles was excited and confident that he had solved the murder mystery.

'Are you sure it was the right buttock? It should be the left buttock to be authentic!'

'I am certain; I now remember. He asked for the left buttock, but he had too much scarring from a skin graft to repair facial burns. He said it was a war injury and by the look of his face, it was a major injury.'

Charles was excited again, in fact euphoric.

This will be proof positive that the person masquerading as Charles Lamont was, in reality, his twin brother, Harold.

Charles paid the old man the ten thousand francs he had promised, with the assurance he would be available to give evidence in a court case if required.

He returned to his hotel with the paperwork from the tattoo parlour and re-examined it. 'This is the first step in proving Charles Lamont is a fraud and a murderer,' he said aloud.

He telephoned Françoise, arranging to meet her at her apartment where she was cooking coq au vin, one of his favourite dishes.

'Hello, cheri. How did you go today?'

'Brilliant.'

He described how he had stumbled upon the old tattoo parlour and discovered 'Charles Lamont' had a tattoo placed on his right buttock in 1920.

'You told me Charles birthmark was on his left buttock. Why did he get it on the right?'

163

Charles explained what he had learned from the old tattoo artist.

'What next, cheri?'

'Well, I now need to find out what happened on the battlefield and how Charles was killed.'

'You don't believe that Charles was shot in battle?'

'If he was, Harold would have become the rightful heir. Why would he go to all the trouble to assume Charles' identity right down to the infamous birthmark?

'Of course you are right.'

'Harold was wounded at the Battle of Amiens in the Spring of 1918. He received a gunshot wound to the right leg. When he was being moved back to the trenches for medical attention, he was caught in a gas attack. This was where he would receive his horrendous facial injuries. This all occurred the day after Charles was killed. It seems a little strange that these events occurred within twenty four hours of each other.'

'The officer's report states there was a Private with Charles at the time of the shooting and it was he who carried him back to the trench.'

'Does the report identify the Private?'

'Sidney Black.'

'Have you tried to find him?'

'No. I only received a copy of the report a couple of days ago.'

'Why don't you place an advertisement in some English newspapers and see if you can find him?'

'I thought of that, but Lamont owns all the major papers. There's a slim chance he may get wind of what I am up to.'

'Why don't you try the regional papers? It's worth a try.'

He took Françoise's advice and placed an advertisement in several regional papers.

Dirty Deeds Done Dirt Cheap

Chapter 35

Information Wanted

Harold Lamont's Death

Large Reward

Information is sought on how Harold Lamont, Second Lieutenant, British Army, died during the Battle of Amiens in France, April 1918.

Information is also sought in relation to his brother, Charles Lamont, and his role in the battle.

Contact Charles Weatherspoon:33 6245 1234 (Reverse Charge)

He also placed a second advertisement:

Seeking Sidney Black

Served in the British army between 1916 and 1918 in France.

If you are Sidney Black or know of his whereabouts, please contact Charles Weatherspoon:33 6245 1234 (Reverse Charge)

Generous Reward will be paid.

Charles was not really hopeful that he would receive a response but it was worth a try.

A week passed without any contact.

Then he received a reversed-charge call from London.

'Hello. Is this the bloke looking for Sid Black?'

That's right. And who are you?'

'Sid Black.'

Charles held his breath.

'Hello Sid. Thanks for calling.'

Charles' heart was racing.

'I read the other ad you had in the paper about the Lamont brothers, I know plenty about that lot too.'

'Do you now? Well, maybe we can catch up and you can tell me all about them.'

'Maybe. You said you'd pay me for any info?'

'Not just "any info." It's got to be useful information.

What sort of information have you got, Sid?'

'You reckon I can earn a big quid?'

'That's right. What have you got?'

'Well I'm not gonna tell you over the dog and bone am I?'

'I suppose not. Can we meet somewhere?'

'Yeah, do you know the "Blind Beggar" in Whitechapel Road in the East End?'

'Can't say that I do, but I'll find it.'

'I'll meet you there tomorrow at say: 5pm.'

'Done.'

Charles caught an early plane from Paris and checked into the "Savoy Hotel".

He decided to do some shopping at Harrods and purchased a "Paul and Shark" jacket and some silk ties. He was still getting used to being wealthy; his father's estate left him with a small fortune. He purchased a large bottle of Chanel Number 5 for Françoise and decided that was quite enough shopping.

He returned to the "Savoy" and made a few phone calls; one was to his newspaper, letting them know he would submit his story on post-war Paris after a week or so.

He asked the doorman to hail him a taxi. He arrived at the "Blind Beggar" at 4.50pm.

166

He chose a secluded booth in the lounge bar and waited for Sid.

At 5pm precisely, in wandered a swarthy short man; he was as skinny as a rake. He looked around in the dim light and spotted Charles. Charles got up to greet the man.

'I presume you are Sid Black?'

'That's right and who might you be, Gov?'

Charles introduced himself and offered Sid a drink.

Once they were settled in the booth, Sid asked.

'So what is it you wanna know about the Lamont brothers? Hold on, before I tell ya, how much are ya gonna pay me, Gov?'

'Well Sid, that depends on the quality of the information you give me. If it is really good, I will give you ten thousand pounds.'

'Fuck me, that's more than Lamont paid me to shoot him!'

'I beg your pardon: what did you just say?'

'Bloody hell, alright I better tell ya what I knows,' said Sid.

Sid recounted in his own words what had happened in 1918, down to the last detail.

'Well, that explains a lot! So you believe that Charles, as you knew him, wanted to be shot, and be shipped back home taking no further part in the war?'

'Yep, that's the way I understood it. Why would you want someone like me to shoot you in the fucking leg?'

'Sid, would you be willing to testify in a court of law telling the jury all that you know?'

'You gonna pay me ten thousand quid?'

'I will, if you testify. The only problem might be incriminating yourself.'

'What's that mean?'

'They may send you to jail!'

'Don't give a flying fuck. I've got lung cancer! The quack reckons I've only got twelve months to live at best.'

'I'm sorry to hear that Sid.'

'Why, you don't fucking know me! Anyways, I want the money to give to me daughter. She's got three kids and no bloody husband.'

'Sid, I'll give you a promissory note. I'll pay you after you testify.'

'Deal.'

The two men shook hands and departed in different directions, Sid headed back to the East End; Charles caught a taxi to the "Savoy".

Back at the hotel, Charles examined the evidence he had gathered and was confident the case against Lamont was strong, but not strong enough; the missing link was evidence from his mother.

It was she who could testify that Charles and she were close friends before they became lovers. She could testify Charles's unique birthmark was located on his left buttock not his right where the French tattooist placed it.

The dinner party at Lord Lamont's Pall Mall mansion was another piece of damning evidence. He did not recognize her!

He had planned to call her in Boston that evening to bring her up to date. He would ask if she was willing to testify and divulge to the world her long-kept secret.

Charles placed the call and his mother answered.

He recounted to her the evidence he had so far accumulated including his conversation with Sid Black. She was delighted. He also explained that her testimony would strengthen the case against Charles Lamont. She agreed.

'Are you intending to take this evidence to the police?'

'Not at the moment. I think it would need to be the French police and I don't want to proceed to that at the moment. The solicitors in London have suggested we bring a civil case against Lord Lamont. When we win that case, the police may want to bring criminal charges against him.'

'Again I will take your advice on that.'

'I will call you in a few days once I see the lawyers again.'

Justice Shall be Done

Chapter 36

Charles Weatherspoon made an appointment with one of London's best legal firms, "Babcock and Green". His intention was to obtain advice regarding Lord Lamont and how he should proceed. He was shown into the chambers of Martin Wright Q.C., a lawyer with a formidable reputation.

'Mr Weatherspoon, how can I help you?'

'Please call me Charles; I would like some advice on a matter that is of great importance to me.'

Charles explained the situation, supported by the evidence that he had accumulated against Lord Lamont.

'Well, you certainly have picked a tough one haven't you? Firstly you are going after one of the most powerful men in the country if not the world! The case is predominantly circumstantial although your evidence is pretty convincing. My initial response would be that this is a criminal case. However having said that, a civil case would be easier to prove.'

'Why would a civil case be easier to prove?'

'Under "English Law" a civil case is based on "Preponderance of evidence". The fact that you have convincing evidence with sworn statements and credible witnesses should convince the judge that this murder did take place and was perpetrated for financial gain. So, we can't charge Lord Lamont with murder in a civil case but we can prove he took an illegal action to deprive you of your rightful inheritance and title.'

'You're saying we should sue him for the fortune he illegally gained?'

'That's right. The end result, of course, would be proof that he murdered your father. I am sure the police and the public prosecutor would be very interested in pursuing him with criminal charges.'

'I would like to discuss the options with my mother before I make a decision to proceed. Would it be OK to get back to you next week?'

'Take your time. Don't underestimate how difficult you life could become taking on the establishment. Lord Lamont has 'first name' relationships with many important people, including the Prime Minister and the Chief Justice.'

'I know it will be tough.'

The Day of Reckoning

Chapter 37

1954, London, England

Lord Lamont had just completed his daily meeting with his editors; there were now six, one for each of the six newspapers he owned.

His secretary buzzed him on the intercom.

'Lord Lamont, there is a gentleman from The High Court who insists on seeing you. Shall I send him in?'

'Send him in'.

The door to Lord Lamont's office opened and a tall man dressed in a double-breasted suit entered.

'Are you Lord Lamont, Sir?'

'You know I am.'

'I am sorry, but you must answer the question; are you Lord Lamont?'

'Yes I am. Who the devil are you?'

'I am an officer of The High Court of England. I am here to serve you with court proceeding papers.'

The man handed over the papers to Lord Lamont.

'I am required to inform you that you need either to accept the claim or defend it. If you intend to defend the claim, you must serve a defence, including any counterclaim, within twenty eight days of today's date. Is that clear?'

'I understand. Is that it? Good, you know where the door is. Goodbye sir.'

Lamont read through the court papers: a cold chill ran down his spine.

'Who the hell is Charles Weatherspoon? I have never heard of him. Why does he think I stole his inheritance? My inheritance. No court can take it away. I am the only living member of the Lamont family; of course it's mine.'

Charles cancelled all appointments for the day and requested Ruth to make an appointment with Sir Geoffrey Randle, his lawyer of many years.

Charles arrived at the rooms of "Randle and Bacon" at 11am and was shown directly into Sir Geoffrey's office.

' Hello, Geoffrey, I seem to be in a spot of bother.'

Lamont handed Randle the "Court Proceedings." He read them carefully and then looked at Lamont.

'OK, what's this all about?'

'I don't bloody know, Geoffrey. I have no idea.'

'Who is Charles Weatherspoon?'

'I don't know! I swear on the Bible, I have never heard of the bugger.'

'So, out of the blue, some chap appears and says I want your entire fortune: it's mine. What's more, I am going to sue you for it in the highest civil court in the land?'

'Apparently.'

'OK, if we are going to defend this claim and I assume you want to, we have to have all the cards on the table. You need to be completely open about your past.'

'I will, I assure you, Geoffrey, completely open.'

'I want you to go home and write down anything you can think of that may have facilitated this claim. We should meet again in a few days after I have done some detective work on this Mr Weatherspoon.'

'Certainly. Should I speak with your secretary to arrange an appointment?'

'Don't worry, I will arrange it.'

Charles returned home and did as Sir Geoffrey instructed. He couldn't come up with anything.

Three days later, he received a telephone call from Sir Geoffrey's secretary asking him to come in the following day at 3pm.

Lord Lamont was punctual and was shown into the meeting room. Sir Geoffrey was there to greet him.

'Hello, Charles, please be seated.'

He had an easel with butcher's paper at the ready.

'OK, I have discovered a little about Weatherspoon.'

He pointed to the first page on the easel.

Born in Boston USA, 28th of April 1921

Father: John Weatherspoon Born Boston

Mother: Emily Scott   Born England

Emily Scott migrated to Boston USA in 1920

Was a war widow and pregnant when she married John Scott.

Emily Scott attended Oxford University from 1914-1917

Charles Weatherspoon graduated in English and journalism at Harvard in 1939

Served with the US Army during the Second World War in Europe

Inherited the majority of his father's wealth estimated to be $40,000,000

Mother still living in Boston

Lamont read the fact sheet; when he came to Emily Weatherspoon's education, he froze. She was at Oxford the same time as his brother. Did they know each other?

Were they friends or maybe even more than friends?

Was his brother Charles actually the father of her child, Charles, the bastard who was suing him?

'Well, Charles, does that enlighten you?'

'Not really.'

'Are you sure you are being open with me?'

'I am, I assure you.'

'Well, one question I have is this: why sue you when he is already worth $40,000,000? He's not going after you for the money; there must be some other motive.'

'Well, all I can say is that I would hope we enter the courtroom with more than we have at the moment. We are talking about your entire estate here. What's it worth?'

'Oh, I'm not sure. It depends on the valuation of the newspapers, but I'd say about 100,000,000 pounds.'

'Well, that's certainly worth safeguarding, Charles. Keep thinking about what motive or reason he may have for bringing on this suit against you. Let's leave it to the week before the case begins, unless there are any major break-throughs we need to discuss. OK Charles?'

'OK, Geoffrey. I expect I shall see you then.'

There was agitation in Lamont's voice as he closed the door and bade goodbye.

Here Comes the Judge

Chapter 38

Lord Lamont returned to his home where he sat in the library contemplating what lay ahead.

The only reason this Weatherspoon bastard was pursuing him was for revenge: it couldn't be for money; he had more than enough of his own.

Revenge, but for what? If he was his brother's bastard son, how could he know what happened at Amiens? Nobody had seen him shoot Charles, not even the bloody Germans.

He knew he couldn't tell Sir Geoffrey the truth; he just had to hope the case against him was weak.

He received a telephone call from Sir Geoffrey a few weeks after their initial meeting.

'Hello, Charles. We have a date for the proceedings.'

'When?'

'26th June at The High Court.'

'The High Court?'

'That's right, in the Chancery Division. That's the court that deals with estate disputes, etc.'

'Well, at least I won't have far to walk. The court is only five minutes from my office.

What time?'

'10am.'

'So, you will want to see me before, no doubt?'

Charles, can you enlighten me on why this case is being brought against you?'

'No, I can't. I'm baffled.'

'OK, then there isn't really any reason to meet before, not much to discuss.'

'As you will, Sir Geoffrey.'

High Court - Chancery Division.
26th June, 1954.

The presiding judge was Justice Muirhead. He was regarded as the most experienced on the bench and was not known for his leniency.

The courtroom was historic, being part of The High Courts opened by Queen Victoria in 1812.

Sir Geoffrey Randle sat with Lord Lamont on the left and Martin Wright Q.C sat with Charles Weatherspoon on the right.

'This court will decide if the plaintiff, Mr Weatherspoon, has a case against Lord Lamont, in relation to the rightful and legal ownership of the Lamont estate and the title of Lord, bestowed by the British Monarchy. Mr Wright, I invite you to begin proceedings with your opening remarks.'

'Thank you, Your Honour'.

'My client, Mr Charles Weatherspoon, claims that he is the rightful and legal inheritor of the entire Lamont estate bequeathed by Lord and Lady Lamont upon their death in 1918.

The plaintiff will present a number of witnesses who will prove that the defendant acquired the Lamont estate by a deed most foul. We propose that the defendant is not Charles Lamont but is in fact Charles Lamont's younger brother, Harold.'

'Present your first witness, Mr Wright.'

'I call to the witness stand Mr Sidney Black.'

Sir Geoffrey leaned over to Lord Lamont and whispered.

'Do you remember him?'

Charles was fidgeting and seemed very flushed.

'I think he was under me in my platoon.'

'Don't worry, I have researched his background.' Sir Geoffrey gave his old friend a reassuring wink.

'Mr Black, or should I call you Sid?' asked Mr Wright.

'Sid will do, Gov.'

'How do you know the defendant?'

'He was an officer in my platoon when I served in the army during The First World War.'

'Where were you stationed?'

'In France.'

'Can you tell the court of the conversation you had with Lieutenant Lamont on or about the 21st June 1918?'

'Well, he, Lamont, came up to me in the trench and said he needed to get home in one piece and fast. He asked me to go out with him into no-man's land and shoot him in the leg.'

'Did you agree?'

'Not at first, but he promised me a bloody lot of money to do the deed.'

'What do you call a lot of money, Sid?'

'Two thousand quid.'

'That was a lot of money. So you "did the deed"?'

'Yeah, we went out saying we wanted to see what the Krauts were up to. It was about 3am, so not much happening.'

'Go on, Sid.'

'Well, we got out of sight from our blokes and then I did what he asked me to do, shot him.'

'Where exactly did you shoot him?'

'In the thigh, from the front, so it looked like Jerry had shot him.'

'Then what?'

'Well, he was carrying on like a girl, screaming and such. I put his arm around my shoulder and started to make our way back to our trench.'

'Then what happened, Sid?'

'Well, we were nearly back, when the Germans started firing gas shells. One exploded close to where we were. I quickly donned me mask but Lamont didn't bring his, silly bugger. He got pretty badly burnt.'

'Did you get your money, Sid?'

'Yeah, he was true to his word.'

'Well that's something in his favour.'

'Enough of the sarcasm, Mr Wright,' Justice Muirhead instructed.

'Thank you, Sid.'

'No further questions, Your Honour.'

'Sir Geoffrey, do you have any questions?'

'Yes, Your Honour.'

'Mr Black, what has been your profession since you were discharged from the army?'

'I've been a labourer.'

'Any other jobs?'

'Nup.'

'I believe you had a career as a petty thief.'

'Well, I wouldn't call it a career.'

'Well I do. You have had more than twenty convictions since 1919.'

'Nothing too serious though.'

'You have spent a total of eight years in jail. Is that correct?'

'Oh yeah, that's about right.'

'Eight years.'

'Yeah, well I had to feed my family didn't I? Anyways that doesn't change things with Lamont, does it?'

''We'll let the court decide that shall we? No more questions, Your Honour.'

'Mr Wright, would you care to call your second witness, please?'

'Thank you, Your Honour, I call Mrs Emily Weatherspoon to the stand.'

Emily looked quite nervous, having never been in a law court before, unlike Mr Black.

She took the oath and sat down.

'Mrs Weatherspoon. You are the mother of the plaintiff, Mr Charles Weatherspoon?'

'I am.'

'Would you tell the court your maiden name and place of birth, please.'

'My maiden name was Scott, Emily Scott. I was born in England.

'When did you emigrate to America?'

'In 1919.'

'What was your year of birth, Mrs Weatherspoon?'

'1900.'

'So you were only 19; that's young to leave your country of birth and emigrate to another country. Don't you agree?'

'Yes, I suppose it was.'

'What was your reason?'

'I was pregnant with my son, Charles. My parents felt it was the right thing to do.'

'I take it you were not married at the time?'

'No, I was not.'

' I know it is difficult for you, but can you tell the court who the father was?'

'Charles Lamont.'

'The gentleman sitting over there?'

'No, not him!'

'Can you explain what you mean? Take your time, Mrs Weatherspoon.'

'Charles Lamont and I were very close friends for three years at Oxford University. We were not girlfriend and boyfriend, just very good friends. I hadn't seen Charles for some time after we graduated. I did see him at a hotel a couple of months later when he invited me to be his partner at his officer graduation. It was on that night that we became lovers and, as a result, I became pregnant.'

'Did you tell Charles of the pregnancy?'

'No, he was already in France, fighting, when I discovered I was pregnant, I didn't want to burden him.'

'So, the result of your romantic night was the birth of your son, Charles?'

'Yes, and I couldn't be prouder.'

'May I ask you an even more intimate question, Mrs Weatherspoon?'

'What is it?'

'Were there any distinguishing marks on Charles Lamont's body? Marks only someone who was intimate with him would know about?'

'Well, it is slightly embarrassing but yes he did have a distinguishing mark.'

'Could you describe it to the court please?'

'He had a large port wine birth mark on his left buttock.'

'What shape?'

'Triangular.'

'Are you absolutely sure that it was on his left buttock?'

'Quite sure.'

' Sir Geoffrey, would you like to question the witness?'

'Yes, Your Honour, if it pleases the court.'

'Mrs Weatherspoon, are you absolutely sure that Charles Lamont is the father of your child?'

'Yes, of course I am.'

'May I ask you if you were a virgin prior to the night of lovemaking with Charles?'

'Do I have to answer that, Your Honour?'

'I'm afraid you do, Mrs Weatherspoon!'

'No, I wasn't. I had one other lover before Charles. I must say that was twelve months before I fell pregnant.'

'I see.'

'You're absolutely sure the gentleman next to me is not Charles Lamont and you have never met before?'

'I didn't say that. I have met him once before.'

'Did you? Where?'

'At a dinner party at his Pall Mall home. My parents had been invited and my husband and I were visiting from Boston.'

'Did you speak to him?'

'Yes, I was opposite him at the table.'

'And?'

'He had no idea who I was.'

'Thank you Mrs Weatherspoon, you can step down.'

'Are there any other further witnesses, Mr Wright?'

'Yes, Your Honour, two.'

'Then you had better call your next.'

'I would like to call Monsieur Jacques Badeau.'

'Your Honour, as we made you aware earlier, Monsieur Badeau does not speak fluent English so we have arranged a court approved translator, if required.'

'That's fine, go ahead.'

'Monsieur Badeau would you tell the court what your occupation is.'

'I own a tattoo parlour in Paris.'

'How long have you owned the business?'

'Since 1912.'

'That's a long time, sir. You must have seen some strange tattoos in your life?'

'Yes, some very strange tattoos.'

'Is there one that particularly stands out?'

'Well, the map of la Tasmanie I tattooed it on that man over there.'

'You mean Lord Lamont?'

'Well, I didn't know he was a lord, but yes, his name according to my records was Charles Lamont.'

'So, you tattooed the shape of Tasmania on his buttock. Is that correct?'

'Yes that is correct.'

'Do you remember on what side?'

'I tattooed his right buttock.'

'Are you sure it was the right buttock?'

'I am sure. He wanted it on the left, but scarring from a recent skin graft made it impossible. So he settled for the right side.'

'Thank you, Monsieur Badeau. You may step down. Would you like to question the witness Sir Geoffrey?'

'No, Your Honour, thank you.'

'Well, Mr Wright, would you like to call your final witness?'

'Yes, Your Honour, I would like to call George Simmonds.'

'Mr Simmonds, would you like to tell the court your relationship with Charles Lamont?'

'We both attended Oxford University together.'

'Were you a good friend of his?'

'Yes, we played in the Oxford rugby team together for a few years.'

'So there were many times when you saw Charles Lamont naked in the change rooms?'

'Well, yes, it's inevitable.'

'Do you remember Charles' birthmark.'

'How could you not! Everybody commented on it. It was on his buttock.'

'Think carefully. What side?'

'It was definitely the left side.'

'Thank you, Mr Simmonds.'

'Do you wish to question the witness, Sir Geoffrey?'

'No, Your Honour.'

Lord Lamont looked at his barrister understanding that further questioning would be futile.

'The key to this case would seem to be what side the birthmark is on. It is with this in mind, I ask the court-appointed doctor to examine the defendant and report back in say, thirty minutes.'

The court adjourned.

Thirty minutes later the doctor and a dejected Lord Lamont returned to the courtroom.

The doctor gave his report to Justice Muirhead.

'I am going to reserve my judgement for fourteen days. This case is not just about deception and inheritance. It brings into question whether murder took place. I will be consulting the Director of Public Prosecutions on my final judgement if I deem it necessary.

'I bring these proceedings to a close to be reconvened in fourteen days.'

Justice Muirhead left the court and the courtroom emptied slowly.

Charles Weatherspoon addressed his counsel: 'What do you think?'

'I think we are in with a very good chance.'

'Well, we will just have to wait and see.'

'That we will.'

The two men shook hands and agreed to meet the day before the judgement was due to be handed down.'

Lord Lamont did not discuss the case with Sir Geoffrey; he was driven home and went into the library to contemplate his future. He poured himself a large whisky and sat in his favourite wingback.

'I suppose it was always going to end like this,' he thought.

'Charles, if you can hear me, you know I didn't plan to kill you, it just happened.

'When I say, "it just happened" I mean I didn't plan it. You were ordering me to leave the shell hole and I was terrified. I just lost it. I loved you as I loved no other human being. I have regretted my actions on that day and every day since. Please forgive me.'

Charles took another sip but the whisky tasted like salt tears.

Judgment Day

Chapter 39

Charles Weatherspoon flew back to Paris to spend time with Françoise before the judge delivered his verdict.

Rather than stay in Paris, they decided ten days in the Dordogne would be more relaxing and give them time to talk and spend time together.

Françoise's parents owned a beautiful old villa in the medieval town of Sarlat.

Charles had recently purchased an Aston Martin DB2, which would be the ideal vehicle to motor through Provence and then on to Sarlat.

On the first night they stayed in the old Roman town of Arles. Their hotel, L'Hôtel Particulier was magnificent; it deserved its 5 star rating. They strolled around Arles and visited the Roman arena, Les Arènes, which is one of the finest examples of Roman architecture in France.

'Françoise, can you imagine sitting here and watching gladiatorial battles and other spectacles nearly two thousand years ago?'

'I don't think I would have enjoyed it too much, all that blood!'

'Well, I suppose it was their entertainment, while we watch soccer!'

'I suppose you're right. I don't think our soccer players could have handled it very well. They get a little kick in the shins and they writhe around on the ground.'

'What do you want to do next?'

'I want to go on the Van Gogh walk.'

The walk, or trail as it was called, followed all the sites Van Gogh had used to set up his easel and paint. Paintings such as "Starry Night Over the Rhône" (1888) were painted in Arles.

It was getting late in the afternoon and they decided to make their way back to the hotel.

They ate in the hotel restaurant; the meal was superb, as was the wine.

The plan was to drive to Sarlat next day. The road was good, the DB2 performed beautifully, taking corners at speed and accelerating out faster than most motor vehicles would dare. They arrived at 5pm and parked the car, before walking up a steep cobbled laneway to reach the villa.

'This is absolutely beautiful Françoise! I imagined an old tumble-down house they used occasionally as a holiday house.'

'You're right about "old"; it was built over three hundred years ago.'

The villa was of sandstone construction as was every other building in the medieval village. It had views over parkland and had a large patio which made alfresco dining imperative.

Charles went back to the car and grabbed their luggage.

He passed many restaurants in the village and a mixture of wine and cheese shops. What really stood out were all the "foie gras" displays.

They ate dinner in a tiny little French provincial restaurant and planned the next few days.

'I think we should just drive around the Black Perigord. There is an old castle every few kilometres. It's said this area has more medieval castles than anywhere else in Europe,' Françoise boasted.

'That sounds good to me. Any excuse to drive the DB2.'

'These roads are for sightseeing not for speeding, cheri.'

'I understand. No drifting around the bends.'

The next few days were spent touring, visiting ancient castles and magnificent chateaux.

It was decided that they should eat dinner on their own in the villa, on the fourth night. They were both accomplished cooks, so together they prepared a meal consisting of foie gras as an entrée and Magret de Canard as the plat du jour. After all, this region was famous for its duck.

Over dinner, Charles pulled a small box from his jacket.

'Darling, I love you very much. Would you do the honour of becoming my wife?'

'Charles, I don't know what to say!'

'A simple 'yes' would be good.'

'Yes, of course. Yes, I love you too. I have loved you since I first met you.'

They embraced and held each other for what seemed an eternity.

'You haven't even looked at the ring yet.'

'Oh, I'm sorry, cheri. It could be plastic for all I care.'

'Great! I'll take it back and get a plastic one.'

'Don't be silly.'

She opened the box; a 3-carat brilliant cut diamond ring was waiting for her finger.

'Charles, cheri, it is beautiful, I can't believe it. Where in Sarlat did you buy this?'

'I bought it in Paris, in a jewellery shop on the Champs-Elysees.'

'So you have been planning this for some time?'

'Of course.'

They retired to their bedroom and consummated the engagement.

The next morning, over breakfast, Françoise suggested they do something totally different.

'I would like to go canoeing along the Dordogne River. My brother and I used to do it all the time when we were kids.'

'Well, that's a unique way to spend our first day as an engaged couple. Why not? It sounds like fun.'

That decision would change their lives.

Love many, trust a few, and always paddle your own canoe

Chapter 40

It was a beautiful warm day in the Dordogne, perfect for canoeing on the river. Charles and Françoise drove to Carsac where they would hire the canoe.

Their intention was to paddle twenty five kilometres heading for Port d'Enveaux.

A bus would then drive them back to pick up the car.

The gentleman who hired them the canoe, explained the safety regulations and both were issued a life jacket.

He cast off the canoe and they started paddling. Françoise was the front paddler.

'So, Charles what do you think so far?'

'It's great, once you get your balance right.'

As promised by the brochure, the scenery was magnificent; the river was flowing at quite a strong pace so they didn't have to exert too much energy.

'Darling, let's get close to the bank, the current is twice as fast and we won't have to paddle much at all. My brother and I used to do it all the time.'

They guided the canoe close to the shore. She was right, it was like being towed.

'Hey Charles, look at that castle way up there!'

She turned to face him with a look of complete contentment; then all went black for her.

A tree branch had struck the back of her head with great force; she fell out of the canoe and disappeared beneath the water. She did not re-surface. Charles jumped in and dived below looking for her, but the strong currents made it impossible and before he knew it, he was two hundred metres down-stream from where she went in.

He struggled to pull himself up the riverbank and lay exhausted for a minute or two. He had to do something! He started running along the bank, dodging trees and rocks, trying to see if she was caught in a tree or some reeds. He found nothing.

He ran back to the drop-off point and drove to the nearest village to alert the gendarme.

'Monsieur, my fiancée fell into the river. I fear she has drowned! Can you come back with me please and I will show you where she fell in.'

With the policeman, Charles drove back in a police car to the approximate spot; they scrambled down the bank and searched frantically. Eventually about four hundred metres down river the policeman found Françoise's body, tangled in a fallen tree; it was too late.

Charles dropped to his knees and screamed as he had never screamed before; his body was shaking uncontrollably and then he cried. His grief was all-encompassing. The policeman tried to console him but Charles was inconsolable.

An ambulance was called and Charles was asked to leave the scene while they extricated the body from the river.

It was decided that he was in no fit state to drive, so the police drove him back to the villa; meanwhile, a tow truck was organised to tow the Aston Martin back to Sarlat.

The police interviewed Charles the next day; they were satisfied it was an unfortunate accident. A coroner's inquiry would be held at a later date.

Charles drove back to Paris and met with Françoise's family. Needless to say, it was a very sad meeting. Charles gave her mother the engagement ring the ambulance officer retrieved from her finger.

'I know Françoise would want you to have this.'

He flew back to London. The judge's ruling in the Lamont case was due in a few days. Charles had lost interest in it but knew he was obligated to attend.

His grief was not over yet: there was more to come.

The Decision of This Court is...

Chapter 41

Charles telephoned his mother; she was devastated, she was not aware he had become engaged. Charles was going to tell her after he returned to London.

'Oh my God, Charles, how must you be feeling? I can't believe it, she was such a lovely girl.'

'I'm still in shock, Mum, I don't know what I'm going to do without her. I was expecting to spend the rest of my life with her...'

'Are you going to continue with the case against Lord Lamont?

'I really haven't given it much thought to be honest, not since the accident anyway.'

'I think you should proceed, darling, you're doing it for your father. He deserves the truth to be revealed.'

'I suppose you're right, I have come this far and I don't want Lamont to walk away from this.'

'Is there anything I can do to help?'

'No, Mum, you've done enough already.'

'Take care, my love, I am thinking of you.'

'Thanks, Mum, goodbye.'

High Court Chancery Division

Court 31

Before Mr Justice Muirhead

Monday, 15 July 1954

At 2:45

Trial List Weatherspoon V Lord Lamont

Part-Heard

Charles and his lawyer entered the court at 2.30pm and sat at the appropriate desk.

Sir Geoffrey was already seated but Lord Lamont was absent.

'Doesn't want to be here to face the music,' Charles thought.

At 2.45pm precisely, Justice Muirhead entered the court room.

He looked around the court and noticed the absence of Lord Lamont.

'Sir Geoffrey, would you please approach the bench. Where is your client?'

'I don't know, My Lord, he was due to meet me outside the court at 2.15pm but as you can see...'

'I see. Well, I will continue and if he turns up, well and good.'

Justice Muirhead began his address to the court, which would culminate in his decision.

'I have heard the evidence from the plaintiff in support of his claim for the entire estate of Lord Lamont, and his title.

I am concerned that a large proportion of the evidence revolved around a rather odd birthmark. The only witnesses I could rely on for identification purposes were Lord Lamont's immediate family. Unfortunately they are all deceased.

So we are left with a very old tattooist from Paris who keeps his record in an ancient shoebox.

We also have a woman of impeccable character, Mrs Emily Weatherspoon; however, she is relying on her memory of one night more than thirty years ago.

As for Mr Black, I have disregarded his evidence entirely. He is not a witness to be trusted.

So, my decision...'

A clerk of the court entered the court and asked if he could approach the bench with some urgent new information.

'Well, this is highly unusual; approach the bench.'

The clerk handed Justice Muirhead an envelope, which he ripped open to read the contents. He looked up at the courtroom and called for Mr Wright and Sir Geoffrey to approach the bench.

The judge briefed them and asked them to be seated.

He then addressed the courtroom.

'I have just been informed that Lord Lamont has been found dead in his library. The police believe it was suicide by strychnine poisoning. He left a very detailed suicide note of which I now have a copy. In the letter he makes a full confession to the murder of his brother, Charles, and falsely assuming his identity and accepting his inheritance. He asks for forgiveness.

Therefore, I rule in the plaintiff's favour.

This court is dismissed.'

The Times, they are a Changing

Chapter 42

Charles, who didn't want to be addressed as 'Lord Lamont', returned from his year of travel and reflection. He had made some life changing decisions. He experienced a catharsis while lying on a beach in Northern Queensland. He realised he owed it to both Françoise and his biological father to take on the Lamont newspaper empire and transform it into a more free-thinking liberal stable of papers. Particularly, "The Times" needed to transform from the conservative Tory paper it had always been, into a newspaper for all the population.

He also committed himself to the protection of the thousands of soldiers' remains scattered throughout The Western Front. These fallen warriors were called 'The Missing.'

His father, Charles, was classified as one of 'The Missing', as his body had never been found. Charles now knew he had died. He created a charitable foundation called 'Let them R.I.P.' The foundation's purpose was to ensure fallen soldiers from all countries involved in the conflict were treated with due respect. If remains were found, procedures to bury them in a military grave should be followed to the letter of the law.

He arrived back in London in June, 1955. If he was going to manage the newspapers, he needed to be based in London. He had inherited the Pall Mall townhouse but had no desire to live there. He instructed Sotheby's to sell it while he was travelling.

He purchased another house at Ovington Square in Knightsbridge; it had a number of reception rooms and seven bedrooms. He wondered why he needed all this space but the townhouse was magnificent and close to his office on Fleet Street. He was about to preside over a newspaper empire during some of the most tumultuous decades in recent history.

Decades of Turmoil

Chapter 43

On 1st July 1955, Charles convened his first editors' meeting. The editors of the various papers were pleased to learn that Charles had worked as a reporter for a number of years and therefore understood how newspapers should be run.

The major stories covered by the papers included:

1955

- Winston Churchill resigns as Prime Minister in England and is defeated for re-election.

- The Soviet Union and its satellite communist regimes in Eastern Europe ratify the Warsaw Pact. Later, Churchill calls this act the equivalent of forming an "Iron Curtain" across Europe. The Cold War deepens.

- Rosa Parks, an African American woman, is arrested after refusing to give up her bus seat to a white person in Montgomery, Alabama. Her arrest sparks a bus boycott led by local minister Martin Luther King, Jr., and sets the American civil rights movement in motion.

- Sony – then known as Tokyo Telecommunications Engineering - produces the first pocketsize transistor radio.

1956

- Dwight Eisenhower re-elected as President of the United States. That same year, he signs the Interstate highway into law.

- Nikita Khrushchev tells Western ambassadors, "We will bury you." He also begins "de-Stalinization," releasing millions of political prisoners and liberalizing Soviet politics. Still, Soviet troops invade Hungary to crush an uprising against the Communist government there.

- The second Arab-Israeli war is fought after Egypt seizes the Suez Canal from the British. Israel invades Egyptian territory east of the Canal with British and French help. However, eventually the UN declares the canal Egyptian property.

- Pakistan becomes an Islamic republic.

1957

- The Soviet Union launches the Sputnik satellite, the first man-made object to orbit the earth. About the same time, the Soviets test their first Intercontinental Ballistic Missile (ICBM) that's capable of delivering nuclear warheads in minutes to the U.S.

- North Vietnam, through the Viet Cong, begins a guerrilla war against South Vietnam.

- Martin Luther King, Jr., forms the Southern Christian Leadership Conference (SCLC) to promote non-violent solutions to segregation.

- The British allow women to become members of the House of Lords for the first time.

1958

- In Cuba, Fidel Castro launches a revolution against the Batista government. Batista flees in 1959, and Castro becomes premier of Cuba.

- The European Economic Community – also called the Common Market – is begun to give Europe the same economic leverage as the U.S. and the Soviet Union.

- The army assassinates Iraq's King Faisal. Iraq becomes a republic, withdraws from the Baghdad Pact and allies itself with the Soviets.

- The former colonies of Madagascar, French West Africa and French Equatorial Africa gain their independence but maintain ties to the French Community.

- NASA, the National Aeronautics and Space Administration, is founded and starts the Mercury project to take the first Americans into space.

- Charles de Gaulle is elected president of France, in large part because he is in favour of allowing former colonies gain independence. He proposes the creation of the French Community giving former colonies the right to independence.

1959

- Fidel Castro installs the first communist regime in the Western Hemisphere. The U.S. breaks off diplomatic relations in 1961.

- In Vietnam, the first U.S. non-combatant military advisers die in a Viet Cong attack. In 1961, the U.S. agrees to supply South Vietnamese troops.

- Alaska and Hawaii become the 49th and 50th states in the United States.

- Yasser Arafat establishes the militant Arab group al-Fatah that is dedicated to building a Palestinian state and to the destruction of Israel.

- Xerox introduces the first commercial photocopier to the market.

- American Airlines launches the jet age in the U.S. transportation industry with the first transcontinental flights with a Boeing 707 aircraft.

- The Soviet Union's unmanned Luna 2 rocket reaches the moon. This same year, the U.S. launches into space and safely retrieves two monkeys.

1960

- John F. Kennedy and Richard Nixon run against each other for the U.S. presidency. In the first televised presidential debate, Kennedy is credited with winning the debate. In November, Kennedy wins a close election, becoming the youngest person ever elected president.

- Leonid Brezhnev becomes president of the Soviet Union.

- A U-2 high altitude spy plane from the U.S. is shot down over the Soviet Union. The pilot, Gary Powers, is captured and later exchanged for the Russian spy, Rudolf Abel.

- The Irish Republican Army (IRA) begins guerrilla fighting against the British to reunite six Northern Ireland counties still under British control. Ireland became a republic in 1949.

1961

- U.S.-trained Cuban exiles attempt to overthrow the Castro government in Cuba with an invasion at the "Bay of Pigs." The invasion fails badly. It's a major embarrassment to the Kennedy administration.

- The Berlin Wall is constructed to prevent East Berliners from defecting to the West.

- First man in space – Yuri Gagarin of the Soviet Union becomes the first man in space, beating the U.S. astronaut Alan Shepard by one month.

1962

- Cuban Missile Crisis. U.S. President John F. Kennedy wins a stand-off with Soviet Premier Nikita Khrushchev, who reverses plans to install missile bases in Cuba.

- Nelson Mandela, deputy president of the African National Congress (ANC), is arrested in South Africa for agitating against apartheid laws.

- Astronaut, John Glenn, is the first American to orbit the earth when he goes around the earth three times and returns successfully.

1963

- Lee Harvey Oswald assassinates President John F. Kennedy on November 22 in Dallas, Texas. Lyndon Johnson is sworn in as president and wins re-election in 1964.

- South Vietnamese president Ngo Dinh Diem is assassinated in a military coup.

- In May, young demonstrators in Birmingham, Alabama, were attacked by police dogs and sprayed by fire hoses strong enough to break bones. Photographs and television news film of the event shocked the nation. In August, 250,000 freedom marchers descend on Washington, DC, and hear Martin Luther King's "I Have a Dream" speech.

- The U.S. and the Soviet Union set up a hotline between the White House and the Kremlin to avoid communication problems that were evident in the Cuban missile crisis.

1964

- North Vietnamese patrol boats in the Gulf of Tonkin allegedly attack U.S. destroyers. In response, President Johnson pushes through Congress a resolution allowing him to greatly increase U.S. troop levels in Vietnam. The escalation of the war begins.

- The U.S. Civil Rights Act is passed, ending legal discrimination in public places, promising equal voting rights and creating the Equal Employment Opportunity Commission.

- Soviet President Leonid Brezhnev becomes Communist Party Secretary, replacing Khrushchev, who is forced to resign after the Cuban Missile Crisis.

- The French detonate their first atomic bomb, which is part of their plan to become independent of U.S. military protection.

- China explodes its first atomic bomb.

1965

- Martin Luther King, Jr., leads 4,000 people on a march from Selma to Montgomery, Alabama. On March 7, state and local police with billy clubs and tear gas attack 600 civil rights marchers. Only the third, and last, march successfully makes it into Montgomery. In New York, Black Muslim leader Malcolm X is assassinated.

- The U.S. Supreme Court, citing the Constitutional right to privacy, strikes down a Connecticut law that prohibits married couples from using birth control pills.

- Soviet Cosmonaut Alexei Leonov is the first person to "walk" in space, spending ten minutes outside the Voskhod 2 spaceship.

- The Gemini missions carry the first two-man crews into space and enable the first spacewalk by an American - Ed White - and the first space rendezvous of two manned crafts.

1966

- In China, Chairman Mao launches the Cultural Revolution that lasts until 1969. Students and workers join the Red

Guard and begin purging so-called intellectuals and imperialists, who are believed to be opposed to Mao's socialist vision.

- The Soviet Union lands the unmanned spacecraft Luna 9 on the moon. The U.S. lands Surveyor I on the moon and transmits TV images of the moon's surface back to Earth.

- Indira Gandhi, the daughter of Nehru, become prime minister of India.

1967

- By year's end, there are 480,000 U.S. troops in Vietnam. The U.S. begins mining rivers in North Vietnam.

- In Washington, DC, 50,000 people protest the Vietnam War at the Lincoln Memorial. Students nationwide burn their draft cards. Mohammad Ali is stripped of his boxing title for refusing to join the Army because of his Muslim faith.

- The third Arab-Israeli war – also known as the Six-Day War – begins after Egyptian president Nasser begins remilitarizing the Sinai Peninsula. Israel routs the Arab forces of Egypt, Jordan and Syria, capturing old Jerusalem, the Sinai, the West Bank and Golan Heights.

- After the Six-Day War, the Suez Canal is closed for security reasons, until 1975.

- Dr. Christian Barnard performs the first human heart transplant operation in Cape Town, South Africa. Hamilton Naki, a self-taught black African surgeon who later receives an honorary degree in medicine, assists him.

- Thurgood Marshall becomes the first African American judge appointed to the U.S. Supreme Court.

- The first automatic teller machine (ATM) is put into service at Barclays Bank in London.

1968

- At the end of January, the North Vietnamese begin a massive series of military operations called the "Tet Offensive" because it is timed to coincide with the celebration of the Vietnamese New Year (Tet). The U.S. military repulse the attacks, but they and the country are demoralized by the ferocity of the attacks.

- In the Vietnamese village of My Lai, U.S. troops massacre 347 men, women and children.

- As the U.S. presidential campaign heats up, President Lyndon Johnson shocks the nation by announcing he will not seek re-election because of frustrations with the Vietnam War. Just before the announcement, Robert Kennedy had entered the race. He won the critical California primary in June, but within minutes Sirhan Sirhan assassinated him. The following Democratic Convention in Chicago nominated Hubert Humphrey, but demonstrations outside the hall dissolved into battles between police and protesters. Richard M. Nixon wins the November election, in part because he promises to end the Vietnam War. After election, he expands the war before reaching a settlement with North Vietnam. South Vietnam is defeated in 1975.

- The U.S. Civil Rights Act of 1968 outlaws housing discrimination based on race.

- James Earl Ray assassinates Martin Luther King, Jr., at the Lorraine Motel in Memphis, Tennessee. Riots erupt across the U.S.

- In Iraq, revolution puts the Baath Party in control of the government with a policy of Arab socialism.

1969

- The Soviets begin Strategic Arms Limitation Talks (SALT) with U.S. President Nixon.

- The U.S. troop strength in Vietnam hits 543,000 but they begin the policy of Vietnamization, turning more of the war over to the Vietnamese Army.

- In Woodstock, NY, 300,000 rock-and-roll fans attend three days of music, "peace and love."

- Apollo 11 lands on the moon. More than 100 million people watch on television around the world as U.S. astronaut Neil Armstrong steps onto the surface.

- In computer technology, the microprocessor is invented.

This miniature set of integrated circuits makes possible the computer revolution. Also, the Advanced Research Projects Agency Network (ARPANET) goes online. This decentralized computer communications network is the forerunner of the Internet.

- The Concorde, the world's first supersonic passenger jet, makes its maiden flight.

Charles' commitment to reporting the facts and ensuring fairness to all, became legendary, not only in the U.K., but also around the world. On more than one occasion, he would take the role of reporter and write a story under a pseudonym. Sometimes being a reporter would endanger his life, as the hot spots he visited were extremely volatile. He was about to experience another one.

Terror

Both terrorism and Insurance sell fear... and business is business

Chapter 44

Charles received a telephone call from Golda Meir, the Prime Minister of Israel, in early December 1973.

She suggested that he come to Israel and interview both her and Moshe Dayan, her Defence Minister, on the basis of life in Israel after victory in the Yom Kippur war.

He agreed, but only on the condition that he also interview Anwar Sadat of Egypt and Yasser Arafat of the PLO.

She reluctantly agreed, but insisted he travel to Israel first. Charles knew this was a major opportunity, considering all that had happened in the Middle East in recent times. If he pulled it off, it would be a coup for his papers and certainly newspapers and television stations around the globe would pick it up.

He researched his facts in relation to the Yom Kippur war.

It had been reported widely that Israel's lack of preparedness for the Arab

201

attack was because it was the holiest day on the Jewish calendar, Yom Kippur.

Charles believed there was more to it, however. The Israeli Intelligence community had historically been one of the most aggressive and successful intelligence networks in the world. So, how were the Arabs able to launch a surprise attack against Israel on 6 October 1973?

Charles's theory was that since 1967, the Arabs had been busy planning and preparing for an attack on Israel. Additionally, the Arabs had incorporated the fine use of deception, denial, and disinformation to disguise their deadly intent. In contrast, Israel had been lulled into a sense of security and laxity. Much of the Israeli hierarchy believed that the Arabs were not prepared for war and if they did foolishly attack, Israel could quickly defeat them as was the case in the 1967, Six Day War. Additionally, Israel's focus on their future adversary was distracted due to internal problems in the intelligence community, funding cutbacks, and an immediate need to respond to terrorist activities.

Although numerous indicators outlined the Arabs' intentions, it was only hours before the actual invasion that Prime Minister Meir agreed to a partial mobilization of the Israeli Defence Force.

The surprise attack was a result of actions from both sides. The Arabs' intense preparation and keen use of deception, denial, and disinformation were certainly factors in their initial success. The Israelis were able to be surprised because of widespread problems in the intelligence community, the lack of perception in identifying the Arabs' intentions, allowing distractions to take them away from their real enemy, and the high regard for their own military ability.

Israel Mobilises

Charles's journalistic pseudonym was Ray Mathews; he used this name on the odd occasion on which he published an article in one of his newspapers.

He decided to fly to Paris to catch up with Françoise's parents to whom he had become very close, since she drowned. He then flew on to Rome where he was to connect to an "El Al" flight directly to Tel Aviv in Israel.

He bought a few magazines, including "Time," to read on the flight; he also purchased a copy of "The Times" to catch up with what was happening at home and see what views the editorial was espousing. It featured the 'three-day week' electricity consumption reduction measures coming into force in the United Kingdom due to coal shortages caused by industrial action.

His flight was announced and as a First Class passenger, he could board anytime. Usually he waited to the very last minute but he decided to board early this time. He boarded the Jumbo 747 and settled down into his luxurious seat. A delightful Israeli flight attendant offered him a glass of Dom Pérignon, which he graciously accepted. He was flipping through the "El Al" flight magazine waiting for the doors to be closed when he heard some sort of commotion in the terminal. He couldn't work out what was going on but there was much screaming and then he heard gunshots from the terminal building.

'Oh my God, there are terrorists taking over the terminal', shrieked one of the passengers.

Just then, two terrorists with balaclavas and brandishing AK 47s ran into the First Class cabin yelling at the passengers to get into the breach position.

They then stood at the front of the cabin, one in each aisle.

'OK, everybody, make sure you have your seat belt tightened and put your hands on your heads. If you obey our instructions, nobody will get hurt.'

While one of the terrorists kept watch on the passengers, the other banged on the cockpit door with the butt of his rifle demanding that the crew open the door. They refused, so he fired several bursts into the lock, allowing him to enter; he fired and killed the three crew members.

Charles and the other passengers were in shock. This human being, if you could call him that, had just murdered three innocent people in cold blood.

The terrorist returned to the passenger cabin, looked over at his comrade and nodded. With that, they started to fire at the passengers. Within a couple of minutes, they were all dead, trapped in their seats, secured by their seatbelts.

It was a scene of total carnage.

Charles had become one of the most powerful media barons in the world; he was also a generous philanthropist and a confidante for some of the most significant world leaders of the day.

The military and political aspects of the conflict

Israel and the Arabs: old wounds reopened

Military: Louis Heren

ESTIMATE OF MILITARY POWER AT START OF FIGHTING

Country	Manpower	Aircraft Total (inc fighters, bombers)		Tanks Total	Heavy	Med	Light	Ships Total (inc subs, dest)		
Israel	300,000	488		1,700		1,700		54		
Egypt	298,000	620	390	1,955	90	1,860	75	108		
Syria	132,000	326	310	990	50	140	100	35		
Iraq	101,900	224	216	1,065		990	75	30		
Jordan	75,650	52		420		420		8		
Libya	25,000	44		27		27				
Lebanon	15,250	18		190		60				

Figures from International Institute of Strategic Studies, London.

Israeli tanks move up to the front yesterday.

Political: Nicholas Ashford

Sounds commercial

Tim Devlin

Towards a new Tory mix

Clive Landa

The author is national chairman of the Young Conservatives.

© Times Newspapers Ltd, 1973.

The Times Diary

Last of the great gas stories?

Out tourist

Unsupported

Revelation

Concession

Pretty plump

A Plump sitting pretty

PHS

He never married. After losing his one true love, he felt he could never commit to another woman.

In his will, he left a significant amount to Let Them RIP (www.letthemrip.com) to ensure the missing soldiers on the Western Front were assured of not being simply re-buried, if dug up by ploughing or excavation work. A significant amount was donated to the Commonwealth War Graves Commission to manage the program and ensure proper military burials.

Let Them RIP was also allocated the task of educating farmers in Northern France and Belgium in relation to the benefits of non-tillage farming. This ploughing method would minimise the chance of disturbing the remains of the fallen.

The Great Ormond Street Children's Hospital in London also received £10,000,000 a year for cancer research.

The six newspapers were left to the staff. Each Editor received ten per cent and the remaining ninety per cent were distributed to staff, based on years of service.

Charles was buried in the graveyard of the family church in Boston, next to his stepfather.

On his gravestone, his mother's, stepfather's and his biological father's names were engraved and their memories immortalised.

The End

Lamont Clan Crest

"Neither spare nor despise"